Happy Birthday 1994

Baseball & The Game of Life

Stories for the THINKING fan!
If you can't watch it,
you must settle for
thinking about it —
but just until next
season or the
strike is over —
whichever comes
first.

Love
Marsha
& Micah

BASEBALL

&

THE GAME OF LIFE

Stories for the Thinking Fan

EDITED BY PETER C. BJARKMAN

VINTAGE BOOKS
A Division of Random House, Inc.
New York

First Vintage Books Edition, March 1991

Library of Congress Cataloging-in-Publication Data
Baseball and the game of life: stories for the thinking fan / edited
by Peter C. Bjarkman.
p. cm.
Reprint. Originally published: New York: Birch Brook Press, 1990.
ISBN 0-679-73141-5
1. Baseball stories, American.
PS648.B37B37 1991
813' .0108355—dc20
90-50501
CIP

Manufactured in the United States of America
10 9 8 7 6 5 4 3 2 1

This book is for
DAVID ROBERT BJARKMAN
who shared baseball's richest memories,
during baseball's finest decade.

Contents

PETER C. BJARKMAN

Introduction:
Baseball & The Game of Life

Poets are like baseball pitchers. Both have their moments. The intervals are the tough things.—**Robert Frost**

With the first crack of 19th-century ash bat against sewn horsehide, baseball flowered as America's unchallenged pastoral national sport, a status it has steadfastly maintained down to the present era. Baseball's growth in the popular imagination was not so rapid as it now appears in the lucid hindsight of history—painstaking evolution from townball folk-ritual, to recreational factory game, to multi-million-dollar electronic media entertainment spectacle. Yet by the end of the 19th century baseball reigned supreme in the land as the nation's favorite leisure-time activity. With its subsequent panoply of incomparable legendary heroes (Ty Cobb to Babe Ruth to

Ted Williams to Willie Mays to Johnny Bench) and its appropriate myth-shrouded origins in the cow pastures outside the village of Cooperstown, New York, the nation's adopted pastime has provided a perfect reflection of New World dreams and an unmatched repository as well for unbounded American pride and self-assurance. This simple "boy's game played by grown men" was from the outset a perfect analogy for American independence, frontier individualism, and a New World spirit of fair play. The massive popular culture industry which today surrounds our national pastime (literature, fiction, music, Hollywood film, bubblegum cards, collectibles of all sorts) lends weighty support to Roger Angell's whimsical observation that baseball seems to have been invented solely for the purpose of explaining all other things in life.

From the first concealed references to the game in Walt Whitman's *Song of Myself*, baseball also seems the favorite of American poets and writers. As early as 1889 Mark Twain saw baseball as "the very symbol, the outward and visible expression of the drive and push and rush and struggle of the raging, tearing, booming nineteenth century" (*cf., Messenger 1981:80*). Today's writers are more apt to reflect Murray Ross' sentimental notion that baseball "was old fashioned right from the start . . . conceived in nostalgia, in the resuscitation of the Jeffersonian dream . . . an artificial rural environment removed from the toil of urban life" (*Ross 1971:31*). Literature instructor James O'Donnell appropriately reminds us that baseball provides both "recreation" and "re-creation"—an imaginative drama of perfect pacing and balanced reflection in which baseball reality stands as an unmatched metaphor for life-experience itself (*O'Donnell 1988:1*). This is so because (in the words of poet Donald Hall) "baseball plays best in the theater of the mind." As redoubtable expression of national optimism (Twain), or as wistful longing for a lost paradise (Ross), baseball has always had its irrepressible literary side.

The ledger of American writers avowing a passion for baseball itself reads like a selective honor roll from an American academy of arts and letters. Novelists who have invented huge metaphors from the game include most of the nation's literary immortals—Wolfe, Faulkner, Hemingway, Roth, Malamud, Frank Norris, Mark Twain, Robert Coover—as well as more contemporary literary super novas like John Irving, Mark Harris, John Updike and Jay Neugeboren. The list of poets known to avow passion (or at least sympathies) for the game include Marianne Moore, Robert Frost, Whitman, Robert Francis, Richard Hugo, Rolfe Humphries, Donald Hall, Jack Kerouac, and dozens more.

Over the past three decades a new literary phenomenon has arisen, the serious adult baseball novel, a legitimate American art form finding most mature expression in the works of Mark Harris (the Henry Wiggen tetrology) and W.P. Kinsella (the Iowa baseball novels). Kinsella and Jerry Klinkowitz have also fostered the baseball short story and lifted the latter genre from the drivel of juvenile fiction to the stuff of avant-garde post-modernist fiction.

The way was first paved by Bernard Malamud, who single-handedly launched the adult sports novel in 1952. With *The Natural* Malamud effectively exploited for the first time the inherent mythic potentials of baseball as literary subject. In his pioneering portrayal of mysterious 38-year-old rookie Roy Hobbs, Malamud seized upon baseball legend to flesh out a modern-day recreation of the Wasteland and Arthurian myths, ancient folklore dramatically transplanted to the heart of America's 20th-century diamond sport. Mark Harris, through his Henry Wiggen stories, in turn demonstrated that baseball fiction could also be populated with full-blown human heroes and serious adult themes of love, jealousy and failure. By the late 1960s and early 1970s two novels, especially, were to elevate baseball culture to the artistic plane of an American pastoral tradition: Robert Coover's *The Universal Baseball Association, Inc., J. Henry Waugh, Prop.* and Philip Roth's *The Great American Novel.* Together they reinvented baseball legend in the guise of often ruthless cultural satire. *The Great American Novel,* especially, is one of our richest modern-day literary satires; Roth's use of baseball history as the stuff of social and political satire is altogether more serious than implied with his tongue-in-cheek rejoinder that baseball was an appropriate enough subject for great American fiction since whaling had already been effectively done (by Melville). Even Roth's title carries a certain ironic appropriateness: It was altogether fitting that a pretentious and weighty novel in the image of Melville or Hawthorne should at long last be devoted to such an inherently literary institution as American baseball.

Once the serious adult baseball novel arrived with Coover and Roth in the late 1960s and early 1970s, the genre literally exploded. Better than one hundred adult novels featuring baseball have appeared since 1973 alone (most of these unfortunately are still not listed in most standard baseball bibliographies like Paul Adomites' "Essential Baseball Library" in *Total Baseball*). The first sign of things to come, of course, was Coover's *Universal Baseball Association,* with its fitting exploitation of the notion of parallel universes which sustain the worlds of imaginary baseball (table-top board games) and real baseball. The true turning point, however, came somewhat later, in 1973, with Roth's enigmatic satirical novel in which he explores the loss of an American Eden through the lost Edens of America's "boys of summer." Now anything was possible and baseball was freed from its sports-action narrative and released into its unbounded mythic and fantasy dimensions. From Jerome Charyn's *Seventh Babe* (1973) to the novels of W.P. Kinsella (notably

The Iowa Baseball Confederacy, 1986) in the second half of the current decade, baseball fiction continually exploits such delightful fantasies as time travel, wizards and shamans, mystical resurrections of yesterday's heroes, impossible hitting and throwing feats by mysterious rookies and phenoms, and magical events of all imaginable sorts. Baseball action is as magical and charmed on the fictional pages of dozens of baseball novels as it often is in the stadiums of big-league play.

By the mid-1980s adult baseball fiction has surprisingly come to provide the finest gourmet *entremets* within the rich annual feast of serious and often scholarly baseball books spread before us each spring. While critics continue to debate the meanings as well as the artistic merits of *The Great American Novel*, there is little doubt that baseball fiction has never been quite the same since Roth irreverently employed our national sport to critique and condemn everything from American politics and sociocultural myths to the esteemed national literary establishment itself. For Roth's novel is as much a lavish joke on *Moby Dick* as it is a thorough deconstruction of hallowed baseball history and lore. After Roth, baseball novels no longer found their subject matter restricted to "that simple boy's game played professionally by grown men" in urban stadia across the land; it was no longer sufficient to reconstitute myths internal to the national pastime, or to repackage virtues inculcated by its real-life or fictional ballplayer heroes. Baseball novels were now more symbolic and sophisticated, treating the broader scope of our collective national lives and our individualized private fantasies. And for all their whimsical fantasy, these latter-day baseball novels more accurately reflected those complexities of real-world baseball which have made the American game so much more than just another sport—which have in fact elevated it to fresh status as the unrivalled national passion. While pre-1973 baseball novels, for all their mythic overtones, focused on the everyday world of major league and/or amateur baseball, after Roth the best of baseball fiction has usually been surrealistic and magical in tone and fantastical in its settings, as perhaps best seen on the pages of Jerome Charyn, John Alexander Graham, and most recently W.P. Kinsella.

But baseball fiction is certainly not an exclusive phenomenon of the second half of the 20th-century. An established tradition of boy's dime novels and juvenile pulp fiction produced enough volumes on the national game between the late 19th and mid-20th centuries to fill over forty pages of entries in Anton Grobani's first extensive bibliography of baseball literature (*Grobani 1975*). The origins of modern baseball fiction lie clearly within the juvenile Horatio Alger formula stories of William Heyliger, Gilbert Patten ("Burt L. Standish"), Edward Stratemeyer ("Lester Chadwick"), Harold M. Sherman, John Tunis, Ralph Henry Barbour, and Zane Gray; no less a figure of literary baseball than Mark Harris has written explicitly about the formative influences of such juvenile works upon his own pioneering attempts at writing the serious adult baseball novel (*Harris 1988*).

The transition to adult fiction came of age with the eight Roy Tucker novels of John Tunis during the late 1940s and early 1950s; these novels present baseball as a unifying thread of New York urban life in the immediate post-war years and express "the communal sense of the game's ritual before television fragmented the audience" (*Bergen 1986*). Yet the first serious adult baseball fiction (if one excludes perhaps Ring Lardner's dozen best stories and one major novel), did not appear until the early 1950s with Bernard Malamud's *The Natural* and Mark Harris' *Henry Wiggen* trilogy. This was more than a full century after baseball had first been crowned the American national game! Why, then, we might inevitably ask, was there such a lengthy embryonic period for the serious baseball novel? In large part the answer is that we could not take our baseball fiction as "serious literature" until the arrival of the 1960s, when television would first physically separate us, as fans and spectators, from the games we watched, removing us by electronic magic from long-accustomed intimate contact with actions and players upon the field. Major novels of the 1960s and 1970s (i.e. those of Coover and Roth) thus began to treat baseball as highly symbolic metaphorical activity—focusing on archetypes of human behavior and on actions that were more appropriate to the imaginary worlds of magic and fantasy. From the rich historical ambiance of Eric Rolfe Greenberg's *The Celebrant* (perhaps baseball's best novel) to the insipid prose and vapid plotting of George Plimpton's *The Curious World of Sidd Finch* (perhaps its most overrated novel), contemporary baseball novels are as complex in symbol and as bold in archetypes as any competing genre of current American fiction.

Baseball novels of the modern age seem to fall neatly into five readily identifiable types. First are the *realistic novels*, crafted in the tradition of Mark Harris' Henry Wiggen trilogy, in which the everyday realities of on-field baseball and locker-room politics are showcased. These are stories in which the ballplayers are all recognizable baseball prototypes (flaky rookie southpaw, grizzled veteran manager, fading veteran star, etc.); the on-field action is always believable and lovingly detailed, and the themes and issues always involve ballplayers struggling for elusive baseball immortality or perhaps merely battling for daily professional survival. Historical novels like Greenberg's *The Celebrant* (1983) or Harry Stern's *Hoopla* (1983) provide perhaps the high water marks of this special and most popular brand of baseball fiction. A second broad type, the *mythical baseball novels* of writers like Bernard Malamud (*The Natural*) and Robert Coover (*The Universal Baseball Association*), provide a stark departure from the more realistic mode, with their highly stylized and symbolic actions and the religious and archetypal importance in which ballplaying is cloaked.

Personal nostalgia novels—of which the best examples are David Ritz's *The Man Who Brought the Dodgers Back to Brooklyn* and Robert Mayer's *The Grace of Shortstops*— focus on the deep-rooted humanizing features of baseball memories and of our own personal baseball fantasies. Often these works unmask the adult male struggling to come to grips with aging and with personal lifetime failures. This third fiction type often focuses more on the fan of baseball than on actual ballplayer heroes, and dozens of adult softball novels fall clearly into this genre. A fourth type is the "magical realism" or *fantasy baseball novel* practiced first by Jerome Charyn and Philip Roth in the 1970s and brought to full bloom by W.P. Kinsella in the 1980s. Here the intention is often satirical, the baseball events are bizarre (even other-worldly) and usually magical, and the thematic impact is far more often genuinely comic rather than intentionally tragic (as with mythic novels like *The Natural*). Finally, there is a whole lesser sub-genre of *baseball detective novels* where the local ballpark (often a minor league park) becomes the setting for murder and mayhem in the best tradition of our finest cloak-and-dagger "who-done-it" thrillers.

It is not surprising that baseball stands out as the most literary and intellectual among American sports. Explanations for the linkage of baseball with literature are legion as well as lucid. Most obvious to the casual observer, perhaps, are parallels between baseball's organizational structure and the rambling architecture of literature's most sprawling narrative form—the novel. Baseball provides the very essence of fictional structure with its perfect pacing of intense action alongside welcomed respite and dramatic pause—the apparent deadtime between pitches and between innings, the leisurely pace of a sun-drenched afternoon's play. Baseball also boasts its symbolic "timelessness," being the only game not governed by the timeclock and thus potentially capable of being played out forever. Extra innings—unlike overtime periods in other sports—can stretch out over ever-expanding and theoretically unending time periods. Then, too, there are the carefully scripted roles of the diamond's few defensive players, who themselves appear—far more than in other games—as distinctive *dramatis personae* within the colorful pageant unfolding—pitch by measured pitch—before the enthralled spectator. Distinct defensive positions are spread out across the panoramic field for easy view, and unique baseball roles (outfielder, infielder, pitcher, catcher, pinch-hitter) provide distinctive personality types as well as contrasting human physical specimens of differing statures and postures. Finally, and most importantly, there are the life-mirroring seasonal and daily cycles of baseball play: the fluctuating pace and repetitive cycles of the long on-going summer season are the very essence and mirror of our daily human existence. "This ain't football," Earl Weaver has reminded us, "we do this every day" (*Boswell 1982:3*).

But above all else, baseball carefully breaks down ("articulates") its delicate balance of segmented actions—pitcher versus batter being only the most central of these dramatic pauses—so that it is always easy to identify villain and hero and to understand moral implications of each hit, error, brilliant fielding play or tragically dropped ball and missed tag-play. Add to the symbolic dimensions of baseball action the detailed "quantification" of a ballgame—its preoccupation with numbers and percentages and with statistical measurements of all sorts—and little doubt is left as to why baseball is the foremost game among acute thinkers, intellectuals and, above all, storytellers and poets. Baseball's entrenched historical connections with American myth and folklore—including the underlying myth about the game's alleged but long-dis-proven birthplace in the charming frontier village lots of Cooperstown—only work to enrich and reinforce the previously deep-rooted literary dimensions of the national game.

Stories featured in this present anthology consistently reflect these deep-rooted literary qualities of baseball, as well as showcasing here some of baseball literature's most accomplished household names alongside some of the genre's most promising new talents. Our volume opens with Robert Coover's "McDuff on the Mound"—one of baseball's most inspired and yet least known pieces of short fiction. Coover's unorthodox recasting of the time-worn "Casey at the Bat" legend is delivered from the triumphant pitcher's perspective. Filled with Disney-like pratfalls and sustained by perhaps the most ingenious lampooning to date of the Casey myth—"McDuff on the Mound" establishes the preeminence of Coover as a practitioner of the serious adult baseball short story.

Other names in our lineup familiar to even casual baseball readers include W.P. Kinsella (*Shoeless Joe*), Jay Neugeboren (author of the fine baseball novel *Sam's Legacy*), Merritt Clifton (purveyor of the hit underground novella *A Baseball Classic*), and David Nemec (*Great Baseball Feats, Facts and Firsts*). Kinsella's previously unpublished story "Lumpy Drobot" is again squarely in the tradition of this author's unique brand of "magic realism" laced with baseball humor. And David Nemec's otherworldly baseball tale which closes the volume is reminiscent, at one and the same time, of the best of Kinsella infused with the ironic wit of science fiction pioneer Rod Serling. "Browning's Lamps" is, in fact, that rare storyline which effectively exploits all of baseball's most familiar and most effective literary themes—unreal time and space and the seductive possibilities of time travel; the naive baseball folk-hero of mysterious rural origin and heretofore unseen hitting or pitching talent; the cyclical nature of the professional baseball career and the inevitable defeat of each summer's heroes at the hands of ceaseless time and aging; baseball's fascination with the mystery and magic of numbers, as well as with the lasting immortality provided with on-field baseball achievement; the nostalgic connections of this boy's game with the richest and most melancholy moments of our lost youth.

Some of the finest writing of this volume, however, is provided by untried rookies and little known literary journeymen who have long toiled unnoticed in the bush leagues of baseball fiction. Irwin Chusid provides a delightful short parody of one of baseball's finest and most widely read non-fiction classics (Lawrence Ritter's *The Glory of Their Times*). Henry Roth, Luke Salisbury, Tom Tolnay, and John Hildebidle summon up fresh treatments of standard baseball tales—stories of the promising rookies and fading veterans grasping at one last opportunity for sudden baseball fame and fortune. The fan's loving perspective on the game, in turn, is at the heart of stories by William Stafford and Jay Feldman. Finally, Leslie Woolf Hedley, Lawrence Watson and James Kissane turn sandlot and schoolboy ballgame experiences into the rich stuff of life-metaphor and elevating personal baseball mythology.

In short, almost everything to be found in the most traditional literary uses of baseball is found under one guise or another in the stories which fill out the roster of the present anthology. There are enough sandlot dreams and memories here to fill a Hot Stove League fiction season for even the most voracious among baseball readers. By volume's end, our readers should be left nodding in firm agreement with Jim Bouton's classic observations about baseball and the essence of its hold on the American nation's popular imagination—"You see, you spend a good piece of your life gripping a baseball and in the end it turns out that it was the other way around all the time." (Jim Bouton, *Ball Four*).

REFERENCES CITED

Adomites, Paul D. "The Ultimate Baseball Library," *Total Baseball*. Edited by John Thorn and Pete Palmer. New York: Warner Books, 1989, 2272–2282.

Bergen Philip. "Roy Tucker, Not Roy Hobbs: The Baseball Novels of John R. Tunis," *The SABR Review of Books: A Forum of Baseball Literary Opinion*, Edited by Paul D. Adomites. Cooperstown: The Society for American Baseball Research, 1 (1986), 85–97.

Bjarkman, Peter C. *The Immortal Diamond: Baseball in American Literature and American Culture*. Westport, CT: Meckler Books, 1990, to appear.

Boswell, Thomas. *How Life Imitates the World Series*. Garden City, New York: Doubleday and Company, 1982, (Middlesex: Penguin Books, 1983).

Charyn, Jerome. *The Seventh Babe*. New York: Arbor House Publishers, 1979 (New York: Avon Books, 1980).

Coover, Robert. *The Universal Baseball Association, Inc., J. Henry Waugh, Prop*. New York: Signet New American Library, 1968.

Greenberg, Eric Rolfe. *The Celebrant*. New York: Everest House, 1983 (New York: Viking Penguin, 1986).

Grobani, Anton, Editor. *A Guide to Baseball Literature*. Detroit: Gale Research, 1975.

Harris, Mark. "Horatio at the Bat, or Why Such a Lengthy Embryonic Period for the Serious Baseball Novel?" *Aethlon: The Journal of Sport Literature* 5:2 (Spring 1988), 1–11.

Malamud, Bernard. *The Natural*. New York: Farrar, Straus and Giroux Publishers, 1952 (New York: Avon Books, 1980).

Mayer, Robert. *The Grace of Shortstops*. Garden City, New York: Doubleday and Company Publishers, 1984.

Messenger, Christian K. *Sport and the Spirit of Play in American Fiction: Hawthorne to Faulkner*. New York: Columbia University Press, 1981.

Neugeboren, Jay. *Sam's Legacy*. New York: Holt, Rinehart and Winston, 1974.

O'Donnell, James. "A Short History of Literary Baseball," *Crosscurrents* (Washington Community College Humanities Association Yearbook) 7:1 (Winter 1988), 4–6.

Plimpton, George. *The Curious Case of Sidd Finch*. New York: Macmillan Company, 1987 (New York: Ballantine Books, 1988).

References Cited

Ritz, David. *The Man Who Brought the Dodgers Back to Brooklyn.* New York: Simon and Schuster, 1981.

Ross, Murray. "Football Red and Baseball Green: The Heroics and Bucolics of American Sport," *Chicago Review* 22:2 (1971), 30–40.

Roth, Philip. *The Great American Novel.* New York: Holt, Rinehart and Winston, 1973 (New York: Viking Penguin Books, 1981).

Stein, Harry. *Hoopla.* New York: Alfred A. Knopf, 1983 (New York: St. Martin's Press, 1983).

Baseball & The Game of Life

ROBERT COOVER

McDuff on the Mound

IT WASN'T MUCH, a feeble blooper over second, call it luck, but it was enough to shake McDuff. He stepped weakly off the left side of the pitcher's mound, relieved to see his catcher Gus take the job of moving down behind the slow runner to back up the throw in to first. Fat Flynn galloped around the bag toward second, crouched apelike on the basepath, waggled his arms, then bounded back to first as the throw came in from short center. McDuff felt lightheaded. Flynn's soft blooper had provoked a total vision that iced his blood. Because the next batter up now was Blake: oh yes, man, it was all too clear. "Today's the day," McDuff told himself, as though taking on the cares of the world. He tucked his glove in his armpit briefly, wiped the sweat from his brow, resettled his cap, thrust his hand back into his glove.

Gus jogged over to the mound before going back behind the plate, running splaylegged around the catcher's guard that padded his belly. McDuff took the toss from first, over Gus's head, stood staring dismally at Flynn, now edging flat-footed away from the bag, his hands making floppy loosewristed swirls at the cuffs of his Mudville knickers. Gus spat, glanced back over his shoulder at first, then squinted up at McDuff. "Whatsa matter, kid?"

McDuff shrugged, licked his dry lips. "I don't know, Gus. I tried to get him." He watched Flynn taunt, flapping his hands like donkey ears, thumbing his nose. The hoodoo. Rubbing it in. Did he know? He must. "I really tried." He remembered this night-

3

mare, running around basepaths, unable to stop.

Gus grinned, though, ignoring the obvious: "Nuts, the bum was lucky. C'mon, kid, ya got this game in ya back pocket!" He punched McDuff lightly in the ribs with his stiff platter of a mitt, spat in encouragement, and joggled away in a widelegged trot toward home plate, head cocked warily toward first, where Flynn bounced insolently and made insulting noises. Settling then into his crouch, and before pulling his mask down, Gus jerked his head at the approaching batter and winked out at McDuff. Turkey Blake. Blake the cake. Nothing to it. A joke. Maybe Gus is innocent, McDuff thought. Maybe not.

Now, in truth, McDuff was not, by any standard but his own, in real trouble. Here it was, the bottom of the ninth, two away, one more out and the game was over, and he had a fat two-run lead going for him. A lot of the hometown Mudville fans had even given it up for lost and had started shuffling indifferently toward the exits. Or was their shuffle a studied shuffle and itself a cunning taunt? a mocking rite like Flynn's buffoonery at first? Had they shuffled back there in the shadows just to make Flynn's fluke hit sting more? It was more than McDuff could grasp, so he scratched his armpits and tried to get his mind off it. Now, anyway, they were all shuffling back. And did they grin as they shuffled? Too far away to tell. But they probably did, goddamn them. You're making it all up, he said. But he didn't convince himself. And there was Blake. Blake the Turkey. Of course.

Blake was the league clown, the butt. Slopeshouldered, potbellied, broadrumped, bandylegged. And a long goiter-studded neck with a small flat head on top, overlarge cap down around the ears. They called him "Turkey," Blake the Turkey. The fans cheered him with a gobbling noise. And that's just what they did now as he stepped up: gobbled and gobbled. McDuff could hardly believe he had been brought to this end, that it was happening to him, even though he had known that sooner or later it must. Blake had three bats. He gave them a swing and went right off his feet. Gobble gobble gobble. Then he got up, picked out two bats, chose one, tossed the other one away, but as though by mistake, hung on to it,

4

went sailing with it into the bat racks. Splintering crash. Mess of broken bats. Gobble gobble. McDuff, in desperation, pegged the ball to first, but Flynn was sitting on the bag, holding his quaking paunch, didn't even run when the ball got away from the first baseman, just made gobbling noises.

Vaguely, McDuff had seen it coming, but he'd figured on trouble from Cooney and Burroughs right off. A 4-to-2 lead, last inning, four batters between him and Casey, two tough ones and two fools, it was all falling into place: get the two tying runs on base, then two outs, and bring Casey up. So he'd worked like a bastard on those two guys, trying to head it off. Should've known better, should've seen that would have been too easy, too pat, too painless. McDuff, a practical man with both feet on the ground, had always tried to figure the odds, and that's where he'd gone wrong. But would things have been different if Cooney and Burroughs had hit him? Not substantially maybe, there'd still be much the same situation and Casey yet to face. But the stage wouldn't have been just right, and maybe, because of that, somehow, he'd have got out of it.

Cooney, tall, lean, one of the best percentage hitters in the business: by all odds, see, it should have been him. That's what McDuff had thought, so when he'd sucked old Cooney into pulling into an inside curve and grounding out, third to first, he was really convinced he'd got himself over the hump. Even if Burroughs should hit him, it was only a matter of getting Flynn and Blake out, and they never gave anybody any trouble. And Burroughs *didn't* hit him! Big barrelchested man with a bat no one else in the league could even lift—some said it weighed half a ton—and he'd wasted all that power on a cheap floater, sent it dribbling to the mound and McDuff himself had tossed him out. Hot damn! he'd cried. Waiting for fat Flynn to enter the batter's box, he'd even caught himself giggling. And then that unbelievable blooper. And— *bling!*— the light.

McDuff glared now at Blake, wincing painfully as though to say: get serious, man! Blake was trying to knock the dirt out of his cleats. But each time he lifted his foot, he lost his balance and toppled over. Gobble gobble gobble. Finally, there on the ground, teetering on his broad rump, he took a healthy swing with the bat at his foot. There was a bang like a firecracker going off, smoke, and the shoe sailed into the stands. Turkey Blake hobbled around in mock pain (or real pain: who could tell and what did it matter? McDuff's pain was real), trying to grasp his stockinged foot, now smoking faintly, but he was too round in the midriff, too short in the arms, to reach it. Gobble gobble gobble. Someone tossed the shoe back and it hit him in the head: bonk! Blake toppled stiffly backwards, his short bandy legs up in the air as though he were dead. Gobble gob—

McDuff, impatient, even embittered, for he felt the injury of it, went into his stretch. Blake leaped up, grabbed a bat from the mad heap, came hopping, waddling, bounding, however the hell it was he moved, up to the plate to take his place. It turned out that the bat he'd picked up was one he'd broken in his earlier act. It was only about six inches long, the rest hanging from it as though by a thread. McDuff felt himself at the edge of tears. The crowd gobbled on, obscenely, delightedly. Blake took a preparatory backswing, and the dangling end of the bat arced around and hit him on the back of the head with a hollow exaggerated clunk. He fell across the plate. Even the umpire now was emitting frantic gobbling sounds and holding his trembling sides. Flynn the fat baserunner called time-out and came huffing and puffing in from first to resuscitate his teammate. McDuff, feeling all the strength go out of him, slumped despairingly off the mound. He picked up the resin bag and played with it, an old nervous habit that now did not relieve him.

His catcher Gus came out. "Gobble gobble," he said.

McDuff winced in hurt. "Gus, for God's sake, cut that out!" he cried. Jesus, they were all against him!

Gus laughed. "Whatsa matter, kid? These guys buggin' ya?" He glanced back toward the plate, where Flynn was practicing artificial respiration on Blake's ass end, sitting on Blake's small head. "It's all in the game, buddy. Don't forget: gobble and the world gobbles with ya! Yak yak!" McDuff bit his lip. Past happy

6

Gus, he could see Flynn listening to Blake's butt for a breath of life.

"Play baseball and you play with yourself," McDuff said sourly, completing Gus's impromptu aphorism.

"Yeah, you *got* it, kid!" howled Gus, jabbing McDuff in the ribs with his mitt, then rolling back onto the grass in front of the mound, holding his sides, giddy tears springing from his eyes, tobacco juice oozing out his cheeks.

There was a loud moist sound at the plate, like air escaping a toy balloon, and it was greeted by huzzahs and imitative noises from the stands. Flynn jumped up, lifted one of Blake's feet high in the air in triumph, and planted his fallen baseball cap in the clown's crotch, making Blake a parody of Blake, were such a thing absurdly possible. Cheers and courteous gobbling. Blake popped up out of the dust, swung at Flynn, hit the ump instead.

"Why don't they knock it off?" McDuff complained.

"Whaddaya mean?" asked Gus, now sober at his side.

"Why don't they just bring on Casey now and let me get it over with? Why do they have to push my nose in it first?"

"Casey!" Gus laughed loosely. "Never happen, kid. Blake puts on a big show, but he'd never hit you, baby, take it from old Gus. You'll get him and the game's over. Nothin' to it." Gus winked reassuringly, but McDuff didn't believe it. He no longer believed Gus was so goddamn innocent either.

Flynn was bounding now, in his apelike fashion, toward first base, but Blake had a grip on his suspenders. Flynn's short fat legs kept churning away and the dust rose, but he was getting nowhere. Then Blake let go—*whap!*— and Flynn blimped nonstop out to deep right field. Gobble gobble gobble. While Flynn was cavorting back in toward first, Blake, unable to find his own hat, stole the umpire's. It completely covered his small flat head, down to the goiter, and Blake staggered around blind, bumping into things. Gobble. The ump grabbed up Blake's cap from where it had fallen and planted it defiantly on his own head. A couple gallons of water flooded out and drenched him. Gobble. Blake tripped over home plate and crashed face first to the dirt again. The hat fell off. Gobble. The umpire took off his shoes and poured the water out. A fish jumped out of one of them. Gobble. Blake spied his own hat on the umpire's soggy head and went for it. Gobble. The ump relinquished it willingly, in exchange for his own. The ump was wary now, however, and inspected the hat carefully before putting it back on his head. He turned it inside out, thumped it, ran his finger around the lining. Satisfied at last, he put the hat on his head and a couple gallons of water flooded out on him. Gobble gobble said the crowd, and the umpire said: "PLAY BALL!"

Flynn was more or less on first, Blake in the box, the broken bat over his shoulder. McDuff glanced over toward the empty batter-up circle, then toward the Mudville dugout. Casey had not come out. Casey's style. And why should he? After all, Blake hadn't had a hit all season. Maybe in all history. He was a joke. McDuff considered walking Blake and getting it over with. Or was there any hope of that: of "getting it over with"? Anyway, maybe that's just what they wanted him to do, maybe it was how they meant to break him. No, he was a man meant to play this game, McDuff was, and play it, by God, he would. He stretched, glanced at first, studied Gus's signal, glared at Turkey Blake. The broken end of the bat hung down Blake's sunken back and tapped his bulbous rump. He twitched as though shooing a fly, finally turned around to see who or what was back there, feigned great surprise at finding no one. Gobble gobble. He resumed his batter's stance. McDuff protested the broken bat on the grounds it was a distraction and a danger to the other players. The umpire grumbled, consulted his rulebook. Gus showed shock. He came out to the mound and asked: "Why make it any easier for him, kid?"

"I'm not, Gus. I'm making it easier for myself." That seemed true, but McDuff knew Gus wouldn't like it.

"You are nuts, kid. Lemme tell ya. Plain nuts. I don't folla ya at all!" Blake was still trying to find out who or what was behind him. He poised very still, then spun around—the bat swung and cracked his nose: loud honking noise, chirping of birds, as Blake staggered around behind home plate holding his nose and splattering catsup all around. Gobble gobble gobble. Gus watched and grinned.

"I mean a guy who can't hit with a good bat might get lucky with a broken one," McDuff said. He didn't mean that at all, but he knew Gus would like it better.

"Oh, I getcha." Gus spat pensively. "Yeah, ya right." The old catcher went back to the plate, showed the ump the proper ruling, and the umpire ordered Blake to get a new bat. Gus was effective like that when he wanted to be. Why not all the time then? It made McDuff wonder.

Blake returned to the plate dragging Burrough's half-ton bat behind him. He tried to get it on his shoulder, grunted, strained, but he couldn't even get the end of it off the ground. He sat down under it, then tried to stand. Steam whistled out his nose and ears and a great wrenching sound was heard, but the bat stayed where it was. While the happy crowd once more lifted its humiliating chorus, Flynn called time-out and came waddling in from first to help. The umpire, too, lent a hand. Together, they got it up about as high as Blake's knees, then had to drop it. Exaggerated thud. Blake yelped, hobbled around grotesquely, pointing down at the one foot still shoed. The toe of it began to swell. The seams of the shoe split. A red bubble emerged, expanded threateningly: the size of a plum, a crimson baseball, grapefruit, volleyball, a red pumpkin. Larger and larger it grew. Soon it was nearly as big as Blake himself. Everyone held his ears. The umpire crawled down behind Flynn and then Flynn tried to crawl behind the umpire. It stretched, quivered. Strained. Flynn dashed over, and reaching into Blake's behind, seemed to pull something out. Sound of a cork popping from a bottle. The red balloon-like thing collapsed with a sigh. Laughter and relieved gobbling. Blake bent over to inspect his toe. Enormous explosion, blackening Blake's face. Screams and laughter.

Then Burroughs himself came out and lifted the half-ton bat onto Blake's shoulder for him. What shoulder he had collapsed and the bat slid off, upending Blake momentarily, so Burroughs next set it on Blake's head. The head was flat and, though precariously, held it. Burroughs lifted Blake up and set him, bat on head, in the batter's box. Blake under his burden could not turn his head to see McDuff's pitch. He just crossed his eyes and looked up at the bat. Gus crouched and signaled. McDuff, through bitter sweaty tears, saw that Flynn was still not back on first, but he didn't care. He stretched, kicked, pitched. Blake leaned forward. McDuff couldn't tell if he hit the ball with the bat or his head. But hit it he did, as McDuff knew he would. It looked like an easy pop-up to the mound, and McDuff, almost unbelieving, waited for it. But what he caught was only the cover of the ball. The ball itself was out of sight far beyond the mowed grass of left-center field, way back in the high weeds of the neighboring acreage.

McDuff, watching then for Casey to emerge from the Mudville dugout, failed at first to notice the hubbub going on around the plate. It seemed that the ump had called the hit a home run, and Gus was arguing that there were no official limits to the Mudville outfield and thus no automatic homers. "You mean," the umpire cried, "if someone knocked the ball clean to Gehenny, it still wouldn't be considered outa the park? I can't believe that!" Gus and the umpire fought over the rulebook, trying to find the right page. The three outfielders were all out there in the next acreage, nearly out of sight, hunting for the ball in the tall grass. "I can't believe that!" the umpire bellowed, and tore pages from the rulebook in his haste. Flynn and Blake now clowned with chocolate pies and waterpistols.

"Listen," said McDuff irritably, "whether it's an automatic home run or not, they still have to run the bases, so why don't they just do that, and then it won't matter."

Gus's head snapped up from his search in the rulebook like he'd been stabbed. He glared fiercely at McDuff, grabbed his arm, pushed him roughly back toward the mound. "Whatsa matter with you?" he growled.

"Lissen! I ain't runnin' off nowheres I ain't got to!" Flynn hollered, sitting down on a three-legged stool which Blake was pulling out from under him. "If it's automatic, I'll by gum walk my last mile at my own dadblame ease, thank ya, ma'am!" He sprawled.

"Of *course* it ain't automatic," Gus was whispering to McDuff.

"You know that as well as I do, Mac. If we can just get that ball in from the outfield while they're screwin' around, we'll tag *both* of 'em for good measure and get outa this friggin' game!"

McDuff knew this was impossible, he even believed that Gus was pulling his leg, yet, goddamn it, he couldn't help but share Gus's hopes. Why not? Anyway, he had to try. He turned to the shortstop and sent him out there with orders: *"Go bring that ball in!"*

The rulebook was shot. Pages everywhere, some tumbling along the ground, others blowing in the wind like confetti. The umpire, on hands and knees, was trying to put it all back together again. Gus held up a page, winked at McDuff, stuffed the page in his back pocket. Flynn and Blake used other pages to light cigars that kept blowing up in their faces. That does it, thought McDuff.

He looked out onto the horizon and saw the shortstop and the outfielders jumping up and down, holding something aloft. And then the shortstop started running in. Yet, so distant was he, he seemed not to be moving.

At home plate, the umpire had somehow discovered the page in Gus's back pocket, and he was saying: "I just can't believe it!" He read aloud: "'Mudville's field is open-ended. Nothing is automatic here, in spite of appearances. A ball driven even unto Gehenny is not necessarily a home run. In short, anything can happen in Mudville, even though most things are highly improbable. Blake, for example, has never had a hit, nor has Casey yet struck out.' And et cetera!" The crowd dutifully applauded the reading of the rulebook. The umpire shook his head. "All the way to Gehenny!" he muttered.

The baserunners, meanwhile, had taken off, and Turkey Blake was flapping around third on his way home, when he suddenly noticed that fat Flynn, who should be preceding him, was still grunting and groaning down the basepath toward first.

The shortstop was running in from the next acreage with the ball.

Blake galloped around the bases in reverse, meeting Flynn head-on with a resounding thud at first. Dazed, Flynn headed back toward home, but Blake set him aright on the route to second, pushed him on with kicks and swats, threw firecrackers at his feet. The fans chanted: *"Go! Go! Go!"*

The shortstop had reached the mowed edge of the outfield. McDuff hustled back off the mound, moved toward short to receive the throw, excitement grabbing at him in spite of himself.

Flynn fell in front of second, and Blake rolled over him. Blake jumped up and stood on Flynn's head. Honking noise. Flynn somersaulted and kicked Blake in the teeth. Musical chimes.

The shortstop was running in from deep left-center. *"Throw it!"* McDuff screamed, but the shortstop didn't seem to hear him. He ran, holding the ball high like a torch.

Flynn had Blake in a crushing bear-hug at second base, while Blake was clipping Flynn's suspenders. Blake stamped on Flynn's feet—sound of wood being crushed to pulp—and Flynn yowled, let go. Blake produced an enormous rocket. Flynn in a funk fled toward third, but his pants fell down, and he tripped.

The shortstop was still running in from the outfield. McDuff was shouting himself hoarse, but the guy wouldn't throw the goddamn ball. McDuff's heart was pounding and he was angry at finding himself so caught up in it all.

Flynn had pulled up his pants and Blake was chasing him with the rocket. They crashed into McDuff. He felt trampled and heard hooting and gobbling sounds. When the dust had cleared, McDuff found himself wearing Flynn's pants, ten sizes too large for him, and Blake's cap, ten sizes too small, and holding a gigantic rocket whose fuse was lit. Flynn, in the confusion, had gone to second and Blake to third. The fuse burned to the end, there was a little pop, the end of the rocket opened, and a little bird flew out.

The shortstop was running in, eyes rolled back, tongue lolling, drenched in sweat, holding the ball aloft.

Flynn and Blake discovered their error, that they'd ended up on the wrong bases, came running toward each other again. McDuff, foreseeing the inevitable, stepped aside to allow them to collide. Instead, they pulled up short and exchanged niceties.

"After *you*," said Blake, bowing deeply.

"No, no, dear fellow," insisted Flynn with an answering bow, "after *you!*"

The shortstop stumbled and fell, crawled ahead.

Flynn and Blake were waltzing around and around, saying things like "Age before beauty!" and "Be my guest!" and "Hope springs eternal in the human breast!", wound up with a chorus of "Take Me Out to the Ballgame!" with all the fans in the stands joining in.

The shortstop staggered to his feet, plunged, gasping, forward.

The umpire came out and made McDuff give Flynn his pants back. He took Blake's cap off McDuff's head, looked at it suspiciously, held it over his own head, and was promptly drenched by a couple gallons of water that came flooding out.

McDuff felt someone hanging limply on his elbow. It was the shortstop. Feebly, but proudly, he held up the baseball. Blake, of course, was safe on second, and Flynn was hugging third. The trouble is, thought McDuff, you musn't get taken in. You musn't think you've got a chance. That's when they really kill you. "All right," he said to Blake and Flynn, his voice choking up and sounding all too much like a turkey's squawk, "screw you guys!" They grinned blankly and there was a last dying ripple of mocking gobbling in the stands. Then: silence. Into it, McDuff dropped Blake's giant rocket. No matter what he might have hoped, it didn't go off. Then he turned to face the Man.

And now, it was true about the holler that came from the maddened thousands, true about how it thundered on the mountaintop and recoiled upon the flat, and so on. And it was true about Casey's manner, the maddening composure with which he came out to take his turn at bat. Or was that so, was it true at that? McDuff, mouth dry, mind awhirl, could not pin down his doubt. "Quit!" he said, but he couldn't, he knew, not till the side was out.

And Casey: who *was* Casey? A Hero, to be sure. A Giant. A figure of grace and power, yes, but wasn't he more than that? He was tall and mighty (omnipotent, some claimed, though perhaps, like all fans, they'd got a bit carried away), with a great moustache and a merry knowing twinkle in his eye. Was he, as had been suggested, the One True Thug? McDuff shook to watch him. He was ageless, older than Mudville certainly, though Mudville claimed him as their own. Some believed that "Casey" was a transliteration of the initials "K.C." and stood for King Christ. Others, of a similar but simpler school, opted for King Corn, while another group believed it to be a barbarism for Krishna. Some, rightly observing that "case" meant "event," pursued this reasoning back to its primitive root, "to fall," and thus saw in Casey (for a case was also a container) the whole history and condition of man, a history perhaps as yet incomplete. On the other hand, a case was also an oddity, was it not, and a medical patient, and maybe, said some, mighty Casey was the sickest of them all. Yet a case was an example, argued others, plight, the actual state of things, thus a metaphysical example, they cried—while a good many thought all such mystification was so much crap, and Casey was simply a good ballplayer. Certainly, it was true, he could belt the hell out of a baseball. All the way to Gehenny, as the umpire liked to put it. Anyway, McDuff knew none of this. He only knew that here he was, that here was Casey, and the stage was set. He didn't need to know the rest. Just that was enough to shake any man.

Gus walked out to talk to McDuff, while the first baseman covered home plate. Gus kept a nervous eye on Flynn and Blake. "How the hell'd you let that bum hit ya, Mac?"

"Listen, I'm gonna walk Casey," McDuff said. Gus looked pained. "First base is open, Gus. It's playing percentages."

"You and ya goddamn percentages!" snorted Gus. "Ya dumb or somethin', kid? Dontcha know this guy's secret?" Gus wasn't innocent, after all. Maybe nobody was.

"Yeah, I know it, Gus." McDuff sighed, swallowed. Knew all along he'd never walk him. Just stalling.

"Well, then, *kill* him, kid! You can do it! It's the only way!" Gus punctuated his pep talk with stiff jabs to McDuff's ribs. At the plate, Casey, responding to the thunderous ovation, lightly doffed his hat. They were tearing the stands down.

"But all these people, Gus—"

"Don't let the noise fool ya. It's the way they want it, kid."

Casey reached down, bat in his armpit, picked up a handful of dust, rubbed it on his hands, then wiped his hands on his shirt. Every motion brought on a new burst of enraptured veneration.

McDuff licked his dry lips, ground the baseball into his hip. "Do you really think—?"

"Take it from old Gus," said his catcher gently. "They're all leanin' on ya." Gus clapped him on the shoulder, cast a professional glance over toward third, then jogged splaylegged back to the plate, motioning the man there back to first.

Gus crouched, spat, lowered his mask; Casey swung his bat in short choppy cuts to loosen up: the umpire hovered. McDuff stretched, looked back at Blake on second, Flynn on third. Must be getting dark. Couldn't see their faces. They stood on the bags like totems. Okay, thought McDuff, I'll leave it up to Casey. I'm just not gonna sweat it (though in fact he had not stopped sweating, and even now it was cold in his armpits and trickling down his back). What's another ballgame? Let him take it or leave it. And without further wind-up, he served Casey a nice fat pitch gently down the slot, a little outside to give Casey plenty of room to swing.

Casey ignored it, stepped back out of the box, flicked a gnat off his bat.

"*Strike one!*" the umpire said.

Bottles and pillows flew and angry voices stirred the troubled air. The masses rose within the shadows of the stands, and maybe they'd have leapt the fences, had not Casey raised his hand. A charitable smile, a tip of the cap, a twirl of the great moustache. For the people, a pacifying gesture with a couple mighty fingers; for the umpire, an apologetic nod. And for McDuff: a strange sly smile and flick of the bat, as though to say . . . everything. McDuff read whole books into it, and knew he wasn't far from wrong.

This is it, Case, said McDuff to himself. We're here. And he fingered the resin bag and wiped the sweat and pretended he gave a damn about the runners on second and third and stretched and lifted his left leg, then came down on it easily and offered Casey the sweetest, fattest, purest pitch he'd ever shown a man. Not even in batting practice had he ever given a hitter more to swing at.

15

Casey only smiled.

And the umpire said: *"Strike two!"*

The crowd let loose a terrible wrathful roar, and the umpire cowed as gunfire cracked and whined, and a great darkness rose up and all the faces fell in shadows, and even Gus had lost his smile, nor did he wink at McDuff.

But Casey drew himself up with a mighty intake of breath, turned on the crowd as fierce as a tiger, ordered the umpire to stand like a man, and then even, with the sudden hush that fell, the sun came out again. And Casey's muscles rippled as he exercised the bat, and Casey's teeth were clenched as he tugged upon his hat, and Casey's brows were darkened as he gazed out on McDuff, and now the fun was done because Casey'd had enough.

McDuff, on the other hand, hadn't felt better all day. Now that the preliminaries were over, now that he'd done all he could do and it was on him, now that everybody else had got serious, McDuff suddenly found it was all just a gas and he couldn't give a damn. You're getting delirious, he cautioned himself, but his caution did no good. He giggled furtively: there's always something richly ludicrous about extremity, he decided. He stepped up on the rubber, went right into his stretch. Didn't bother looking at second and third: irrelevant now. And it was so ironically simple: all he had to do was put it down the middle. With a lot of stuff, of course, but he had the stuff. He nearly laughed out loud. He reared back, kicking high with his left, then hurtled forward, sent the ball humming like a shot right down the middle.

Casey's mighty cut split the air in two—*WHEEEEP!*— and when the vacuum filled, there was a terrible thunderclap, and some saw light, and some screamed, and rain fell on the world.

Casey, in the dirt, stared in open-jawed wonderment at his bat.

Gus plucked the ball gingerly out of his mitt, fingered it unbelievingly.

Flynn and Blake stood as though forever rooted at third and second, static parts of a final fieldwide tableau.

And forget what Gus said. No one cheered McDuff in Mudville when he struck Casey out.

JAY NEUGEBOREN

The Zodiacs

WHEN I WAS in the seventh grade at P.S. 92 in Brooklyn,
Louie Hirshfield was the only one of my friends who
wasn't a good ballplayer. Which is putting it mildly.
Louie was probably the worst athlete in the history of
our school. He was also the smartest kid in our class and you'd
think this combination would have made him the most unpopular
guy there, but it didn't. He wasn't especially well-liked, but
nobody resented him. Maybe it was because he let you copy from
his homework—or maybe it was just because he didn't put on any
airs about being smart. Louie didn't put on airs about anything. He
was one of the quietest kids I'd ever met.

The only time I ever saw him excited—outside of what happened with him and our baseball team—was when our fathers
would take the two of us to baseball games at Ebbets Field. Louie
lived one floor under me, in my apartment building on Lenox Road,
and we'd grown up together, so I knew lots about Louie that
nobody at school knew. He was an interesting guy, with lots of
hobbies—tropical fish, rocks, stamps, Chinese puzzles, magic tricks,
autographs.

Collecting autographs was the one thing the guys did know
about. I don't know how many days he'd waited outside Ebbets
Field to get them—all I know is he had the best collection of baseball
players' signatures of any guy in school. Lots of them were
addressed personally, too—like "To Louie, with best wishes from

Jackie Robinson." What amazed me most about Louie, though, was that he could figure out a player's batting average in his head. If a guy got a hit his first time up in a game, Louie would say, "That raises his average to .326"—or whatever it was—and sure enough, the next time the guy came up, when the announcer would give the average, Louie would be right.

Louie had no illusions about his athletic ability—he was never one of those guys who hangs around when you're choosing up sides for a punchball or stickball game so that you *have* to pick him. Whenever he did play—like in gym class at school—he did what you told him and tried to stay out of the way. That was why I was so surprised when he came up to my house one night after supper and asked if he could be on our baseball team.

"Gee, Louie," I said, "we got more than nine guys already—anyway, we're not even an official team or anything. We'll be lucky if we get to play more than five or six games all year."

"I don't really want to play," Louie said. "I—I just want to be on your team."

"Well, I suppose you can come to practices and games," I said. "But I can't promise you'll ever get in a game."

"Honest, Howie—I know all the guys on your team are better than me. I wasn't even thinking of playing.—What I'd like to do is be your general manager." His eyes lit up when he said that. I looked at him, puzzled.

"Look," he said. "What do you think makes the Dodgers draw almost as many fans as the Yankees? What was it that made people stick with the Dodgers when they were hardly in the league?"

"I don't know," I said. "They were just Dodger fans, I guess."

"Sure—that's it. Don't you see? Being a Dodger fan means something because being a Dodger means something colorful to the fans. And you know why? Because the Dodgers have what my dad calls 'a good press'—they know how to get headlines in the papers whether they're winning or losing."

I nodded. "But what's that got to do with us?"

"What's your team like now? I'll tell you. It's the same as ten thousand other teams of guys our age all over Brooklyn. Nobody cares if you win or lose—except maybe you guys. If I'm general manager, Howie, I promise you this—your team will be noticed. Guys won't say, 'We got a game with Howie's team.' They won't come to the Parade Grounds to see all the older guys play. They'll come to see *The Zodiacs!*"

"The who—?"

Louie stopped for a second and I realized that I'd never heard him speak so fast before. "That's—that's the first thing you have to do, it seems to me." He spoke more hesitantly now, the way he usually did, not looking right at you. "You have to have a name that's different."

"What's wrong with calling ourselves the Sharks?"

"Nothing's wrong with it—but don't you see, nothing's right with it, either. I'll bet there's a hundred teams in Brooklyn alone called the Sharks. Sharks, Tigers, Lions, Phantoms—every team has a name like that. But calling ourselves—I mean, your team—*The Zodiacs,* will make them different—"

"Sure—but giving us a crazy name isn't going to win us any games."

"Right. What will win you games? I'll tell you. A good pitcher. I've been going down to the Parade Grounds to watch games, making a study of the teams there, and I've found that pitching is about ninety percent of winning. Especially at our age, when we're not fully built up yet. Did you know, for example, that on high school teams pitchers average about eleven strike-outs a game? It's like with baseball teams in spring training—the pitchers are way ahead of the hitters, because the hitters' reflexes aren't developed yet."

"Izzie's a pretty good pitcher," I said. Izzie was my best friend, and the pitcher for our team.

"Sure, but let's face it, he's not a real top-drawer pitcher. He's just not big enough to be. He's got good control, I'll admit that—but his fast ball is almost a change-up. If you let me be general manager, Howie, I'll get the best pitcher in our school to play for us."

"Who's that?"

"George Santini."

I gulped. *"Him?"*

"That's right."

George Santini was a year ahead of us at P.S. 92 and he was always getting in trouble with the teachers and the cops. He was about six feet tall, had black greasy hair which was long and cut square in back, and the biggest pair of shoulders I'd ever seen on a guy. He was also the best athlete in our school. The coaches and teachers were always talking to him about going straight and being a star in high school and college, but George never seemed to care much. He was the leader of this gang, which, as far as everybody in our section of Brooklyn was concerned, was the most dangerous gang the world had ever known.

What made George's reputation even worse was his older brother, Vinnie. Vinnie was about nineteen years old and he'd already spent two years in jail. He was a skinny guy—not at all like George—and the word on him was that he was really chicken. To listen to George, though, you would have thought that Vinnie was the toughest guy ever to hit Brooklyn. Whenever he wanted an audience, George would sit down on the steps of the school—on Rogers Avenue—and start telling tales of all the jobs he and Vinnie had pulled off. Sometimes, if we'd bother him enough, he'd tell us about the gang wars he had fought in with Vinnie—in Prospect Park, in Red Hook, in Bay Ridge. If he was sure no teachers or cops were around he'd show us his zip gun, the gun that Johnny Angelo—one of George's lackeys—claimed George had once used to kill a guy with.

"I don't know," I said. "If my mother ever caught me hanging around with him, I'd really get it—and, anyway, how would you get him to play for us?"

Louie smiled. "You leave that to me."

A few days later I got all the guys together at my house and I let Louie speak to them. He told them what he'd told me about how he would make our team special, maybe famous—and he also told them that George Santini had agreed to pitch for us. A few of the guys reacted the way I did to this news—they were scared. But

20

when Louie insisted he'd be able to handle George, Izzie and I backed him up.

"I say it's worth a try," Izzie said. "Even though I'm pitcher and he'll take my place. I'll bet we could beat lots of high school teams with him pitching for us."

"Sure," I said. "You ever see the way he can blaze a ball in?"

A few more guys followed our lead, and after a while we all agreed that we'd probably be invincible with George Santini pitching for us.

"One thing, though," asked Kenny Murphy, our second baseman. "How'd you get him to play for us?"

"Simple," said Louie. "I offered him the one thing he couldn't refuse—fame. I told him I'd get his name in the newspapers. It's not hard. All you have to do is telephone in the box score to the *Brooklyn Eagle* and they'll print it. My father knows a guy who works there."

For the next few weeks Louie was the busiest guy in the world—calling up guys at other schools, arranging games, getting permits from the Park Department, coming to our practices . . . . When he started giving us suggestions on things, nobody objected either. He may have been a lousy ballplayer, but he knew more about the game than any of us. Izzie and I gave up playing basketball in the schoolyard afternoons and weekends and spent all our time practicing with *The Zodiacs*.

Our first game was scheduled for a Saturday morning the second week in April. Louie had gotten us a permit to use one of the diamonds at the Parade Grounds, next to Prospect Park, from nine to twelve in the morning, and we were supposed to play a team of eighth-graders from P.S. 246. I was at the field with Izzie by 8:30, but the other team didn't get there until after nine. We ran through infield practice and then let them have the field for a while. Kenny Murphy's father, who'd played for the Bushwicks when they were a semi-pro team, had agreed to umpire the game. By a quarter to ten neither Louie nor George had shown up and the other team was hollering that we were afraid to play them.

Since George had never come to any practices, some of us were

21

a little worried, but at about five to ten he showed up. He was wearing a baseball hat like the rest of us, with a Z sewn on the front, and he looked a little embarrassed. He was smoking and he didn't say much to anybody. He just asked who the catcher was and started warming up. He wore a T-shirt, with the sleeves cut off. Looking at him, you would have thought he was too muscle-bound to be a pitcher, but when he reared back and kicked his left foot high in the air, then whipped his arm around, he was as smooth as Warren Spahn, only righty, with the natural straight overhand motion that every coach spends his nights dreaming about. Stan Reiss, our catcher, had to put an extra sponge in his mitt, but he was so proud, catching George with all the guys looking at the two of them, that I think he would have let the ball burn a hole in his hand before he would have given up his position.

"C'mon," George said after a dozen or so warm-ups. "Let's get the game going."

"We were waiting for Louie," I said. "He should be here any minute."

"Okay," George said. "But he better hurry. I got better things to do than spend all day strikin' out a bunch of fags."

He said the last thing loudly, for the benefit of the other team. Then he turned and spit in their direction, daring one of them to contradict him. No one did.

A minute later I saw Louie. He was getting out of his mother's car, on Caton Avenue, and he was carrying this tremendous thing. From my position at shortstop I couldn't make it out, but as he came nearer, running awkwardly and holding it in front of him like a package of groceries, I realized what it was: his old victrola.

"Hey, George!" Louie called. "You ready to break Feller's strike-out record?"

George laughed. "Anytime they get in the batter's box—"

"Wait a second," Louie said. He put the victrola down next to the backstop. He started fiddling with it, cranking it up the way you had to to get it to work, and then he started playing a record. At first it wasn't cranked up enough and you couldn't tell what kind of music it was. But then Louie cranked some more—and I whipped

22

off my hat and stood at attention as the strains of "The Star-Spangled Banner" came blasting across the infield. I looked at George and he was smiling as broadly as he could, holding his cap across his heart, standing rigid, at attention. The team from P.S. 246 must have been as shocked as we were, but by the time the music got to "and the rockets' red glare" both teams were standing at attention, saluting, listening, while Louie kept cranking away so that the music wouldn't slow down. People sitting on benches, guys playing on other diamonds, men and women walking along Caton Avenue, a few park cops—they all stopped and started drifting toward our diamond. When the record was over, Louie—in the loudest voice I'd ever heard—shouted "Play ball!" and we started the game. We must have had a crowd of over fifty people watching us play our first game, and I told myself that if George had been pitching for a Major League team that day he would have pitched at least a shut-out.

He struck out all but two of their men—one guy hit a grounder to me at shortstop, and another fouled out to Corky Williams at first base. He also hit four home runs. I got a double and two singles, I remember. We won, 19–0, and the next day, as Louie'd promised, our box score was in the *Brooklyn Eagle*.

Louie got us six more games during the next two weeks, and we won all of them. George gave up a total of seven hits in the six games, and he was a pretty happy guy during that time. He had clippings of the box scores of all the games in his wallet, the way we all did. Clippings of the box scores—and then, the first week in May, the best clipping of all: an item in Jimmy O'Brien's column in the *Brooklyn Eagle* about our team, mentioning George, and Louie's victrola. I think I carried that clipping around with me until my third year in high school.

After that we began getting even more attention and teams from all over Brooklyn were challenging us to games. We played as many of them as we could—and George kept shutting out every team we played.

In the meantime Louie devised another plan. He called a meeting of the team the second week in May to discuss it. He told us that a team with our ability and prestige had to live up to its name. We said we were—we were winning games, weren't we?

"Sure," Louie said. "But what do you look like out on the field? People are starting to come in pretty large numbers to see us play—they hear about us, we got a reputation—and then when they see us, we look like a bunch of pick-ups." He lowered his voice and went on. "What we have to do," he said, "is develop some class. And I've got the plan worked out. It's not new, I'll admit—lots of the high school guys use it. I say we run a raffle and use the money to buy ourselves jackets and uniforms."

We all liked the idea of jackets and uniforms, naturally, but they cost a lot of money—especially the kind of uniforms and jackets we wanted to have.

"I got it all figured out," Louie said, pulling out some pieces of paper. Then he started talking about numbers, and once he did that, I knew we'd get those uniforms and jackets. It turned out that Louie could get a clock radio at a discount from an uncle of his. Then he said he could get Levy's Sporting Goods Store, on Flatbush Avenue, to donate a glove and ball for the raffle. He also said they'd sell us the uniforms and jackets at cost if Jimmy O'Brien would mention them in his column sometime. Louie said his father could take care of that. We'd make the radio first prize and the glove and ball second prize, but we'd tell the kids at school that if they won first prize we'd give them the glove and ball anyway. There were fifteen of us and if we each sold five books of ten chances at a quarter apiece, that'd be almost two hundred dollars. Louie said that he himself would sell at least fifteen books, and he expected most of us to sell more than five. If we took in three hundred dollars in the raffle, we could have the uniforms and jackets.

George was at the meeting this time—in Louie's house—and he volunteered to get his gang to sell chances. All of us were pretty glad then that we'd be on the selling end of the raffle during the next few weeks. Louie smiled and said he'd already had the raffle books printed and that the drawing would take place on Friday afternoon, June 1. On June 2, we all knew, we had a big game with the Flatbush Raiders, a team from P.S. 139 that had lost only one game. Louie said that if we could give Levy's a down payment of one hundred dollars they'd go ahead and get the uniforms and jackets made in time for the game against the Raiders.

We only had two games during the next week, and the rest of the time all of us were running around getting everybody we knew—friends, relatives, neighbors, teachers, store owners—to buy chances. By the following Friday, Louie reported that we had more than a hundred dollars and that Levy's had already started making the uniforms and jackets. The uniforms would be gray with orange lettering and the jackets were going to be made of an orange and black material that felt like satin, with *The Zodiacs* written across the back in bright yellow.

By the middle of the following week Louie reported to us that if we went over three hundred dollars—and it looked like we would—the extra money would be used to get Louisville Sluggers and official National League baseballs for the team. Louie also told us that his father could probably get Jimmy O'Brien to come down to see our game against the Raiders.

On Wednesday afternoon, two days before the raffle drawing, Louie rode out on his bicycle to Marine Park, where the Raiders were playing a game, and when he showed up at our big meeting on Friday, June 1, he had a stack of scouting notes.

"Before we get to our skull session on the Raiders," he said, "we have to get this raffle business over with. First, some of you haven't given me all the money—or the leftover raffles."

While Louie took care of the final accounts on the raffle, George stayed by himself in a corner, looking through Louie's sports magazines. Although he spoke to a few of us a little more, you couldn't really say that any of us had become pals with him. At school he stayed pretty much with his gang, and after school—on the days when we didn't have games—we knew that he still hung around with his brother.

"Okay," said Louie. "I got it all figured out. Just a few things don't check. You, Marty, you took out seven books and only gave me fifteen dollars."

"I forgot," Marty said. He handed Louie a book of tickets. "I didn't sell these."

Louie crossed his name off. He seemed to be stalling, because he kept adding and subtracting figures and I knew that he never had that much trouble figuring things out.

"George?"

"Yeah?"

"According to my records you gave me raffle stubs from sixteen books, which means you owe forty dollars."

"So?"

"You only gave me twenty-eight so far."

We were all quiet. George wasn't looking straight at Louie. He had a magazine out, with a picture of Sal Maglie on the cover, and he made believe he was thumbing through it.

"Maybe you didn't give me sixteen books," George said.

"I did. It's right here in writing."

"Hell, anybody can phony up figures."

"I didn't phony them up." Louie's voice was loud. "You still owe twelve dollars."

"Prove it."

"Prove it? It's down here in black and white."

"Oh yeah? My word's as good as yours."

"It's not!"

"Are you callin' me a liar?" George stood up now and walked toward Louie.

"I'm just saying you owe twelve dollars. You better pay up, or—"

"Or what, smarty?"

"Or—" Louie stopped. "—Or you can't play tomorrow."

George laughed. But his laugh was forced. "Who needs to play with you guys, anyway? You can't win without me and you know it."

"You pay up or you don't play. I mean it, George. You won't get your uniform and you won't get to play in front of Jimmy O'Brien either . . ."

"I don't give a damn," George said. He walked up to Louie and pushed his fist at Louie's face. Louie didn't move. This surprised

George. "I never should of given you the twenty-eight dollars either. And you know what you can do with your raffle—"

George didn't finish his sentence. Instead, he picked up the clock radio, raised it over his head, and then flung it to the floor, splattering its parts all over the room. Louie leapt at George, screaming curse words, but with an easy push George shoved him to the floor. Then he kicked him a few times and Louie started crying. He got up and went for George again, and this time I was ready. I grabbed George's right arm.

"C'mon, you guys, help me hold him." Izzie jumped on George's back and got him in a stranglehold. George tried to throw him off, but by this time Kenny and Corky and Stan and the other guys were all holding George. He fought and it took all our strength to hold him, but it was fifteen to one and these odds were too much, even for him.

"C'mon, Louie," I said. "Give it to him now."

"Yeah, c'mon," the guys yelled. "Let him have it ... right in the gut ... he deserves it ... give it to him good ..."

Louie was still crying, but he came at George. "You're—you're nothing but a *bum!*" he screamed.

George spit at him.

"C'mon," Kenny said. "We can't hold him all day. Just give it to him—"

"Yeah, c'mon, ya little sawed-off runt—I hear they're gettin' up a girls' team at school for you to play on."

"You're just a big bum," Louie said, whimpering. He was breathing heavily. "I wouldn't waste my knuckles on you. Just get out of my house. Get out. We—we don't need crooks on *The Zodiacs.* Get out. Get out ..." Then Louie started crying again. We all pushed and pulled George to the door and somehow we managed to slam it with him on the other side.

We ran off the raffle anyway. Louie said the money that was going to go for bats and balls would be enough to get another radio—and a few hours later we left Louie's apartment. I was glad I lived in his building.

The next morning there were over two hundred people gathered around the backstop and baselines at the Parade Grounds. Izzie warmed up and he looked good. I think the new uniforms made us all play a little over our heads that day. The pitcher on the Raiders was very fast, and our only chance, we knew, was if his control was off.

When Louie cranked up his victrola before the game, most of the onlookers started laughing. We ignored them. In fact, I think hearing the National Anthem, the way we had in all our other games, made us play even harder, because in the first inning Izzie held the other team and, in our half, Kenny Murphy doubled and then I hit a single which drove him in. That was the last time we had the lead, though. The Raiders tied it up in the third inning and went ahead in the fourth, by 4–1. The final score was 7–2.

When we were picking up our gloves and stuff, and changing out of our spikes, nobody said anything. And nobody looked at Louie. We waited for each other and were walking away from the diamond when Stan spotted George.

"Uh-oh," he said, pointing. "He's got his gang with him."

We all looked and we saw about ten of them—all in motorcycle jackets and pegged pants.

"Hey," George shouted, coming nearer. "Ain't those guys got pretty uniforms."

"Yeah," said one of his guys. "And look at those jackets. They look like my mommy's underwear—"

This seemed to strike George's gang as a pretty good joke.

"Hey, you bunch of fags," George said. "Who won the game?"

Nobody answered. George and his gang had almost reached us now.

"Aw, c'mon—you don't mean you let those other fruitboots beat you, do you? How could anybody beat a team that's got a manager like Louie? He's real smart, ain't he?"

George was in front of us now, about fifteen feet from Louie, his hands on his hips. Louie stopped.

"C'mon, smart boy. Cross my path, I dare you—"

"Don't do it, Louie!" I shouted. I looked around, hoping a policeman was nearby. Louie put down his victrola.

"I don't want any trouble," he said.

"Hey, listen to this, guys. He says he don't want no trouble. Ain't that nice. I don't want none either, see. Only I say you called me a liar and a crook and I don't take that from nobody."

"I—I didn't mean to call you that," Louie said. "Why don't we just forget the whole thing."

"I don't forget easy."

I was holding one of the bats and I gripped the handle firmly. The other guys had already let their gloves and equipment drop onto the grass. I spotted a cop about a half block away. He was moving toward us. I tried to stall.

"What's the gripe, George?" I asked. "You mad 'cause you didn't get to pitch today?"

"You keep your trap shut, Howie. Can't Louie fight his own battles—?"

"We just don't want any trouble, that's all."

The guys in George's gang began to move toward us and then George shoved Louie. I ran at him, the bat raised over my head. "We got bats, George. One of you is gonna get a bloody head."

"You don't scare us with your toothpicks!"

Somebody grabbed my arm and then the fight was on. It didn't last long—probably less than a minute—but by the time the cop got there and started bopping guys on the head with his nightstick most of us, myself included, were glad it was over. I had managed to get a leg-scissors on George and even though he was blasting me in the gut I held on long enough so he couldn't get at Louie. More cops were on the scene by then and when we were separated they asked the usual questions about who had started the fight. When they saw that nobody was going to give them any answers, they told us to beat it.

"Okay, all of you—get on home. You, kid," the cop said, pointing to Kenny. "You better get some ice on that eye in a hurry."

George's gang started to move away, and then George turned and called to us. "We'll get you guys at school—"

One of the cops ran after George and grabbed him by the front of his jacket. "Okay, tough boy," he said. "If I find out that one hair

29

on the head of any of these kids was touched, I'll throw you and every one of your cronies in jail. You hear that?"

George nodded.

"Hey," the cop said suddenly. "I know you. You're George Santini, ain't you? Vinnie Santini's brother—"

"So what?" George tried to squirm out of the cop's grip.

"It figures," the cop laughed. "He's that punk we had down at the station last week. I never seen a guy turn yellow so quick."

"*It's a lie!*" George shouted. He almost broke away. "You shut your damned mouth!"

George kicked at the cop and the cop whacked him across the arm with his club. Another cop held George while the first cop put his nose right up to George's face and continued. "I never seen a guy turn yellow so quick," he said. "We didn't have the light on him more than ten minutes when he started ratting on every petty thief this side of Bensonhurst. And you're probably the same."

George didn't say anything. He just sort of hung there, held up by the cop. "Get goin', punk," said the cop, shoving George. "And I better not hear that you touched these kids."

George and his gang walked away. We all picked up our stuff, Kenny and Marty carrying Louie's victrola, and then suddenly Louie started running after George. "Hey, wait a minute! Wait—"

George turned and waited till Louie caught up to him. "Yeah?" George said.

Louie stopped, as if he'd forgotten why he had told George to wait. Then he spoke, in that slow, hesitant way of his. "I was going over the records last night," he said. "And I discovered that I made a mistake yesterday. You really only owed eight dollars. I was thinking that if you gave me the eight dollars, then—then you could pitch for us against the Raiders. We play them a return game next week."

"Who'd wanna play on your sissy team?" said one of the guys in George's gang.

George looked at Louie, then at the guys in the gang, then back at Louie. "I'll let you know," he said, and walked off.

The next day he gave Louie the eight dollars. On the following

Saturday, with George pitching and wearing his new uniform, we beat the Raiders, 4–0. We were the happiest group of guys in Brooklyn, George included. We won about a dozen more games that month. At the end of June, though, lots of the guys, myself included, went away to camp or to the country and the team had to break up. The next year when George was a freshman at Erasmus Hall High School he didn't play for us.

When he was a sophomore at Erasmus—I was a freshman that year—he played fullback on the football team and was starting pitcher on the baseball team. In the middle of his junior year, though, he quit school. The next time I heard about him, somebody said he had taken off for Florida with his brother.

W. P. KINSELLA

Lumpy Drobot, Designated Hitter

I F THERE'S ANYTHING I hate more than my nickname, it's my manager, the guy who hung it on me.

Lumpy.

Lumpy Drobot, designated hitter.

"Lumpy runs with all the speed of water finding its own level," the manager is saying to a reporter from the local newspaper. Then he guffaws, spraying spit. He was a shortstop in the Bigs for seven years, a powderpuff hitter, but feisty and mean-spirited, nicknamed "Surgeon" because he spiked more runners sliding into second than anybody else in his era—that's why Cleveland kept him in their organization, made him a manager. And when he was running out an infield hit, his filed spikes would land like a cat on the instep of any first baseman who didn't get out of his way. The rumor is that the day he spiked Johnny Mize for the second time in a game, Mize waited for him under the grandstand, which explains why the Surgeon's nose is crooked and leans dangerously to the left, as if it might tip over.

He called me Lumpy even before I got hit-by-pitcher five times in five games. He called me Lumpy to be mean—to motivate me. The Surgeon's theory is that if us players hate him enough, we'll play well to spite him, we'll play so well we'll get moved up to Triple A and away to hell from him, and from his drinking buddy, our pitching coach, Beanball Monaghan, who, if anything, is meaner than the Surgeon. That's what he figures.

The Surgeon is sixty-seven years old. The reporter asks him why he's managing here in the boonies in Double A when he earned enough money in his career, and has had enough years in management, that he could afford to retire comfortably.

"Baseball kind of gets under your skin," he says, and guffaws spit past the reporter, who has learned not to stand in front of him when doing an interview. The reporter doesn't notice that the Surgeon is glancing sneakily at me all the time he's answering the question. Figures he's smart, the Surgeon does.

I've never been crazy about Drobot as a name. But I was born to it; it's a good Polish name and I wouldn't change it, even though when I was in grade school the kids used to call me Drobot the robot and stupid things like that. John is a nice, neutral first name, and Stanley isn't the worst second name I could have. When I proved myself a star hitter in high school some of the guys took to calling me Stan the Man, after Musial the most famous Polish baseball player of all, and I certainly didn't mind that. My old man called me Stash, but only at home, he knew it embarrassed me if he yelled it out at a game, or used it when my friends were around. The old man knew I had feelings; knew I was a human being.

But not my manager. The day I reported to the Double A franchise in Chattanooga, he wandered into the locker room, looked me up and down and said, "Drobot, I hear you run with all the speed of shit moving through a long dog."

After everybody had stopped laughing I said, "You hear wrong. I'm not that fast." And I put out my hand to shake, but he ignored it.

"Listen, you lumpy son of a bitch," he said, "you better be one hell of a designated hitter, 'cause you sure don't look fit for nothin' else." Then he guffawed, spraying brown spit.

I have to admit the Surgeon was ahead of his time. He called me Lumpy before I decided that getting hit-by-pitcher was the way to make a name for myself. Before the miracle.

I am Lumpy. I admit that. I'm 5'7", 190 lbs., and never would have made it as a professional baseball player if it wasn't for the designated hitter rule. Because of my size I just can't cover much ground in the outfield, and I'm too short to be a first baseman, so that leaves designated hitter or nothing. Being a designated hitter is something I'm good at; I've never hit below .300 and I've got good power to all fields. I can stay with an outside pitch and slap it off, or over, the right-field wall. I love the feel of connecting solidly with the ball, knowing by the tingle that begins in my hands, and runs up my arms like electricity, that the ball will clear the fence, that I can stand for a second and watch it go, knowing I can relax and not have to chug around the bases like an overheated engine, but that I can ease into a home run trot, my extra weight bobbing over my belt. I hit .331 my first two weeks with Chattanooga, but the Surgeon wasn't happy.

"Your on-base percentage is too low," the Surgeon barked at me the morning after I'd hit a two-run homer in the bottom of the 10th inning to win a game for us.

"You're short," he hollered, as if I didn't know that already. "Short-assed players need to draw a lot of walks. Your strike zone is too big. And a short, lumpy bastard like you should get hit-by-pitcher more often. When they come inside on you, don't back off, you've got bones like fucking plumbing pipes, you can take a shot without breaking anything. You're built like Don Baylor, only shorter and lumpier."

He sure knew how to make a young ballplayer feel good about himself, but some of what he said stayed with me, and the next time I came up with the bases loaded, when the pitcher came in on me I stood my ground. I took one on the left bicep, trotted to first as the go-ahead run crossed the plate. And the Surgeon was right, even though the ball had hit me solidly the pain was hardly noticeable.

As I took a short lead off first, I remembered something I'd heard back in Legion ball—little guys have to prove they belong, while big guys belong until they prove they can't play. Well, I thought, I'll always be a little guy, nothin' I can do about that. So I'm gonna do whatever I have to to prove that I belong. If it means gettin' hit, it means gettin' hit.

"Easiest RBI I ever got," I said to a reporter after the game.

"Guess the skipper hollered 'Get a hit,' but I thought he said 'Get hit!'"

"Lumpy here is doing what he has to do to win ballgames," the Surgeon said to the reporter, clapping me on my bruised arm.

I'm gonna hate my way right up to Triple A and the Bigs, I said to myself.

The next morning my name appeared in the newspaper as John "Lumpy" Drobot, by the end of the next week the John had been dropped and I was plain Lumpy, without quotation marks. My teammates started to call me Lumpy, too, hollering from the dugout, "Get a hit, Lump," or "Bang it out there, Lumpy." And from the far corner of the bench I'd hear the Surgeon's high-pitched, piercing voice, "Get on base you lumpy son of a bitch."

Over the next few weeks I became fearless at the plate. I'd crowd the plate, daring the pitcher to throw at me. It was a real feeling of power. Me, John Stanley Drobot, was intimidating pitchers. If they tried to move me off the plate I'd just turn into the pitch and take my base. If the pitch was outside I'd take it for a ball. If it was over the plate I'd hammer it.

In spite of my success, a .300+ batting average, lots of walks, and being hit-by-pitcher 12 times, I wasn't happy. The Surgeon still treated me like I smelled bad, while his buddy, Beanball Monaghan the pitching coach, ridiculed me at every opportunity. I didn't have a friend on the team.

Everyone came to call me Lumpy. All except the Christians. They never called me Lumpy; they called me John; the Christians were this little clique of players who wouldn't say shit if their mouths were full of it. They addressed *me* as John, and none of *them* had nicknames; they were Dean, Robert, Alvin, Vernon, all guys who could slide into second base without getting their uniforms dirty.

They belonged to something called A*C*E, Athletes of Christian Endeavor. These guys got together and prayed in the corner of the locker room before every game. They praised the Lord if they made the game-winning hit and said it was God's will if they butchered a double play ball to allow the opposition to score the winning run.

The Surgeon hated them at least as much as he hated me, maybe more, because though they did everything they were told—never sulked, never talked back, never cursed or fought, or got arrested, or sneaked girls into their rooms, or stayed out after curfew—they didn't accept the Surgeon's word as final authority. When the Surgeon ranted and raved and called one of them out for a mistake, the offender nodded and smiled, but didn't play any differently the next game.

Our pitching coach, Beanball Monaghan, had been hand picked by the Surgeon. They were longtime friends. In his playing days, Beanball Monaghan had been busting skulls in Triple A for a couple of years, and was on his way to the Bigs when, one night in Columbus, his inside fastball ruptured the ear drum of the Yankees' number one draft choice.

The number one draft choice never played again, and in what seemed an uncharacteristic move, the Yankees bought Beanball Monaghan's contract from Oakland for a lot of money, demoted him to Double A, and left him there to rot for his whole career, refusing to trade or promote him. They figured the best punishment was for him to get paid peanuts for being a star in Double A, while, just in case he went stagnant, they continually hinted that he was about to be forgiven and promoted, or traded to a team who would promote him. I could understand why *he* had the personality of a buzzsaw.

When the Christians would get together to pray before a game, the Surgeon and Beanball Monaghan would stare at them like they were some kind of exotic animals; then management in tandem would spit darkly on the locker room floor and stalk off to the field, their cleats grinding on the cement.

One of the Athletes of Christian Endeavor was named Angel Correa; his first name was pronounced Ann-jell, and though he was a sensational shortstop he spoke little English, and was more fervent than the other Christians in his dedication.

One night, after making the game-winning hit and being interviewed on the field after the game, I returned to the locker room just in time to see Beanball Monaghan take hold of Angel Correa by the gold chains around the shortstop's neck. Correa had the unfortunate habit of going around the clubhouse after a game, handing out three-colored religious tracts, small as credit cards.

"Hey, you habla the English there, Chico?" said Monaghan.

Correa squeaked. His answer could have been either yes or no.

"Don't matter. Even if you don't understand all the words you'll get my drift," and he raised Correa another foot off the floor and held him at arm's length.

"Now I don't want you to take this personal, boy, and I sure wouldn't want you to consider this an infringement on your civil rights. I know that freedom of religion gives you the right to believe in whatever damn fool thing you choose to believe in. However, personally, I feel that freedom of religion also encompasses freedom from religion, and that's what I want to discuss with you."

Correa, whose skin was very black, seemed to be developing a bluish tinge.

"So, if y'all want to live long and die happy and don't want your carcass nailed to the clubhouse wall, you'll never flash any of that literature around here again. The only time I want you to speak to me is if you need advice on throwing the curveball, but since you're a shortstop, I don't expect you'll ever need that advice. And. . ." he paused and shook Correa side to side a few times, "if you ever tell another reporter that it was the Lord's will that you popped up with the bases loaded to end the game, I'll personally cut your life expectancy by about 57 years."

Shaking Correa one more time he set him down, and when he noticed the shortstop's knees buckle as his feet touched the floor he laid him carefully on the cool concrete, smiled amiably and made his way to his own locker.

When a player is a long way from home and when his manager and coach, who, at least in the minor leagues, are supposed to be sort of father figures, hate him, he has to turn somewhere. Some of the players pounded the Bud, some had wives or girlfriends they could turn to for comfort, confide in, sometimes abuse. I didn't drink, or have a girlfriend. But with events taking the turns they were, I needed a friend, but friends were few and far between. Yet, when I looked around there were the guys from A*C*E, just waiting, ready and willing as fly paper.

I reached out a hand, tentatively, and once they had me, like fly paper, they wouldn't let me go.

"I'm gonna turn crazy if I don't talk to somebody," I said to a lanky outfielder named Robert Eager. We were dressing in the locker room. "You guys seem to have a cozy little group. What do I have to do?"

One of the other members of A*C*E was standing behind me, combing his brick-colored hair down across his forehead. His name was Vernon Smith and he was a freckled, horse-faced third baseman with a slow, Texas drawl.

"Y'all don't have to *do* anything," said Smith. "Come along with us, we're headin' over to the Perkin's Steak and Cake for a bite to eat."

"I could eat me a buffalo," said the fourth member of A*C*E, a relief pitcher with the unlikely name of Dean Breadfollow.

"I don't know," I said. There was something *too* nice about them; that made me suspicious.

"You don't have to be afraid of us," said Robert Eager. "We're not much different than anybody else, except we believe our lives are guided by the Lord. We're merely vessels, listening vessels," he went on. "Come along with us. You obviously need somebody to talk to, and we're good listeners."

"Good listen, man," said Angel Correa, who appeared from nowhere, dressed in a silver shirt, a half dozen gold chains around his neck.

"I promise you, John, no one's going to try to convert you to anything," said Smith. By calling me John he had already won me over. I'd been Lumpy to everyone for the past several weeks.

And they kept their word. The five of us went to Perkin's and chowed down. I laughed for the first time in weeks.

"What's bothering you?" Robert Eager asked. "What is it you really want to know?"

"I don't understand why I'm doing what I'm doing. Am I punishing myself by getting hit all the time? Or am I just so ambitious that I'll do anything to succeed? Or. . ?"

Vern Smith cut me off.

"We believe there's an answer to every question somewhere in the Scriptures." He held up his well-thumbed Bible. "Let's just do a little exploring together. We'll start in the obvious place, the Book of John."

That evening and the next we read through several chapters of John, but nothing, even when we stretched our imaginations to the utmost, seemed to apply to me.

It was Angel Correa who suggested Revelations.

"Written by St. John the Evangelist," said Correa, smiling, pleased at his knowledge.

I'd gone two for three that evening, and been hit twice, once on the thigh, once in the ribs on my left side.

It was while reading the second chapter of Revelations that, like pieces of a puzzle, like tumblers of a lock clicking into place, some answers seemed to appear. The second and third chapters of Revelations are John's letters to seven different churches.

In each of the seven letters there were admonitions to those who had sinned, but also in each letter rewards were offered "to him who overcomes." It was one of those "rewards" that Robert Eager seized on. And it seemed so right. I know this will sound odd, but we were all really tired after a long road trip and an extra-inning game. And as Vern Smith said, his face shining, "There is no accounting for *fervor*."

"'He who overcomes shall be arrayed in white garments, and I will not blot his name out of the book of life. . .'" read Robert Eager.

"Amen to that," shouted Correa.

"The home team uniform," said Dean Breadfollow, making one of his infrequent comments.

"Sure," said Bob Eager.

It seemed logical to me. Our home uniforms *were* a blazing white.

"What is it you hate most about what's happening to you?" asked Vern Smith. It was the next evening and we were all in Robert Eager's tiny basement room.

"My name," I said without hesitation. "Nobody likes to be called Lumpy."

"Then listen to this," said Vernon Smith. "Revelations 2:17 'To him who overcomes I will give him a white stone, and in the stone a new name written, which no one knows except him who receives it.'"

"That's what I need," I said. "A new name."

"A white stone?" said Angel Correa.

"A baseball," said Robert Eager. "As you must well know, they're hard as stone when you get hit," he said to me.

"Spalding?" said Vern Smith.

"My new name will be Spalding?"

We all laughed uproariously. In our own way we were high as the players who drank too much, or smoked dope.

"Lumpy Spalding," I said, as we all doubled over with laughter.

"Spalding Drobot," said Robert Eager.

"Sounds like something from a snooty prep school, Spalding Drobot, counselor at law."

"Or the handsome hero of a romance novel. 'Spalding Drobot crushed Melanie's pale body in his tanned, handsome arms.'" We shrieked like grade schoolers.

"Actually Rawlings makes the baseballs these days, and they're manufactured in Haiti on assembly lines manned by relatives of Papa Doc Duvalier," said Robert Eager.

We kept on laughing. Dean Breadfollow read from another chapter in Revelations, and I have to admit that in the heat of the moment it made sense. "'To him who overcomes I will give

41

authority over nations.'"

"You'll become Commissioner of Baseball in Japan. . ."

". . .Or Cuba."

". . .Or the Dominican."

". . .Or Haiti. They don't play baseball in Haiti. They play soccer. They'll make you Commissioner of Soccer for Haiti."

"There *is* an answer to every question," intoned Robert Eager, trying to bring us back to earth. I could picture him in years to come as the evangelist he planned to be, arms raised high, exhorting Jees–HUS to perform miracles. And he'll have a pretty wife, and several pretty children behind him, all dressed in white, and he'll own a cat named Lefty as his one concession to being a baseball player in his youth.

The emanation of the miracle began about the twentieth time I got hit-by-pitcher (a reporter later pointed out to me it was the twenty-fifth), but it was the strangest and the most painful. The fans roared as the pitch hit me; I was fast becoming a minor celebrity. ("A geek who bites the heads off live chickens is a minor celebrity," Robert Eager had pointed out to me a few days earlier.) I was batting left handed; the count was 0–2, and the next pitch tailed in on me at the last second. I could have gotten out of the way, but I helped things along by almost stepping into it, in order to protect my neck, which is where I thought it was headed. I took the pitch full on the right bicep, midway between elbow and shoulder. As good a place as any to be hit.

But that time being hit felt incredibly strange. Instead of the dull pain of ball bruising muscle, intimidating bone, it was as though the ball had exploded when it struck me. It felt like what I imagined a shotgun blast might feel like. I could feel the shards, like tiny needles, spray to the furthest points in my body. My scalp prickled, my fingers tingled, my tongue felt as if I had bitten it sharply.

I went down as the pitch hit me, but bounced to my feet quickly. Ballplayers are taught to be macho about being hit by a pitch. In spite of wanting to run off to first base I stood stunned for several seconds, trying to get my bearings, trying to understand why I hurt all over instead of just at the point of impact.

I used every ounce of self control to keep from rubbing the spot. I waived off the trainer who was lumbering toward me, carrying a can of spray to deaden the pain.

My arm was sore and slightly swollen after the game. I didn't look at it too closely, there was no reason to; there was the beginnings of a bruise, a small mottled area with pinpricks of red and blue, like a huge, superficial vaccination mark. But instead of clearing up in a few days, the way a bruise should have, it stayed sore. I could feel the soreness through my uniform; I could feel the swelling and feel my pulse throbbing in the wounded area.

It was about the fifth day after being hit that, in the shower, I touched the swollen area with my fingertips, felt the puffiness on my upper arm, then looked closely at it. What I saw frightened me, but because of the steam in the shower I couldn't be certain of what I had seen. When I got to my room I checked the arm carefully. The skin was puffed up nearly an inch and the seams of a baseball were clearly visible on my bruised skin.

A week later, the next time we played Knoxville, their catcher told me they never found the ball that hit me, the one that felt as though it disintegrated and entered my body, the ball that, though I hate to use the word, impregnated me.

"I thought it just dropped and rolled to the backstop," I said.

"Since there was nobody on base, I didn't pay too much attention," said the Knoxville catcher. "But when I looked around it was nowhere to be seen, and the ballboy was still sitting by the corner of the dugout. I didn't have time to worry about it because the ump slapped another ball into my glove and the game went on."

I wonder if the ball didn't go straight into my arm like an injection, and then, like an injection, disperse to every part of my body.

My joining ranks with the Athletes of Christian Endeavor was, as far as management was concerned, the final straw. The Surgeon and Beanball Monaghan treated me with more contempt than they did the regular members of A*C*E, though they also tended to heap new abuses on the A*C*E members, more because they resented whatever influence they had on me.

"You don't want to become a freak. You don't have to become a freak by getting hit by pitches; you can make the grade on your own ability," said Robert Eager. We were sitting in a circle in what the other players and management called the Christers Corner of the locker room.

By now the lump was so big it was scary. It distended the loose sleeve of my uniform.

"I want to show you something," I said. "I want you to tell me what you think it is."

I gently pushed up my sleeve so they could see the huge carbuncle on my upper arm.

"You said it was just a boil," gasped Vernon Smith.

They stared at it, left their fingers suspended in midair as they almost touched it. It was clear that the boil contained a baseball.

"It's a miracle," said Robert Eager. The other members of A*C*E concurred.

"And in the stone a new name written," said Dean Breadfollow.

"You don't have to be hit intentionally to be a great ballplayer."

"You never gonna be Lumpy to nobody no more once you find out your new name," said Angel Correa.

Everyone in the locker room gathered around us.

"What the fuck are you guys doin'? You got a whore in there?" said Beanball Monaghan, pushing his way into the circle.

The boil was as large as it was ever going to get. The ball was recognizable under the translucent skin of my bicep. It was like the ball was covered by the thin whiteness of surgical-glove rubber.

"Hey, Skip, come look at this," Beanball Monaghan called to the Surgeon. "Fucking Drobot has baseball in his blood." Monaghan and everyone except me and the members of A*C*E were laughing.

"Have you been to the doctor?" asked a black outfielder.

I shook my head.

"And he ain't gonna," snarled the Surgeon. "This is a minor league, low-budget team, we need the baseballs." He guffawed like a fool.

Robert Eager got a tiny knife from the trainer. He poured rubbing alcohol over the blade, then touched it gently to the distended skin of my upper arm, which was the color of skim milk. I felt a pinprick of pain, less than a mosquito bite, and the pale skin peeled back leaving a glistening, mucous-coated baseball, a radiant, luminous white.

With its protective coating gone the ball balanced for a few seconds then dropped to the floor of the locker room. We all stood gaping at it; no one made a move to pick it up.

"What a bunch of pansies you guys are," said Beanball Monaghan. He picked up the ball, wiped it up and down on the front of his uniform, clearing the wet glaze from it.

One or two players made sounds of disgust.

"I used to deliver calves back in Oklahoma. What the fuck is there to be queasy about?" He tossed the ball back and forth, hand to hand.

"Let me see it," I said.

Monaghan held it up to the light, turned it slowly as a globe in his big hand.

"Regulation baseball," he said. "Perfect condition. Something mighty fishy here." He turned it some more, paying no attention to my repeated requests for it.

"Hey, it's Lumpy's baby," said one of the players. "Give it over to him to hold."

"Maybe he wants to nurse it."

"Yeah, you got resin in your tits there, Lumpy?" said one of the black players.

"At least the lumpy son of a bitch has got tits. He won't have to bottle feed it," said the Surgeon, spraying tobacco juice.

Monaghan picked up another baseball off a bench, he tossed

both in the air, then flipped them back and forth.

"Don't do that," I said, as several other players echoed my sentiments, especially those from A*C*E.

Monaghan bounced both balls off the wall, catching them on the rebound. He dribbled first one then the other, like miniature basketballs. But he kept on tossing them around until the baseballs were hopelessly mixed up. With an evil laugh he tossed them both into a wire basket of batting practice balls.

"You're young an' healthy," said Monaghan, "you'll produce other offspring." Everyone except those of us from A*C*E roared with laughter.

I rubbed my hand over various spots on my arms, thighs, buttocks, the spots where I had been hit by pitches in recent weeks. I could feel the slight puffiness of the skin in each area. I was indeed going to produce more baseballs. But the first one was the important one. Surely the first one would be the baseball with my new name in it.

The game doesn't start until 7:30 tonight, but I'm at the park before noon.

"That's a fine lookin' equipment bag," the old man at the players' gate says to me.

"Carried a few bats home for sanding and taping," I say.

He doesn't notice that the bag says *McCulloch* in big red letters all down one side, and I'm sure not about to point it out to him.

Just as I figured I'm all alone in the ballpark; it's dark and damp down under the grandstand, smells moldy the way a grave must. It takes me only a couple of concentrated shoves to break open the door to the equipment room. The snapping of wood sounds loud as gunshots to me and my stomach grinds and gargles, but there's only me here and the old man is a hundred yards away at the players' gate in left field.

The room is poorly lit by a sick little pimple of a bulb that swings back and forth on a dark cord, casting eerie black shadows. The bases are stacked up like pancakes against one wall. There are bats all over the place, some in racks, some in boxes, some bumping my ankles like huge matches; I breathe in their varnishy smell, and the leather odor of the baseballs. In the corner are a couple of buckets of "mud" so the umpires can rub the shine off new baseballs before each game.

The used baseballs are all collected in one place. New ones are still in boxes stacked on simple pine-board shelves along the back wall. There must be 300 balls, all loose, like a cache of eggs, in what looks like a child's playpen with chicken wire sides. There are also a couple of wire baskets half full of batting practice balls.

I fire up the *McCulloch*. If I thought breaking the door was noisy! The odor of burning oil tickles my nose. One of those baseballs is mine: conceived, grown to term, birthed. It will take me a few tries to get used to the saw. But I have all afternoon. I pick up a ball, one with grass stains and bat marks; it will be good to practice on. I carry it to a waist-high shelf, hold it gingerly with my left hand, approach it with the saw. It is easier to halve than I imagined. I reach for another ball. One of them has my new name in it, and I'm gonna find out which one.

LAWRENCE WATSON

Pinstripe

ROY HATED THE UNIFORM. He hated the brand of beer they served in the clubhouse. He hated chewing tobacco wrapped in bubble gum. He hated hotel food. He hated stewardesses. He hated Country Western singers coming to spring training. He hated afternoons with nothing to do but watch soap operas. But more than anything he hated the uniform.

It was not the specific uniform he hated. In fact, as uniforms went, it wasn't bad—traditional white, with a blue pinstripe. Maybe it didn't have the class of the Yankee pinstripes or the Dodger blue, but it sure was a hell of a lot better than those Viet Cong black pajamas the White Sox wore. No, it wasn't the *look* of the uniform, it was the *idea* of it. When spring training came around this year, he could take the thought of doing all those laps and sprints and calisthenics in the Florida sun, of pitching batting practice, and of meeting young guys who were making more in one year than he had made in the last eleven. He was even ready to sit through the sessions with that sports shrink who was going to talk to each of them about "developing and nurturing a winning attitude." He could make himself get up for all that, but he hated the idea of putting on the uniform again.

He tried avoiding it every way he could. Early in spring training it was easy. Roy had a few pounds to lose, so he wore a rubberized sweat shirt. Then he went to regular sweat shirts and a wind-

49

breaker. When he had to wear the uniform top, he wore it with sweat pants. Since the opening days were more workouts than anything else, he could get away with wearing Nike running shoes instead of spikes. When the intrasquad and exhibition games began, and later when the season itself began, he had to develop other ways to avoid putting on the full uniform—and do this while still making it look as though he was dressed like every other ballplayer on the field.

He started on the inside and worked his way out. He quit wearing a jock and a cup and just wore briefs. (The closest a line drive had ever come was the middle of his right thigh.) He wore his own T-shirts instead of the gray ones with the team name. If the weather was cold enough for an undershirt he wore one of his own cotton turtlenecks instead of a jersey. He wore his own sweat socks under his stirrups, and he wore the stirrups as seldom as possible. In Seattle, he bought one of those white boating caps, a kind of modified sailor's cap that you squashed down on your head and turned down the brim all the way around. He wore that before the games and eventually he even wore it in the bullpen, switching to his regular cap if he had to get up and warm up or if he was called in. In Minneapolis he bought a pair of moccasins, and if he was sure they weren't going to call him, he wore them in the bullpen. He quit wearing his contacts and wore his horn rims. Conrad, his roommate, told him he looked just like Bob Griese. Only ugly.

One night in May after they lost to Cleveland 6–5 in thirteen innings, the manager called him into his office. Roy didn't know why, but they always talked to you after losing a close one, when you *almost* won. When you went down 12–2, they just shrugged. Roy changed into his street clothes before he went in.

"What I don't figure," the manager said, "is that we both want the same things."

"What's that, Skip?"

"Not Skip. Not Skipper. Ed. Just Ed."

"Ed."

"We both want to stay with this ball club. And we both want to win some ballgames. And those two things go together. To stay here we got to win ballgames. Agreed?"

Ed was right. They both needed the job. Ed had been with three teams in four years. He thought he was always being let go because of his religion. Five years ago in Phoenix he gave his life over to Jesus, and he thought the owners had it in for him because of his religious convictions and his evangelistic activities in the off-season. In fact, owners had it in for him because every team he managed had a losing record. They prayed a lot, but they still lost ballgames. Roy needed the job, too. He had been knocking around this league for a long time, and he was now with his fifth team in eleven years. He hadn't had an E.R.A. under three-five for four years, and last year it had been over five. He couldn't go over three innings, and he was one of the only short-relievers who needed two days of rest. The next time a team let him go it wasn't going to be another big league club. Yes, what Ed said was true.

"Agreed," Roy said.

"Okay," Ed stood up. It was his way of saying his speech was over. "So why don't we work together."

"Sounds good to me." Roy left the office.

And it did sound good to him. He had nothing against winning games. In fact, even after all these years, in spite of the uniform, he still enjoyed playing the game. He liked anything having to do with a bat and a ball and a glove. Hell, he liked to play pepper (though fewer people played now), and he liked to hit fungoes. If they ever started to give out awards for skill with a fungo bat, he figured he was up for one of the first. And out on the mound he felt that in some ways he was getting better. The statistics didn't agree and neither did the hitters, but it was still the way he felt. Maybe it had something to do with the way you grew up. From the time you were a kid every year you got older you got better. It was automatic, programmed. Every year, you got taller, stronger, smarter. It didn't seem right that this pattern should reverse itself without any warning, that you kept getting better until you hit twenty-five and then you started getting worse and you never felt the difference.

But the difference was there. The other night in Chicago, Roy came in in the eighth, and they were up 6–4. There were runners on first and second, one out, and all he was supposed to do was get that kid Carter to hit the ball on the ground. Roy worked him pretty good, and then he threw what he thought was the best pitch he had thrown in a year, a fast ball, plenty of smoke, on the outside corner and right on the knees. Carter pulled it, he *pulled* it, and when it went out of the park it was still moving so good Roy was surprised it didn't kill somebody out in the left-field grandstand of Comiskey Park. And then the sonofabitch had to run around the bases with his fist in the air.

Still, there were times Roy could get the job done. Maybe his fast ball didn't have much juice, but he could get it to move around more, make it come in on right-handed hitters and tail away from left-handers. And his curve ball was better, he knew that for sure. When he first came up, he didn't dare throw a curve ball in the strike zone. It was good for wasting pitches and nothing else. He could throw a screwball now and a forkball and a knuckler. More junk than K-Mart was what Conrad said, but Roy didn't care. His control was good, he knew the hitters, he could change speeds, and if that was what would get people out, he'd take it. They said the legs were the first to go, but his legs didn't feel any worse than they ever had. There was only one time he remembered having trouble with his legs, and that was last summer in Kansas City. It was a hot night, the humidity was around 99 percent, and when he walked from the golf cart to the mound, his legs felt so heavy it was as though they were filled with water. No bone, no muscle, just skin and water. When he was warming up, he expected to slosh when he kicked. He lasted one-third of an inning, and he was just glad he got out of there before something happened when he had to move quickly—cover first, pick up a bunt—and he revealed that he simply couldn't do it. If his legs hadn't felt all right the next day he would have quit.

The uniform, however, had nothing to do with baseball, with the game itself. It was *of* the game, but it was not the game. Over the last two or three years Roy had been carefully picking out those things that were essential to the game and those things that were not. It was difficult, because though certain elements, like sports-writers and exploding scoreboards and ballgirls and general managers, obviously were not necessary, there were other elements that did not so quickly declare themselves as non-essential. But the list here was extensive, and it included such things as: umpires, coaches, freshly-limed basepaths, grandstands and bleachers and the spectators that filled them, batboys, trainers, managers, and uniforms. Definitely uniforms. Roy's point was not that these all detracted from the game. It wasn't that at all. He was sure, in fact, that many of these added a good deal. He would not want to eat french fries without salt. But neither did he wish to deceive himself into believing that potatoes could not exist without salt. It was important to him to make certain distinctions.

In the middle of June the manager called him in again. They had lost eleven of their last thirteen games.

"What do you think, Roy?" Ed asked him. "You've been around this league for a while. Why aren't we winning ballgames?"

Roy was fairly certain Ed wasn't interested in his opinion, and he suspected the question was a leading one, but he went along. "I don't know, Skip. Ed. We're not scoring enough runs, I guess."

"That's what pitchers always say. 'Not enough runs.' It's either that or 'the defense isn't backing us up.' One or the other."

"Now that you mention it, our defense is horseshit. You ever watch Bradley take infield?" Roy knew Ed never watched the team work out; he left that to the coaches. "He can't catch a ball that's hit right at him."

"Nah, that's not it. Kansas City's defense is worse than ours and they're in first place. Defense is overrated."

"Well you asked," Roy shrugged. "That's just my idea. Hell, I don't know why we're losing ballgames."

"Then let me tell you why *I* think we're losing."

Roy knew everything had been working toward this. "Okay," he sighed. "Tell me."

"I can give it to you in one word: attitude."

Oh Jesus, Roy thought. When that shrink was talking to them during spring training it looked as though someone did listen. "I don't know," Roy said. "Could be."

"And the problem with these kids," Ed went on, "is that they can't be taught something like attitude. They can learn it, but they can't be taught."

"Yeah, you might be right about that."

"And the way they learn is to see it, see it in action. See it in somebody they respect."

"Uh-huh."

"And that somebody is you, Roy. I want you to work on your attitude. These young guys look up to you, you're a veteran, and when they see you wearing a winning attitude, they're going to put one on too."

Roy had to try not to laugh. First of all, there was that "veteran" shit again. He gave up last year counting the number of times he was ready to check his birth certificate to make sure it didn't say "Roy Falk, Seasoned Veteran."

And if he had been getting batters out with any consistency it would be "wily seasoned veteran." As for respect. Everyone in the bullpen spent his time trying to give Roy a hotfoot, he found dog shit in his glove in Anaheim, twice analgesic was put in his jock (the jokers not knowing he didn't wear it anymore), and someone took a Peggy Lee tape of his and recorded Donna Summer over it. Respect. It was hard not to laugh.

The team continued to lose, and Roy pitched less and less. For a few weeks after his last talk with Ed, Roy was still called on to get up and throw, but he wasn't put into any games. Then even that pretense dropped away, and Roy never even warmed up. A young kid came up from Toledo who threw sidearm, and Ed pitched him so much Roy was sure the kid's arm was going to be ruined before he finished his first year in the majors. There was a time—perhaps even last year—when Roy would have said something. He would have gone into his manager's office and demanded to pitch. "Play

54

me or trade me," he would have said, and he would have pronounced even that cliché with conviction. But not now. Now, he was just riding it out, and as long as he wasn't playing he wasn't being noticed, and he could show up at the ball park as late as possible, sit in front of his locker in his street clothes for as long as possible before changing into what little of his uniform he still wore, and after the game he could get out of his uniform quickly—no need for a shower—and leave.

Roy sat in the dark hotel bar in Minneapolis. It was raining, and when Roy looked out the rain-streaked window at the cars going by it looked as though their headlights and taillights were melting in the warm rain. Roy had enough of a buzz on that the effect was pleasant, and he purposely blurred his vision to accentuate it.

Standing in front of Roy, staring at him, was the bartender, a short stocky man with a butch haircut who looked like a garage mechanic dressed in a short red jacket and black bow tie. The bartender was drying glasses with deft, clockwise motions of his wrist, as if he were screwing the towel into the glasses.

When Roy looked back at the man, the bartender said, "Sort of took it up the ass today, didn't you?"

They had lost that afternoon, 2–0. The Minnesota pitcher had gone the distance and held them to two hits. So much for offense. But the painful part of it was *their* pitcher had held the Twins to three hits, and both their runs were unearned. So much for defense.

Roy wondered how he had been spotted. He was sitting alone at the bar in a seersucker suit, and he wasn't aware of having said or done anything to indicate he was a ballplayer. Certainly he was not the type who was recognized on the street; once he was out of the ballpark gates (and seldom enough inside) he rarely had to contend with autograph seekers. Worse, he had always hated this part of baseball, being isolated and having to speak for "the team." Let the manager do that. And Keen, their leftfielder, who loved to give interviews almost as much as Ed, and both of them always had theories on why the club lost. Of course, neither of them could do a goddamn thing to prevent it from happening, but their theories were great.

Roy took a long drink before answering the bartender. "Yeah. Sort of."

"Don't that get old after a while? Losing, I mean?"

The bartender seemed more sympathetic than Roy had at first imagined him to be. "No *while*," Roy said. "It's old right from the start."

"But what? You get used to it?"

"I don't know, I guess. It's not the end of the world."

"Tomorrow's another day—right?"

"That's the way it's worked out so far."

The bartender flipped up another glass to dry. "Only tomorrow you guys are probably going to take it up the ass again."

In the middle of August, during a five-game home stand against the Yankees, the city had its hottest weather in fifteen years. The temperature hit a hundred every day, the public pools were so crowded you had to wedge yourself into the water, the sidewalks around the city were splattered here and there with eggs because jerks were always trying to see if it was hot enough for the eggs to fry, and fans came to the ballpark to drink beer, fight in the stands, and yell obscenities at the ballplayers—home *and* visiting. Their next road trip was going to be to Toronto, and Roy could hardly wait. There, you could already feel fall in the air in August, and last summer Roy was sure, one cool night about this time of year, that he could smell woodsmoke in the air.

On the field, conditions were as bad as in the rest of the city. The park never got a breeze, and the air was so fetid and heavy it was as if a lid had been placed on the stadium. When Roy stepped out onto the field, it felt as though all the fans were panting their breath down onto the field, and it was all bad. Night games weren't much better than day; the park stored all the day's heat.

In the sixth inning of the third game of the series—they lost the first two—it all came apart. Earlier, in the third inning, Keen had been hit in the arm by the Yankee pitcher, and, Roy was sure, Keen went back to the dugout complaining about how his pitchers did nothing to protect him. Keen thought he got hit often not because he got his head out over the plate and stepped into every pitch, but because his pitchers would not throw at opposing batters. In this, Ed supported Keen. Ed was big on "retaliating"; he believed it was an expression of team unity. To balance this attitude with his religious beliefs, he quoted Scriptures: "an eye for an eye ..." Roy never knew the context of this passage, but he was fairly sure it was from the Old Testament, and he was fairly sure it was not meant to apply to keeping batters away from the plate. So, in the sixth, Spanaker, their left-hander, probably as a result of Keen's whining and Ed's urging, hit Rowse, the Yankee clean-up hitter, in the ribs. The pitch was perfect: Rowse fell right back into it.

Rowse lay by the plate for a moment, for that moment of breath-holding stillness that you use to inventory your body for broken parts. Then he got up quickly, without ever touching his ribs, and began to jog down to first base.

Roy was watching, and even from the bullpen he thought he could see the instant Rowse's mind changed. He—Rowse—was looking down at his shoes or the chalked ground as he went down to first. Then, his head jerked up just a bit, no more than a few inches, as though he heard something, and halfway up the line, as if there were a corner there to be turned, without breaking stride, Rowse took off for the mound. Roy had to give that kid Spanaker credit; he stood his ground even though Rowse must have had three inches and thirty pounds on him. Against Rowse's charge, Spanaker put up his glove as though Rowse was a line drive to be caught.

Then, as if a giant picked up the field at the edges and tilted it toward the middle, the players poured out of the dugouts, marbles in a kids' game spilled out of their slots.

When the benches emptied, it was expected that everyone get out on the field. Ed didn't care if you mixed it up or tried to act as a peacemaker, just as long as you got out there.

Roy, however, decided to pass. It was a long way in from the bullpen, and by the time he got there, the umpires would probably have the situation controlled. Besides, the last time this happened, two years ago at Boston, Roy had been on his way out onto the field when someone grabbed him by the sleeve of his uniform, spun him around to the ground, and Roy had jammed his shoulder so badly he couldn't throw for a week. So Roy just watched, and from the distance of the bullpen, when the pale dust rose and he let his vision blur just as he had that night in the Minneapolis bar, it became difficult to tell his own team's white uniforms from the visitors' grey.

In the clubhouse after the game (they lost 7–2), Keen approached Roy at his locker while Roy was trying to hurry out of his uniform and the ballpark. Roy was down to his jockey shorts and a T-shirt. White.

Keen had a bottle of beer in one hand and an ice pack in the other. He held the ice pack to a cut over his left eye, a cut caused, Keen insisted, by a lucky punch delivered by a Yankee who was implausibly wearing his World Series ring. Keen swore it was true.

"Where was you, fucker?" Keen angrily asked Roy.

"When?" Roy asked.

"When? You know goddamn good and well when—when the rest of the team, the *team*, was out there trying to show them they can't walk all over us."

Roy looked up and down Keen. Keen's shirt and spikes were off, so he stood in front of Roy in uniform pants, stirrups, and cap, the cap tilted back to accommodate the ice bag. Keen's torso was bare, and Roy could see plainly the results of the weightlifting Keen had been doing in the off-season. Muscles like that should be producing more than the 40 RBI's and 12 home runs Keen had so far this year.

"Lot of equipment out in the bullpen," said Roy. "I thought somebody should stay with it."

"That's bullshit, man, and you know it."

Roy shrugged. He wondered if Keen was bucking for team captain, but since it didn't pay extra, Roy doubted it.

"I wonder," Keen said, stepping closer to Roy, "if you know what the hell *pride* means, if you know what it means to be part of a fucking *team*."

Roy reached for his shirt and put it on. He tried to comprehend what was happening. Keen was going to beat the shit out of him, someone on his own team, because he—Roy—wouldn't run out on the field and try to beat the shit out of someone on the other team. Somehow, it wasn't coming out right. Roy had a pocket computer that he used to figure out his E.R.A. and his retirement checks. When the batteries started going bad even the simplest problem produced a crazily wrong answer, the numbers blinking like a Vegas neon sign. That was what was happening between Keen and him—2+2=17,467,914.

Just then, Majeski, the trainer, came over to them. "Hey Falk," he said to Roy, "Ed wants to see you in his office."

Keen backed off, content, Roy was certain, to let Ed have the first piece of him. That was all right with Roy; he preferred dealing with the manager. Roy finished dressing.

Ed had his right foot up on his desk, an ice bag wrapped to his foot with an Ace bandage. Ed lit a cigarette, a Salem, when Roy walked in.

"What happened to your foot?" Roy asked politely.

"Ahhh, some sonofabitch stomped on it. Never even saw who did it."

Shortly after everyone had charged onto the field, Roy had seen Ed down on his hands and knees by the third base line.

"Anything broken?"

"Majeski says no but it sure is puffing up." He shifted the ice bag's position. "It's cut too. If we would have been on astroturf the guy wouldn't have had spikes on."

"Well. Ice. That ought to do the job."

"Yeah, they use it now on everything but hemorrhoids. Back when I was playing ball they'd probably have me soaking this in hot water." Ed had a brief major league career as a utility infielder. Lifetime batting average .217. "But I didn't ask you in here," Ed continued, "to talk about the ice bags or my aches and pains."

"No, I didn't think you did."

"I want to know where you were today. We could have used you out there."

Too bad, Roy thought, Ed didn't mean out on the mound. They sure as hell could have used some help in the eighth inning when the Yankees got to them for five runs, all of them earned.

"You're the second person who's asked me that," Roy said. "I was out in the bullpen. Right where they're paying me to be. Unless you tell me otherwise. Which you haven't done for a few weeks."

Ed ignored the remark. He put out his cigarette and then he clasped his hands together, interlocking his fingers as though he were going to play "here's the church, here's the steeple" with a child.

"Come here," Ed said to Roy. "I want to show you something." Roy stepped closer. "Now here," said Ed. "Try to pull my hands apart. Go ahead."

Roy gave it a lackadaisical, one-handed effort.

"No. Come on. With both hands."

Roy pulled with both hands, but he still did not pull as hard as he could. Ed's hands stayed together.

"Okay," Ed separated his hands but left them hanging in the air. "*Now* try to move my hand."

Roy pushed Ed's hand, and since Ed put up no resistance, the hand easily flopped to the side.

Ed kept his hands up and shook them like tambourines. "All right. Now here's my point. That's what a team should be. Everybody together. When we're together, we're strong. When we're not together, we're going to get pushed around."

Behind him, Roy could hear the sounds of the clubhouse. Two guys were arguing about who had the highest lifetime batting average against the Yankees. Someone else was complaining about the fit of his uniform pants, how come they were so loose, how come they couldn't be tight, you know, *tight*. There was a noise that sounded as though someone was rhythmically slapping a wet towel on a tabletop. Someone else wanted to know who was driving over to Mickey's, a nightclub across the river. A bat, with its muted wooden clatter, fell on the tiled section of the floor. A question was shouted across the room—"so are you fuckin' her or what?" And threaded through it all, the sound of water running, the showers you didn't even know you heard until the last one was turned off and the sudden silence startled you. Roy had always thought that when he finally had to quit baseball he would miss as much as anything else the clubhouse, its sounds and smells, and the rough struggling friendships that went with the place. But no more. Roy knew now he could walk out of Ed's office and out of the ballpark, and aside from a convenient place to which he could bring his laundry, he would miss nothing of the clubhouse.

Once in mid-winter in the northern Michigan town where Roy grew up there was an uncharacteristically warm day, a January thaw they called it. The temperature rose into the fifties, people went out in shirt sleeves, and the melting snow ran like new rivers through the gutters. At the time, Roy was eleven years old, deeply into a love affair with baseball, at the age when winter was usually a long torture for him because it kept him from playing ball. Roy and Steve, his best friend from three houses down the block, went out into the street on that January day, and they played catch. Between the high banks of snow, under the flat southern arc of the bright winter sun, on the wet street, they played catch. When one of them missed the ball it went into a snow bank, a puddle, or the gutter, and as they played the ball became waterlogged and it grew heavier and heavier. The ball splattered into their gloves, soaking the leather. Their shoulders and the insides of their forearms ached from the weight of the ball and the use of muscles unused since fall. Still they played. For hours, until their parents called them in, they threw the ball back and forth. For Roy, that day had come to represent the most pleasurable ball-playing experience of his life, and as he stood in Ed's office, with the sound of his teammates behind him, he realized that when he left baseball what he would miss would be that simplest of actions, that purity of motion, throwing a ball back and forth.

Ed stared expectantly up at Roy. Roy could tell that Ed had thought a long time about his little hand demonstration and had high hopes for its effectiveness. "I get the message," Roy said.

"I hope so." Ed reached down and readjusted the ice bag. "Now get out of here and let me hurt in peace."

"And Falk, just one more thing—"

"Yeah?"

"Stop wearing that goofy goddamn sailor's cap."

In September they were so deep in the league's cellar that their position there seemed a part of the order of the universe, as though they had evolved nature's perfect last-place ball club. One day in the bullpen, Madden said he had this vision, "nuclear war, World War III, the end of civilization. And when it's over, a couple hundred years later, the papers come out again and they got us in last place, $27\frac{1}{2}$ games out of first."

Boston, who had been fighting for the league lead a few weeks earlier until they lost nine of eleven, came to town for a four game series. The weather had cooled. The only fans who came to the games were those who loved baseball in any of its manifestations and would attend an American League game if it were the only game being played. These fans, usually older retired men, were, however, quiet, and playing a game before them was like playing in a vacant lot where the crack of the bat and the thump of the mitt echoed and vibrated and lost itself out across empty, sun-lit spaces.

Roy had still not played. Two weeks earlier he had gotten up and started throwing in the seventh inning of a game against Kansas City, but instead of using Roy, Ed sent in a left-hander, Holman, to pitch to Collins. Holman got Collins and the rest of the Royals he faced.

In the first game of the series they beat Boston, 4–2. The next two games were a twi-night doubleheader, and in the first game Boston, full of pennant-blowing, empty-handed, season-ending misery and frustration, exploded. By the fourth, they had scored eleven runs, and Ed was desperately going through pitchers like a man with a cold goes through Kleenex. He had started calling in short relievers in the third (having used all the long relievers in innings one and two), and by the fifth he was down to barely-rested starters. Roy was up and throwing and ready, but Ed wouldn't call him. By the seventh Boston had scored seventeen runs, all the hitters taking advantage of the opportunity to add points to their averages and perhaps improve their contract-bargaining positions in the off-season. Roy wondered who was going to pitch the second game of the doubleheader.

In the eighth, Boston scored two more runs, and with only one out and runners on second and third, Ed went out to the mound. Roy reached for his jacket; he was sure Ed would call him now—who was left? Roy was going to take it easy, throw strikes, try to get them to hit the ball on the ground. If they got a couple more runs, so what, the ballgame was lost; this was no longer a matter of pitching but of surviving, and Roy knew how to do that. Knuckleballs, plenty of off-speed stuff.

Ed didn't call him. He put Pay, the third baseman, on the mound. Pay had a strong arm, and he pitched batting practice from time-to-time, but Jesus! putting an infielder on the mound? And with Roy left in the bullpen, warmed up and ready to go? The fans, you could tell, loved and hated the move. They laughed as Pay began to warm up, but the laughter was tentative, uneasy, suspicious, as if they were not quite sure this was all right.

Roy sat down, disgusted. Not being put in the game was not what bothered him. If Ed was going to be that petty, that bush, well, all right. Roy could live with that. He was going to get paid if he played or sat in the bullpen. But putting Pay on the mound, pitching an infielder when a pitcher was available, that was a circus move. That was bad baseball.

Pay threw to three batters. He walked the first two on eight pitches, and he hit the third in the ankle.

With the bases loaded Ed went back out to the mound. On his way out, he tapped his right arm, the signal that he wanted Roy, the righthander. Roy didn't move.

"Hey," Madden said to Roy, "he wants you."

"Fuck him," said Roy. "He's not getting me."

Out on the mound Ed stood gripping his right arm as though he had been wounded. In his right hand he held the ball like a piece of meat that he thought had gone bad.

Madden said, "Jesus, he's waiting."

"Let him wait. Better yet, let him pitch. He's tried everyone else."

Ed suddenly let go of his right arm and raised his left. Spanaker, the left-hander who had been scheduled to start the second game, grabbed his jacket and headed for the golf cart.

"Oh man," Madden moaned. "Your ass is grass. I wouldn't want to be in your shoes for nothing. Oh man."

"That makes two of us," Roy said. "I don't want to be in my shoes either." Roy gathered up his glove, his jacket, his sunflower seeds, and his sailor's cap.

"You all right?" asked Madden.

"Yeah, I mean no. No, I'm not. I've got the shits. When Ed or Kinney calls, tell them I had to split. Tell them I got diarrhea." Roy left the bullpen.

The clubhouse was empty, and Roy's spikes clattered so noisily on the tile that he walked on his tip-toes. Roy wanted to be as quiet as possible, to change and get out unnoticed. He watched for Ed but figured that Ed would probably not leave the dugout but would wait for the break between games to approach him. As Roy took off his uniform, he disinterestedly considered for a moment that it might be for the last time. He thought back to the first uniform he had ever worn. He must have been about ten years old, a Little Leaguer playing for Bailey's Rexall. For most of the season they had no uniforms, only red T-shirts and blue caps, each with an ironed-on white 'B'. It was customary for the Little League teams to play a final, end-of-the-season game under the lights at Bock Field, the home of the Bock Barons, a Class "C" minor league team in Roy's home town. That game, in that park, was very important to the kids, and Mr. Bailey, in a move that elevated him to the status of hero, bought the members of his team, because they were leading the league, new uniforms. Roy remembered that uniform very well. It was cream-colored flannel, hot and ill-fitting. The pants had a button fly, and Roy had trouble making the buttons stay buttoned. He worried constantly about them, and while he was crouching at his shortstop position or in the on-deck circle he would sneak a look down at his crotch to make sure the buttons were holding. The buttons never came undone, but Roy went 0-for-3 that night, and he messed up a double play ball late in the game that let in two runs. He started pitching the next summer, and he'd been pitching every summer since. A lot of summers. A lot of uniforms.

What Ed would probably do, Roy figured, since it was late in the season, too late to trade him, put him on waivers, or bother suspending him, would be to fine Roy and assure him that he wouldn't be playing for this ballclub next year. Roy could afford the fine, though he wouldn't be happy about it, and since Ed wasn't likely to be managing this ballclub next year, he was hardly in any position to say who would be playing for it and who would not. Anyway, Roy had known for a long time this would be his last season. Of course, Ed would continue to see to it that Roy would not pitch in these final weeks.

Outside in the parking lot, the dew was already beginning to form on the windshield and vinyl top of his car. Roy looked up at the night sky. The sky was cloudless, but the lights of the city and the stadium kept all but the brightest stars from being visible. It was still early in the evening, the night of a doubleheader, and he had no place he had to be.

LESLIE WOOLF HEDLEY

The Day God Invented Baseball

F *OUL—STRIKE ONE! (that's what i wanted now he's going to get anxious now i've got the edge)*

There should be a law against beautiful girls chewing gum. They become common and ugly. Especially those whose crayon mouths masticate rubbery soft and juices boil over like sour jam. When teeth on thick slices of bubble gum crack *crack CRACK* amplified against my ears, all my natural worship of women, that prime esthetic fuel, glory of life, sinks and vanishes.

I held a Napoleonic stance on the pitcher's mound. Just to the left of my catcher's head I could see ruminating young cow jaws ripping at their gum, distracting my focus from the game. Quickly I forced my attention to the catcher's glove and his naked hand making signals. We were winning 4–2 in the last inning. Back to the ritual. I leaned over to study these finger signs, a semiotical language for heroes, creating a poised fakery on the baseball diamond. This was traditional form, a kind of stiff ballet, an *opera buffa* which stills baseball action, relieves tense muscles, allows for a relaxing inhalation of oxygen. Eyes are frozen on concentrating, studious pitcher: modern age David with slinging shot.

My art of pitching baseball, however, wasn't too closely related to my catcher's signals. That was diversionary. His wiggling fingers meant nothing. I was more concerned with the position of his ecru glove, my destined target. My pitching wasn't part of Coach Smith's orthodox baseball bible. Having no genuine fast ball, curve or slider, I fashioned other rhythmics, kinetic illusions. I threw three different ways: side-arm, three-quarters, and in surprising moments straight over-hand. The ball rotated somewhat beyond generatrix norm. I would turn my back to the plate, expectant batter waiting, wheel and throw from various angles, the ball arching directly toward the batter's chin or waist. He would often flinch, and I had a strike. My teasing ball ran toward their fists, and that split second of discomfit served my advantage. I disconcerted the opponent—and Coach Smith. Having uncanny control, I used means of timing, motion, psychology.

BALL ONE! (*i can afford to waste one pitch nibbling at the corners of home plate*)

I was more deceptive and zealous than greatly talented. I was, let's confess, so desperate for the need to play, that I did it well. When not pitching I played shortstop and covered the infield with speed and a whip arm. Although hitting over .300 average I rarely got more than pesky singles and a few doubles. "You don't have strong enough wrists," Coach Smith gleefully pointed out. Because I could place hit easily to right field, advancing runners, he put me second in the lineup. I played hard like a soldier bent on victory or death. Baseball was my way of escaping hermetic libraries where I was addicted to devouring books. I didn't want to become a useless intellectual. Coach Smith, of course, was convinced that reading was bad for athletic eyes and probably the sign of obscene sexual habits.

We were a doomed team under a dark calendar. Time was against us. Politics riddled us. Economics crippled us. Our truncated campus was bombarded by priests of reaction and priests of revolution. We were all in a great hurry to destroy ourselves. Now we're a cemetery.

Our catcher, Anderson, mesomorphic, sullen, was our most knowledgeable player and most aggressive. "Sure I'm tough," he said with feisty beer breath, cicatrix marks around his eyes. "Life is tough. If you guys don't like my way, it's tough shit." "Okay," we always placidly agreed. "That's the trouble with you guys," he usually added. What he meant we never understood. Grim, taciturn, he was killed early in the war.

Albano, our center fielder and best pitcher, was erratic. He was loose limbed, talented, lazy. A left-hander scouted by major league clubs, he lacked disciplined temperament. "Like that goddamned game against Michigan State. Man, I had that guy eating from my goddamned hand! That fuckin' umpire!" He would edge toward tantrum territory. "Forget it," I told him. "That was a week ago." But it was acid inside him. "Sure, *you* can forget it, but *I* got a loss on my goddamned record!" Later he was listed by the Navy as missing.

Christian, our third baseman, was ectomorphic, angular and rangy, hitting line drives shot from guns. He was exceedingly bright and cared only for challenges of higher math. We cut classes to hitchhike the countryside, purlieu roads leading to or away from remote and mundane farms or villages. He did complex math problems in his head while hiking. "I don't know why it's so easy," he shrugged. "I can't even get it on paper," I lamented. "Nah, it's so easy. There's nothing to it," he used to say. Hating the city, he was trapped by it. Poverty was invented to destroy talent. Lacking funds to study he tried drugs and died from an overdose.

Birch played left field, was sturdy, modest, strong and quiet. He hit long flies that were caught or went for triples. He, however, preferred chess and wanted to be a veterinarian. "Are gloves really genuine cowhide?" he wondered. His plane was shot down and disappeared.

Nickelau was a broadshouldered first baseman with the easy power of a home run leader. He was coaxed to play because, being Phi Beta Kappa, he looked on us with gentle disdain. "You fellows don't understand money," he instructed with detached, superior air. And it was superior. We all knew it. "College ball is a kid's game. If there was money in it . . . then . . ." he explained business to us. He viewed us from his nepotistic plateau of guaranteed success, knowing every rule to break. Toward me his attitude was ambiguous, having discovered that his younger sisters, girls born naked no matter what they wore, were concupiscent friends of mine who saw my baseball bat with ithyphallic simplicity. He became a sour and deadly multi-millionaire locked in levantine intrigue.

Jones played right field, did occasional relief pitching and was only as good as he wanted to be. Always requiring encouragement, his chief interest was girls, only Caucasian ones. "Sure she likes you," I would nudge him. "Then why ain't she at the game?" he would pout. "Maybe she's got a late class," I slapped his back. "Look at that girl in the yellow sweater," I pointed. He was one of the first Negro cross country champions. When he became a policeman he was murdered by a sniper.

On second base we had an adroit soccer player from Prague. Radek moved with grace and agility, was an excellent scholar. "Soccer is better game, more beauty," he said with careful English. "But you're a *natural* at baseball," we told him. "My heart," he replied seriously, "is not in this game. How I wish to play against Dynamo!" "Wait until we get into the national championship series, then you'll be stimulated," I promised. He smiled. As an intelligence officer he was killed on a mission.

Other team members were of minor ability with occasional high moments. Six of our secondary players entered military service and two returned, one minus a leg. Ours was a period of synoptic disasters.

STRIKE TWO! (now i've got it going take it easy i've got him let him get anxious)

Coach Smith had studied for the priesthood but was now married with three children. He wanted a championship team to get a promotion. His knowledge of baseball was limited. When he first met me he was impressed with my hustle, my ability to win. I had accidentally been elected team captain only because Anderson, who deserved the role, was anti-social. But Smith's enthusiasm for me as an All-American archetype was ephemeral. This initial warmth disappeared when, out of baseball uniform, he noticed that my sportscoat had two election buttons: VOTE COMMUNIST on one lapel, and VOTE DEMOCRAT on the other lapel. That was my growing-up politics, my balancing act.

Coach Smith's ordinarily sun-brightened face became livid. Speechless, his expression swiftly altered from shock to nausea to loathing. Never could Smith conceive that anyone like me would be playing baseball, a game he loved, worshipped next to the Church. If Smith truly detested anything it was Communists and Democrats. Protestants, Jews and a strange assortment of less-enlightened foreigners he had learned to tolerate in small doses. But how someone playing that divine game of baseball, a serious non-game which Smith needed to survive as a man in civil service society, feed wife and children, could be so ... degenerate, insulted his life. Smith felt betrayed, crucified, lungs pierced. Choking, he restrained a verbal hemoptysis. He swallowed his own blood. "Jesus," he said. Coach Smith honestly believed that God had invented baseball.

BALL TWO! (that's ok i can afford to waste it keep calm this is my game)

At first, when the coach instituted prayer meetings after every game won, in order, he wrote on the bulletin board, "To thank God for the blessings of victory," several of us ignored this. It was his awkward way of creating team concinnity. We also felt he needed some means of asserting authority. But the more games we won—and this was our best season, leading the entire conference—the more insistent Coach Smith became regarding our attendance at his prayer meetings. "This isn't a Catholic or Protestant or Jewish thing," he informed us. "It's non-denominational, ecumenical. Anyway, no prayer has ever done harm. It sure can do us all a lot of good. Guys, when we go to the series we face Yale, maybe Arizona State and Southern Cal," he grinned. "It's going to be tough! We'll need every prayer we can say!" Some laughed along with him. I wasn't around or tried to make out I wasn't around. "You," Coach Smith later told me, "are always in the showers during prayer meetings." "I want to be clean," I cracked. "No," he countered. "I want you here. You're team captain. I want you here." "I'll think about it," I said, my stomach throwing sharp curves against my nerves. He said with an angry flush, "You better be there next time. That's my ruling!"

To hell with chewinggumgirls. I finally could make out three other girls I adored sexually, poetically, theatrically, artistically, my literary girls from the school magazine, sitting between third and home. Would they write olympic odes about me? My romantic adrenalin flowed. I stared blankly at the opposing batter. He fidgeted, thinking. Good. Let him think, the last out of the game haunting him. I was boss. I felt it in my fingertips. The umpire cautioned me to hurry. Then I deliberately stepped off the mound. Let them all get nervous. Good. I wasn't nervous. I knew I had the game, knew I had to face Yale next week, knew I had beaten Yale the year before, knew I would beat them again. Anderson trotted toward me. "What the fuck you waiting for?" "Let the bastard get antsy," I said. "He's worried. I'm going to throw a slow ball that'll take six months to get over the plate." "Aw ..." It was my moment.

STRIKE THREE—YOU'RE OUT! (he finished he fished looking like an old lady swinging a broomstick it was beautiful)

Coach Smith pounded most backs, not mine, no not mine. Yet I was elated, realized. We trotted toward the club house. But first I had to talk to my three literary girls. One of them I would see over the weekend, a Saturday night (hopefully), so I could rest all day Sunday. The longer I spent chattering with the girls, in this their most plebeian excursion, meant that the prayer meeting would be over when I got to the club house. My insides churned.

Of course Coach Smith had no intention of prayer meeting being over. He waited. When I entered I could hear no showers, no loud jokes, no bacchanalic voices. Everyone sat subdued. I walked to my locker, took off my shoes and began to undress. A few players slapped and kidded me. "Okay," Coach Smith announced. "Simmer down, guys. Let's begin our prayer meeting." My back was turned and I undressed, placing a towel around my waist. "You too," his voice bounced off my back like a ground ball. "Excuse me," I said, my voice too thin, "I'm going to take a shower." "*After* the prayer meeting," he said. Radek studied me.

"Come," he whispered. "Do it once." "No," I heard myself decide. "Hey, man," Jones jabbed my shoulder. "It don't mean nothing." "No," I said and walked into the shower room. Before I turned on the water I heard Coach Smith shout in a loud crisp voice: *"You're off the team!"*

Alone in my loculus retreat, hot water cascaded over my head and mixed with a few tears. Angry tears or hurt tears or stupid tears, I can't say. What did it matter.

"Nickelau is now team captain," they told me later. "Why did you do it? It's just Coach Smith's way." "What about *my* way?" I wondered. "You're not coach," Radek logically explained. "Tell him you're sorry," Birch said, "and then we can go on as before. You're the guy who loves baseball so much." "No," I told them. "Never. I've got a right to pray or not pray, as I see fit." "What you do, man," Jones laughed, "pray under water? Hell, it don't mean nothing! I go to church with my mom every Sunday and it don't mean nothing!" "No," I tried, drenched with beads of moral agony. "It means something, that's why Smith does it. I won't be forced to do it. Prayer has nothing to do with baseball." It was Nickelau's turn to laugh. "Of course not, but Smith thinks it's a good psychological gimmick. He's probably praying for a fat raise in salary. It doesn't cost anything to amuse him. He's simple. You've got nothing to lose kneeling for a couple minutes." "What about my pride?" I asked him. He beamed, "Pride isn't worth two cents!" "You're a crazy sonofabitch," Anderson wrote me off quickly. "I always knew it. Fuck you." Albano leaped with passion. "But what the hell are we going to do with Yale? How the hell can we win the playoffs now? You, wise guy, are going to cost us the national championship!" He almost cried. "All the goddamned big league scouts will be there!" "You're a great pitcher," I told him. "You can win." "How?" he sputtered, "with only a couple pitchers and a shitty shortstop? Oh . . . the whole goddamned season right down the drain!" "It's not my fault," I said defensively. "Smith threw me off the team. I'm not begging him or anyone else to get back on. He made the decision, not me!" Everyone moaned.

I didn't want any more conversation and therefore lowered my jockstrap flag in retreat. The library had ample philosophical axioms defending my attitude. Should I show them to Coach Smith? I felt alone in a chaos of trivia. At night I dreamed of working out a brilliant compromise, but in the morning I knew it wasn't possible. It was a period of elegant gestures usually hiding in elegant deceptions. One thing worse than being old and phony is being young and phony. Uncertainty itched.

My literary circle heard all this campus talk, but sports they considered a subject unworthy of attention. Wanting both worlds, I stumbled within the silent zone between the two. The next few days we played intellectual games with heavy erotic weapons. Seconds chewed through books. I exercised by running daily, unlimbering my arm, awaiting a compromise agreement. It never came. Why did I expect an athletic coach to be less vicious than my intellectual friends?

On the day of the playoff game I went hitchhiking with a flame haired sephardic girl with insatiable sexual curiosity. We examined flowers, trees, historic places. A baseball flew through the sky. With small, intent face she described her trip to Spain. She loved bullfighting. Adored it! "It's a highly religious and symbolic act," she said. "Some people in Spain actually contend that God invented bullfighting." "No," I told her, counting the amazing sincerity of her freckles. "No," I repeated, knowing otherwise from a punishing season, "God invented baseball."

TOM TOLNAY

A Rookie Southpaw, With Talent

I N THE FIRST HALF of this century your classic minor
league baseball manager was a miserable soul who
used up most of his years in dire county capitals, eating
statistics for breakfast, diamond dust for lunch and raw
crow for dinner, straining his aorta to win ballgames for a pack of
fans who'd sooner lynch him than call him a bum. You know the
type of field skipper I mean—foulmouthed, opinionated, cigar
smoking, feisty, hard drinking.

But as America matured, another type evolved. He had a
college education, with a major in engineering or economics. Not
physical education. He didn't curse, or not as much, and gave up
smoking. He was strong enough to load trucks, and smart enough
to know better.

When you add up their respective scores, though, the new
ruling class in the minors is not all that different from the old. I
ought to know. Here I am in Portland, feeding off the same black
birds as those unschooled (if more colorful) managers of yore, and
sharing their eternal dream. It goes something like this: One fresh
morning some kid materializes at the ball park, from nowhere,
looking for a tryout. . .more a pelican than a person, toting a
pasteboard suitcase in his left hand, with a tattered fielder's glove
jammed up his armpit and reeking with talent.

From spring training on down the home stretch—even in these
days of lost innocence—we get a couple of young fellows hanging

around the dugout, shy but strong, itching to show their stuff. Some managers give them the heave-ho because they figure they will recognize true talent like true love when it comes along. Me, I give all of them a shot because last place is a permanent condition with us, so we can't get any worse. Besides, you never know. You just never know. And the screwier they look, the better, because that's the kind that still thrive in this game, the kind that made us realize baseball is the purest form of democracy. The only trouble is, the great ones are about as common as a pearl at the center of a hardball.

Well, steering clear of liquor and women, and keeping my nose in books instead of other people's business, finally paid off. After twenty-five years of managing on the farm, my dream boy showed up at Parker Field, home of the Portland Clams. And this kid certainly scored big when it came to looking weird—all 6'6" of him weighing less than a hundred pounds, held to the ground by new yellow suction sneakers, with blue knees poking through the splits in his striped railroad pants. His head was topped by cold, blond spaghetti. His ears belonged in the Hall of Fame. A character straight out of Ring Lardner; a walking proof of matter over mind; a neoclassic of American mythology. A living foul ball.

"Sure, kid," I said, "go on out there and chuck a few."

Now I've got as much pride as your old-time boondocks field boss, and even with a degree in economics (minoring in accounting), no one has ever accused me of being a softy. But I'm secure enough to admit—I'd even confess it to those hot dogs from the *Portland Express,* off the record—that when I saw this aluminum-boned southpaw kick that stilt up over his ears, and wheel his whole body into the pitch—blazing it right down the pipe—so help me God, tears came to my eyes.

In all my days I've never read a novel or looked at a painting that could match the sheer esthetics of that single pitch. And the most beautiful thing was that the kid kept rearing back and firing one masterpiece after another. Every time I heard the ball—it was too fast to see—smack into Red McGinty's mitt, my heart jumped a full foot in my chest. Which is exactly what's supposed to happen when you're face-to-face with great art.

A Rookie Southpaw, With Talent

In this game it doesn't take long to recognize Triple-A talent, and even those shell-heads on the Clams climbed up off their tails and stood staring bug-eyed at this baby-cheeked phenomenon—throwing darts. My ace chucker Rod Beastley (3 wins, 10 losses) had turned either very studious or a bit jealous of that flame-thrower, staring with his mouth open as round as a goose egg on the scoreboard. Suddenly I became nervous that a spy from the Troy Dragons might be sniffing around, so I bounced out to the mound and grabbed the kid by the hand (not his pitching fingers!), towing him very gently (so he wouldn't break an ankle and have to be shot) into the dugout, through the damp tunnel to the moldy locker room, into that filing cabinet they call my office.

Slamming the door behind me, and shoving the army supply locker against it, I said as sweet as a bride on the first morning: "What do they call you, son?"

"Butch."

"Do you have a last name, son?"

"Byrd."

It had to be something like that. "How old are you, son?"

The boy hesitated. "Eighteen?"

Eighteen! I'd forgotten anyone could be 18 anymore. "Where are you from, son?"

The kid looked confused, and I became concerned I might spook him with questions that were too intellectual. "Skip that one," I said, pitching right at him: "How would you like to have one of these fine baseball outfits for your very own?"

"How much do they cost?"

"Why, son, I'd be proud to give you one free, and without any charge—except you're responsible to keep it washed." I decided I'd better let him know right off that this wasn't one of those hotsy-totsy ball clubs with valet service. The owner, old Pop Parker, would've been better off in the dry-cleaning business, for there hasn't been a pennant in Portland in 30 years, and fans don't buy tickets to see losers. Except the real addicts, of course, the ones with horsehide for skin.

Then the pelican asked, "Would the uniform have a number on

77

the back of it?"

I placed my hand on my heart. "You have my word."

"What number?"

"Why, son, you could have just about any number that fits."

"Three's my lucky number," he confessed.

"Just like three strikes—you're out," I chuckled, stalling. He would have to pick Moose Brodsky's number, but I was determined to lock this kid up tighter than Koufax' grip on a fastball: "That could be arranged."

"Okay," said the kid, "when do I pitch?"

Just like that! Here I was sweating because I thought for sure he'd hold me up for 200 a week, and then the owner would nix the deal; here I was scheming how to cut him down on his price tag, and this stupid son of a batboy didn't even bring up money. I could've taken him for the biggest ride this side of Disneyland. But talent must be respected, because that's the one thing that separates one body from another in this life. Not education. Not environment. Not brains. Not lineage. . .Talent is class. Talent is power. Talent is beauty. Talent is money. . . .Talent is *eternal*. And this kid had it coming out of his knuckles.

"Seventy-five bucks a week," I spouted, "and not a nickel more."

I could tell from the way he sighed "Wow!" that I could've had him for half that. His jelly-bean eyes seemed surprised to be getting paid anything at all. He was so innocent he believed it was a sin to take money for doing something that came so easy; for something he loved doing. But it was a moot point. There wasn't any money for bats and balls, much less players. (Soon I might have to start doing other people's income tax again to pay my rent and to keep the Mrs. from having to take in laundry—instead of doing what I know and love. . .running rotten teams into the cellar, where they belong.)

That course in business law finally paid a dividend: I devised a contract on the back of a Genesee Beer® calendar and got Butch Byrd's John Hancock on the crooked line. Good thing he could write his name, because there was no way he was going to get out

78

of my cubbyhole in good health without putting ink on the back of July. It turned out the kid wasn't 100-percent jackass: He held out until I added in the wording that No. 3 would be stitched on the back of his uniform.

The next afternoon I had two No. 3s prancing around my outfield, loosening up those last-place muscles. It wasn't until the Byrd hitched up on the mount to pitch batting practice that Moose woke up and came stomping over to me with a "What's-the-big-idea-of-the-kid-wearing-my-number?" jut to his square jaw.

"Listen, Moose," I massaged, "this boy is superstitious. He can't throw strikes unless there's a No. 3 on his shirt."

"Aah don't give a hoot if he cain't throw the ball," grunted Moose. "Three's maah number—always been maah number. That was Lou Gehrig's number, too," he said, like there was some connection between the Iron Horse and this iron head, who didn't even know Gehrig was No. 4.

"Feel that fond of Lou's old number, do you?"

"Damn right," said the Moose.

"Tell you what, you're twice as good as any ballplayer on this club, so I'm going to put *two* No. 3s on your back."

Moose's hard mug froze a moment, as his mind drifted into a reasonable approximation of thought. Then his thick lips loosened into a grin that looked like a slice of watermelon from his home state. At last he waddled off to the batting cage, puffed up like he'd just scored the winning run. That's how I keep going around these losers—by making monkeys out of them, grabbing a laugh or two in between the ulcer attacks. But Moose wasn't smiling for long, because the Byrd was throwing smoke and the best my big pinch hitter could do was dribble a couple foul. Moose walked out of the cage dragging his bat after him. "Dat kid is quicker'n greased lahtnin'!"

The same went for Prestone Filch, the fastest eating, slowest moving first sacker in the league; Gimp Turney, shortstop with the short left leg; right fielder Jack-in-the-Box Rigby, who was red hot with the women and ice cold at the plate; Ping Pong Figaro, third baseman with a paddle for a chest; Leroy Coogan, the fleet, but flaky, center fielder; Frank Plaster, the no-hit, no-field, know-nothing utility infielder; Jim "Slap-Happy" Slipper, who led all second basemen in the league in brawling; and Stu (short for "Stupid") Stuckney, left fielder famed for his ability with a beer bottle—he can down a quart in one gulp.

The same went for the whole mob. Even Red McGinty (the one athlete on this club who's a threat to pole one out of the park every so often) couldn't touch him, and he got so hot over being fooled by a green lefty that he chucked his bat into the empty stands—and almost crowned Pop, who was sweeping up peanut shells in the aisles.

The Byrd really showed me something, and since I had nothing to lose—except another ball game—I decided to start the raw rookie against the Manchester Lumberjacks, who were due in the next day. When I broke the news to him, all the kid said was, "Gee!" But I felt like I weighed 190 again—solid all over, and was getting ready to play *my* first pro game. That night I don't think I slept two hours, the Mrs. elbowing me to "stop bouncing around." By game time I was so nervous I thought I was going to chuck up that gritty American cheese on white.

Awfully bad I wanted the Byrd to come through. Just four or five respectable innings is all I asked. But I had my doubts about him. Maybe he'd used up everything in practice, and in a real game would blow up higher than a Ted Williams home run. So I sat there chewing the skin off my thumbs as the southpaw got Bugs Aker to bounce to Prestone, unassisted. Bryan Fillmore fouled back of third to Plaster, who finally held onto one. Then Charley "Brick Wall" Jones spanked a "seeing-eye" single between second and first. But the kid closed strong by whiffing Sniffy Johnson on a swinging strike.

Feeling his Wheaties® after getting through the first with all his spaghetti still on his scalp—and none yet on his chest—the southpaw struck out Barnaby, Krock and Narum in the second: one swinging, two on called strikes. I was *amazed*. It's those called third strikes that tell a manager plenty: They weren't able to dig in on the kid; he had them off stride. They needed radar to pick up his hummer!

The third and fourth innings disappeared like a six-pack on an August afternoon. And the kid logged three more strike-outs. But in the fifth he gave up his first walk of the game—to the lead-off batter. No manager in any league can sit still when his pitcher—particularly some bone-brained hotshot—dishes out a free pass to the lead-off batter. A nasty situation it was, and it got nastier: The offender on first swiped second, sliding in half a mile ahead of Red's peg.

I started gouging up the hard dirt in the bottom of the dugout with my cleats, stomping back and forth, sitting down, getting up like when I was waiting for my first kid—a girl—to break into the line-up of life at Oklahoma City General. But the Byrd boy loosened those old, stretched-out muscles of mine by striking out two more Manchesters and getting a tough Lumberjack to ground back to the box. The kid snapped it up and flipped him out.

By the sixth inning my uniform was soaked with nerve waste, but the kid was as dry as slate and really putting on a one-boy show—he mowed them down again: one, two, three. "I knew it," I piped out loud, mostly to myself. "As soon as I saw those long knobby fingers, I knew this kid had stuff. Some other journeyman could work 10 hours a day for 20 years and still never nip corners that way." My coach Skeeter nodded, squirted tobacco juice on my shoe and I didn't even chew him out: It needed polish anyway.

In the seventh the Byrd racked up two more strike-outs before the Lumberjacks finally hit one over the infield—a sleepy fly ball that couldn't make up its mind whether to come down or just hang up there awhile. Finally it floated into Stuckney's paws like a big white balloon. Even "Stupe" couldn't boot *that* one. . . . Watching the kid work made me feel as if my hair were turning black again, as if me and the Mrs. were just getting started on our lives together.

The three or four dozen locals in the rickety splinter bleachers suddenly stopped scorching our hides, and started to cheer the rookie at the end of each inning. Even Pop, peddling hot dogs and soda pop, stopped to see what all the fuss was about—to observe the creature he had refused to pay 75 a week. (Me and the Mrs.

decided to pay him out of our retirement savings, at least until he proved himself.) Well, I was glad, because the kid deserved the attention. But it also worried me. Fans can go to a ballplayer's head quicker than Four Roses, so I made up my mind to look after the kid—personally. One thing that I'd learned over the years—no matter how much talent you're blessed with, lots of things have to be right to put it all together. Timing. Health. Hard work. Confidence. Good coaching. Love. God knows what else. And I wanted to do my part to help give this talent a chance to go all the way. Who knows? Maybe one day he'd pitch in the World Series! Maybe he'd send me and the Mrs. a pair of tickets!

To get him started in the right direction, I was convinced he needed a win in his first outing, but the lazy dumbbells on my club had only scratched up three hits—and no runs—off Rex Crimson: We were no better off than when we'd started. Wait, I take that back. At least we weren't behind. Now Crimson is no water boy— we just couldn't sit around expecting him to hand us the ballgame. We had to go out and take it. At the bottom of the seventh, with us coming to bat, I charged into that pack of lead-foots like a one-man gang of umpires, trying to fire them up.

"Come on, you lazy snakes," I yelped, "get the lead out and crack that pill! Swing that lumber like you mean it! Beat the brains out of the ball! Hit it where you live! Start a rally! Get something going! For the love of Jehovah, do *something*."

Do you think it did any good? They stared at me like I was batty, as Coogan and Rigby tapped sissy grounders to the infield. My hopes fluttered when Filch walked and "Slap-Happy" slapped one on the nose—but skied straight to Bridges in center.

Even though Plaster booted a routine bouncer, the boy south-paw kept right on wheeling through the top of the eighth. We entered the bottom of the inning in a flat-footed, scoreless duel. Zeke Borkenstock, Manchester's bark-faced manager, sat stunned on his bench, like it was all a bad dream. The kid was leading off for us, and when he marched up to the plate I went for my crew's throats again. I guess I *was* batty by then—crazy with desire to win one for the kid, for the team, for the fans, for Pop. . .for me. "That kid's pitching a whale of a ballgame for you bush leaguers!" I roared. "The least you could do is chip in with a couple of runs. This is his first pro game. So help me, if you bums lose it for him, I'll send the whole dame bunch of you back to the Little League."

Wiseguy McGinty piped up, "Hey, Boss, when you say 'pro,' do you mean he's getting *paid* for this ballgame?" and the other half-wits giggled at McGinty. The jerks didn't realize they were laughing at themselves, all of them playing without pay for the past month. But I knew why they played. I put up with them for the same reason—for the game.

Just then I looked up and there was an angel dashing toward second sack—the kid himself had poked one to left, and it hugged the foul line like teenagers in love. And when the dust simmered down, Blotto the ump was holding his palms flat—"Safe!" I jumped so high I hit my head on the sagging roof of the dugout. But what did I care if I had a broken skull? I had a man—a boy—in scoring position in the eighth inning. And the score was tied, nothing–nothing. And the top of the batting order was coming up. And, in total defiance of this team's history, there were no outs!

My hopping around like an umpire who'd had a ball fouled off his corns seemed to wake up the lugheads, and they started shouting: "Way to show 'em, kid" and "Beautiful, baby, beautiful" and "Let's pin Crimson's ears to the mound." The Lumberjacks were too shocked to razz back. My heart jigged with joy to see that collection of buffoons pulling together for a change, getting stirred up over the chance of coming out ahead. Ballplayers have to taste winning once in a while, just to continue getting up in the morning. . .and we'd lost 14 straight.

For the first time in weeks, I had a chance to try out some real strategy. While Coogan was moseying up to the plate, I scratched my left ear (that's the bunt sign on this club) at Skeeter in the third base coaching box. He scratched his ear at the batter. And on the first pitch Leroy laid one down between the hot corner and the mound, his round rear flashing toward first. The ball trickled into the overgrown grass and died there, and I blessed the lazy ground crew—"May your soul go straight to heaven, Pop." All I'd prayed for was a clean sacrifice, but I ended up with runners on first and third. Still no outs!

By then my chin felt like satin instead of leather as I rubbed it like the 'Ole Perfessor,' Casey Stengel, deep in calculation. But inside I knew it was the kid that was making me look good, which is perfectly legitimate, because that's one of the things talent can do—make everyone around it come up smelling like rosin, too. In the yellowing bands of sunlight the Byrd looked more like an ostrich than a pelican, but he had showed pretty fair speed on the paths, so I figured we might be able to score on a hit *or* an out. Tag up after a long fly. Even a deep grounder. And I had a man coming up who at least made contact with the ball. Rigby nicked one foul, and out of the corner of my eye I saw Pop wrestle the ball out of the grip of a girl in the stands. But Crimson—the show-off—got tough, kicking off the pitching rubber hard to strike out the Jack-in-the-Box.

With one down, I could almost feel the last few dark hairs on my scalp turning white. That's because this Crimson has this dandy of a sinker that has ruined many a rally with a ground-ball double play. Making it worse was that my next batter, Prestone Filch, runs like he's walking in water. What I needed was a body that could walk *on* water. The closest I could come to a savior was Moose Brodsky, who's even slower than Prestone, but who gets his share of base hits. So I jabbed Brodsky with my elbow: "Double 3, you're swinging for Filch."

Brodsky looked scared because we hadn't been this near winning since the Dark Ages, and he didn't want to end up as the game's goat. But he grabbed a stick and tiptoed into the batter's box, because he knew I'd find some way to humiliate him if he didn't. At least I'd pleased Filch, who was grinning as he came back to the bench. "You better save that smile for a rainy day," I said, and though I don't have the faintest idea what I'd meant, it wiped away his gutless smirk.

Crimson fell behind, two balls, no strikes, and I got to dreaming that maybe the pitcher was tiring and he'd hang a curve ball, or even walk the Moose. But then the bum fired a pair that cut the heart of the plate, and Brodsky stood there blinking at them like they were bright headlights in the night. Two balls, two strikes. "Your arms made of stone?" I moaned inside, while outside I cheered, "Come on, Moosey, slam one. Just a single is all we need," and then to myself again, "You big fish."

When you've been in this game as long as I have, you learn to expect the worst. Crimson sprang one of those double-crossing, death-dealing sinkers, and the Moose—after all, he's just human—tapped a slow bounder to their slick shortstop Narum, who charged it, scooped it up, flipped to second for one, and Johnson's relay to first beat Moose to the bag. Just as I was about to die with disappointment, I saw the ball squirt through the first sacker's mitt, and Moose thundered in safely as the kid scrambled home. The run scored! So help me, I stopped breathing a full minute before gasping. . ."Nice going, kid," and "Good stroke, Moose," like he'd homered with the bases loaded. (The goon had almost given *me* a stroke.) In the meantime, Stuckney struck out and ended the inning.

I could hardly believe the scoreboard:

	123	456	789
LUMBERJACKS	000	000	00
CLAMS	000	000	01

I kept staring at it, wondering if Pop was drunk, or had gone loco behind the scoreboard. After all, the Lumberjacks were riding high in second place and had whipped us eight straight. (A look at the record book would've proved we hadn't topped them in two years.) But it finally came through to me that we actually had a chance to win. Everything rode on the kid's left wing. I didn't even have my ace reliever Luke Brill (earned-run average 7.23) warming up. It was the kid or nothing. Win or lose. Live or die.

In the top of the ninth, I almost swallowed the baseball in my hand when they got their second hit off the Byrd: a "cheapie" Baltimore chop over the shortstop's head. But the kid bore down and struck out the next batter on three pitches, and got the second out on a pop-up to the Gimp. Two down, one to go.

Yes, I thought, this kid sure has talent. That's right. Once upon a time I carried a floppy old glove into a dump just like Parker Field—only it was down in Oklahoma City, 35 years ago. I was a lot taller then. And a lot smarter. Look at me now, collecting splinters in my double-wide behind in this clam burg, all for a bunch of clowns who should've faded away like the five-cent Coke.

Even after I'm dead and buried, I suppose, a band of misfits like this will show up on a lot like this and take their swings. They were timeless, and I was growing old. But I'm not complaining. At least I've had something only a handful around this game ever had. I had a taste of The Bigs—you bet your pearly dentures I did.

The Athletics called me up late in '39 after they were a good 50 games out of it. Connie Mack, the grand old man of baseball, was already thinking about the next season and wanted to see what he had on the farm. Hitting .281, I was brought up with two or three other green hands for that August and September. I even rapped a couple of hits in The Bigs, including a long double to right center (off Joe Krakauskas). But the A's backstop Frankie Hayes had banged out 20 round-trippers that year, and the front office claimed I needed seasoning.

So the next spring came and went, and so did the next, with Hayes hitting over .300, and I was still down on the farm. If he'd hit .200, who knows? I had a pretty good year with Elmira in '40—batted .274 with 12 homers. But the war had broken out. I was yanked into the army, and stayed for the duration. By the time I got back into shape for the '46 season, I'd lost something. The A's took me back into the organization, but each year my average slipped; so did the home runs. No sooner had I put on my cleats, it seemed, than my knees were turning to rubber, crouching down behind the plate.

One day I woke up in Wheeling, managing the Polecats. . .But that's all part of the game. At least I didn't end up in a cramped, airless office, adding up long columns of numbers that had very little to do with real life. Sure, I had talent—plenty of it. My name is in the record books. *Bud Margin: Lifetime Major League Batting Average, .198. 33 Official At-Bats: Five Singles, One Double, Three*

Walks, Two Errors. Those errors, incidentally, don't bother me at all. How many of us get to bobble a couple in The Bigs?

The ump roared "Ball three!" yanking me back to Parker Field. The kid had a full count on Motley Bridges. A walk would put the tying run on second, in scoring position, and the winning run on first. A single would put the knotter on third. A double...I held my breath as the Byrd wound up, kicked that size-14 spike into the clouds and dealt. Bridges stirred the air with 36 ounces of Louisville lumber—long after the ball had cracked into McGinty's mitt. There was only one way to interpret what had happened, the rule book being especially clear on this point: He was out.

The game was ours, I mean, the kid's. . . .

I sat as straight as the flagpole in center field, knocked out but still upright. A 14-game losing streak over! A one-game winning streak started! A two-hit shutout for the kid! Fifteen strike-outs! Something to look forward to in the pitching rotation! And a good night's sleep for the first time in a month!

I wanted to collapse on the bench from exhaustion. I wanted to dance on the roof of the dugout. I wanted to run over to Zeke, slumped on the Lumberjack's bench, and thumb my nose at him. I wanted to call the Mrs. and tell her our investment had paid off. I wanted to kiss the kid's left hand. I wanted to do a lot of things. But I just sat and waited for Butch Byrd, the kid from nowhere, to come in. And when he reached the dugout I stood up, spit in the dust, yawned, and said, "Pretty good game, kid."

"Thank you very much, Mr. Margin."

I wanted to say more to the southpaw, much more, but I didn't dare. I didn't want to be part of that thing—whatever it is—that brings talent to its knees. I didn't want to weaken his chances by telling him he'd accomplished something great. All he did was win one ballgame. Sure it came when we needed it bad. But Cy Young had won 500 ballgames, and some of them had clinched the pennant. Anyway, there's no reason why I can't tell you what I couldn't tell him...at that particular moment, I loved the kid more than my wife, I loved him more than my life.

IRWIN CHUSID

The Glory of Their Haze

RIBBIES" CRAWFORD CLAIMS to have been a utility infielder on the 1907 Chicago White Sox. Though we can find no record of him in the Macmillan Encyclopedia, he assures us he was there, that historians and statisticians have overlooked certain boxscores in which his name appeared. We sat with the ageless "Ribbie" one evening watching last October's fall classic on TV, and he seemed provoked by the proceedings and the attendant fuss. We switched on our tape machine and captured some rather dubious but nonetheless fascinating recollections from this "legend," absolutely none of which can be substantiated by available data.

"Nowadays, manager's got forty-nine coaches and a computer helpin' him run the team. Plus the clubowner second-guessin' him next day in the papers. They got one coach don't do nothin' but teach how to use pine tar. 'Nother one specializes in how to squat in the on-deck circle.

"I'll never forget that 'ought-7' ('07) season. All we had was a manager runnin' the club, all by himself. His name was 'Dummy' Clarke, a Cherokee deaf-mute. He had it real tough, keepin' control in the dugout. If you missed a bunt signal or played a ball lazy in the field, you come back to the bench and he'd try to chew yer hide without actually bein' able to say anything. Clarke'd be there, and the ump would call one against us, and Dummy'd go rushin' out there and argue with the ump in universal sign language. It was a real pathetic sight, him makin' all these hand gestures. Ump'd just turn around and brush off the plate. Dummy would get real mad and go red in the face. One day we was playin' the A's and after another of these wordless tirades, Clarke flashed ump Cal Adams a complicated sign that coulda been done easier with one finger. Ooh, poor Dummy, he didn't know Adams could read sign language. It was a second inning shower for Dummy.

"You know they didn't have relief specialists in those days. Now a guy comes, pitches to one batter, gives him an intentional walk, and they pull him. Gets paid a quarter-million for that. We had this one guy in '07—never forget him—old 'Iron Arm' McNulty. He pitched and won nine straight shutouts in seven days, including two doubleheaders. And all with no sleep. He'd stay up all night, dealin' aces and smokin' Havana ceegars. McNulty always said he tried not to drink anything stronger than gin mornin' of a game. I'll never forget in game six of the '07 series, McNulty threw a pitch so hard he pulled his arm right outta joint. Snapped right at the elbow. You could hear it in the stands, like a branch breakin' off a tree in a cyclone. But he was a gamer, old Iron Arm was. He didn't complain, just went right on pitchin'. Between innings, they patched him up with a hammer and a 3-inch nail. Finished the game, too. AND WON! And he'da been ready for game seven the next day if they'da needed him.

"Nowadays, guy hits .249 with 25 homers, they give him a five-year contract with deferred payments. And what's all this crap about bonus clauses? Some prima donna on a second-division club gets an extra $2,000 for every foul ball he hits after August 1st? We didn't have nothin' a-that back in '07. No sir. I'll never forget old Jake Bockfuster, sluggin' first baseman we had. Hit .313 and led the league with 14 homers in '07 (those was dead ball days—guy'd lead the league with seven or nine homers—old Jake hit 14 that year!). Then in '08 Jake signed for a contract that gave him about $9 a week, plus 50 cents a day meal money. And he had to launder his own uniform—they only issued one. This was in the days before teams was put up in hotels. Jake useta sleep in bus stations or abandoned buildings between games. It wasn't real comfortable (raises voice) BUT JAKE DIDN'T COMPLAIN! He was a gamer. That was the life of a ballplayer in those days. They was tough. Sometimes they'd just go out and make a royal ruckus and spend the night in the slammer, but they'd still make it to the ballpark the next day, no excuses.

"And what's all these safety precautions they got nowadays? Ear flaps? In '07 we didn't wear HELMETS! Only thing protectin' yer noodle was a cotton cap with yer team's initial on it. You didn't need to protect yer coconut in those days. They wasn't college kids—you didn't have no pre-meds in the bullpen or guys studyin' for their real estate license in the off-season. They was SERIOUS BASEBALL JOES! Didn't matter if they got hit—they was SOL-DIERS and baseball was WAR, dammit. If they got beaned, they could stand it! They'd get clobbered by a Burleigh Grimes spitball (according to Macmillan, Grimes did not enter the big leagues until 1916), be knocked unconscious fer a few minutes, whiff some smellin' salts from the batboy, then back on yer feet and standin' in with a 2–2 count. You'd be hemmorhagin', but you wasn't goin' down without yer cuts.

"Speakin' of spitballs, remember old Luke Busby? (Uh, no, actually.) He was the BEST OF 'EM! 'Ol' Leatherneck' we called him. His won-loss record wasn't that great cause he played with the old Washington Senators. Those Senators in '07 were so bad. They lost 133 straight games, from April 25 to September 16. But they had Luke Busby. The spitball was legal in those days, you didn't have to hide nothin'. Luke'd go out there with a big chaw of Day O'Work chewin' tobacco. He'd be standin' out there on the mound, lookin' mean, six days' a stubble on his chin, four nights' a no sleep under his eyes. He'd be starin' down at you, bring the ball up to his mouth, and (loud spitting sound), and he'd put a loada tobacco juice on that ball; it'd look like icing on a cupcake. Then he'd throw that thing ninety miles an hour, trailin' spit the whole sixty feet–six inches, and damned if that thing didn't splash in yer puss and blind you for a moment. STRIKE ONE!

"Busby led the league three years in a row in strike-outs. He only won six games in that stretch, lost 72. But the Senators was one of the worst teams of all time, so Busby did the best he could.

"But those Senators wasn't as bad as the old St. Louis Browns. Let me tell you about this one guy they had, a blind left-fielder with a hook named..."

Unfortunately, at this point our tape ran out, and since we'd been dozing off and on, the rest of the interview was lost.

MERRITT CLIFTON

Exploding Curve

I TURNED TWENTY-ONE IN PRISON, doing life without parole . . ."
I glance toward the clock-radio. The ballgame starts in a few minutes. Pamela comes home in perhaps half an hour. With my work done, I mellow myself for both. And take a moment's reverie, turning the country-western music down, drifting backward to the exploding curve.

First there came the pain and humiliation. I turned twenty-one as a first baseman, outfielder, and long relief pitcher for the Fuji Clippers, a San Jose-based Class B semi-pro team. It would be my final season, I knew, partly because afterward I would be out of college and would probably move away, partly because a ballplayer isn't a prospect after twenty-one if he hasn't been professionally drafted. The Athletics, Giants, Reds, Orioles, and Brewers all had scouted me in turn, beginning at age fifteen, but none of them ever put my name on their draft list, much less offered a contract. Semi-pro isn't just a place to play baseball. It's a showcase for aspiring professionals, a meatrack, the jock equivalent of singles bars, where scouts for the orgies case young flesh, seeking those willing and able to crawl through the dust and sweat of the minor leagues, to cut their hair and wear their clothes just so, to stimulate aged, alcoholic, overweight voyeuristic club owners and still more voyeuristic fans. I wasn't a prospect, perhaps, because I understood the dugout as gay bar; because like the rare Mike Marshall or Bill Lee, I played for the game, divorcing myself from sexual politics. Some, the Marshalls and Lees, are either good enough or lucky enough to get away with it. I wasn't. I ignored the leather-trade orders to wear my Fuji cap while shagging flies in the outfield, because I enjoyed the rare Santa Clara Valley breeze, a warm breeze, riffling my longer-than-permissible hair. I ran for distance, five miles or so, instead of the prescribed one mile of wind-sprints, because I loved the rhythm and motion of running itself, not frothing and panting and writhing for breath after half an hour of obeying a coach's whistle.

I say I played for the game, but not as a Pete Rose does. Competitive, yes, I was; I fought hard on the mound and at bat, enjoying the struggle. But afterward I always left the game itself behind me. Victory or defeat never mattered. I remembered instead the sensual experiences. Baseball was always primarily sensual for me, from when I first played seriously in early puberty. Some of my private joys were almost clichés: the crack of good wood connecting, the supple flex of a well-oiled mitt, scooping a skidding grounder. Others, unmentioned in the sports pages and diamond novels for adolescents, I found downright orgasmic. Catching a high line drive to the outfield on the run, for instance. First the explosion of anticipation into action, with the bat's crack as signal, the beginning of a private dance. The fast, fluttering glide of the baseball, singing through the air toward me. My long jolting strides, racing after it. My lunge, or dive, or stab to meet it, and at the instant of impact, loss of bodily and emotional restraint, carried a few strides farther by momentum before snapping into the next sensual experience, the throw.

But best, and yet most disappointing, the exploding curve, a treat either to pitch or bat against. It comes up hard and close, like a thunderbolt fastball, then as if finding a time-warp, veers and re-emerges two feet away just a split-second later. The art of pitching it lies in locating the time-warp on the inside edge of the strike zone, for a right-handed pitcher to a right-handed batter, and then throwing the ball with just the right velocity and spin to enter. Thrown either too slow or with too little spin, it might still break, bringing back a dribbling grounder, but to get a man out this way is always an inferior encounter, involving nothing done to perfection. Thrown too fast or with too much spin, the pitch becomes either fastball or second-rate slider, overpowering some batters but a cripple to the quick-wristed and strong. Batting, I hit the exploding curve just as I pitched it, by finding the time-warp, then holding my own explosion back a half-second longer than most hitters could, until the ball burst out the far side of it. I never saw the ball actually move from one place to the other. During that almost timeless interval, it vanished into the fourth dimension. When it did reappear, I was the rare hitter who could usually rip it, though straight fastballs of not much greater velocity often handcuffed me—and even when I couldn't rip it, I knew I could always bunt it up the first base line and beat it out for an infield hit.

At age twenty-one the exploding curve had been my chief sensual indulgence for almost half my life. With monomaniacal self-discipline, I lived like a Spartan and worked like a monk, unremittingly, at whatever I judged important. I loved and admired women, but always from a distance, to the point that even girls I saw socially seemed ethereal and unreal. My sexual experience remained confined to imagination while I read all the world's greatest poets and novelists, pored over convoluted Latinate epistles by the early Christians, Gnostics, and heretics, absorbed military history from ancient times through Vietnam, and of course worked out regularly on the diamond. Life appeared passionate and beautiful, but for whatever reason I felt excluded from it, armed with an exceptionally keen critical mind and physical hardihood, while lacking any capacity to give and receive warmth. I wasn't cold, nor inconsiderate, merely emotionally unable to respond as I desired to, as I felt I ought to; where I could willingly, enthusiastically abandon myself to the moment in a ballgame, I remained taut among people, wary, always watching for the knife concealed in loose clothing, the co-conspirator waiting in ambush around the corner, in the closet, or eavesdropping through the ventilator screen.

I turned twenty-one in metaphorical prison, aware my own emotional isolation would inevitably prevent me from accomplishing all I'd studied to do. I had to learn to reach out and hold hearts, as well as minds; effecting social change and appealing to the best in people couldn't succeed if approached one-dimensionally. Nor was I happy, and where that hadn't mattered once, where in my middle teens baseball provided joy enough, now I needed companionship, something fuller and closer than either infield chatter or bookish conversations over beer. I felt a frustrated life within me, beginning to push and blossom out; a tenseness, like my expectation swelling in the batter's box at recognizing the exploding curve begin, just before I blasted into it. But this permeated my whole existence, and one cannot live with such sustained tension. Something would soon erupt. My baseball career, doomed, no longer offered escape or solace. Worse, whether from lost desire or lost faith, I'd lost my batting stroke.

Two out, bottom of the ninth, bases loaded, the Clippers behind a run—the classical clutch situation, facing an A-league team from Santa Clara. I'd come in during the sixth inning and kept us close, pitching brilliantly. The Santa Clara pitcher was exhausted now, hanging curves, grooving fastballs. Confident, I dusted my hands, picked up my bat, a Roberto Clemente model, and settled into the box. But my reputation preceded me. Already the Santa Clara manager called time out, waving his right fielder to the mound—a Chicano kid who'd already pitched a one-hit shutout against us in the first game of this Sunday exhibition doubleheader. He threw the exploding curve and the best fastball I'd ever seen, faster than my own, once clocked at over 90 miles per hour.

For the first time since childhood, I felt helplessly overpowered. I couldn't find the time-warp, and missed the curve twice on his first two pitches. I choked up on the bat handle. Took a couple of fastballs, wide. Took an inside display-case curve, a piece of bat-busting sucker-bait. Full count, I knew what he'd throw, the exploding curve, shooting from point to point like chain lightening following electrical lines. I remembered my old trick, the bunt up the first base line. It wouldn't be expected. I could easily beat it out. The tying run, coming down from third, would be running with the pitch, and both pitcher and catcher would have to act quickly to force him. I found I no longer could conjure up my old relish for challenge. I would take the easy out: bunt. And run. I called time, dusting my hands again, surreptitiously studying the patch of ragged grass where I'd dump that curve, seeking the softest possible spot, the spot most certain to deaden the ball and keep it fair. If it rolled foul, I'd strike out for bunting unsuccessfully with two strikes against me.

But as I found my place, then squinted about the outfield toward the setting sun beyond, as if contemplating the heroic home run I wouldn't hit, I remembered what that exploding curve had once meant to me. I remembered pitching it, and the sinking feeling of having poured all my best into emptiness as batters swung and missed it by a foot. I remembered hitting it, rocketing it cleanly and purely on a line either off or over the concrete clubhouse in right centerfield, or golfing it over houses beyond left-center. I remembered the single most sensual experience of my life so far: perfect contact. Just that, the fat of the bat connecting with the fat of the ball, producing a euphoric, weightless sensation from my fingertips through my hands, wrists, forearms, and shoulders, moving down my spine into my hips and all the way to my knees as I swung into my follow-through, eyes searching out the ball's flight into open spaces. I had thrilled to perfect contact perhaps two thousand times. It ceased to come often after I ceased finding it satisfactory, for reasons I could still not clearly contemplate.

But it occurred to me there, sifting dust through my fingers, that hitting was a form of pushing away, of excluding, and that perfect contact meant no contact at all. It wasn't love, just sex, an explosion, self-dominated and kept as brief as possible. I still enjoyed hitting and always would, but now needed a further dimension. It could no longer seem important, a necessary pleasure.

I returned to the box, picked up the pitch, the time-warp, swung my hardest—and missed. I'd lost it. Finished. Two months past twenty-one. I vaguely recall boos from the sparse crowd, and some mockery I barely heard. Teammates passed, jogging in from the bases or swarming out of the dugout to pick up equipment. Some spoke to me. I mumbled back, not caring or seeing, lost in my disappointment. In all my career I'd never struck out before in the bottom of the ninth with the bases loaded. I'd never failed to rise to a climactic moment. I'd never felt as impotent, or as desolate over what was, after all, a trivial failure: the game didn't even count in our standings.

And the night tide lapped against the narrow beach somewhere along the eastern shore of Reviligado. Sixteen miles from Ketchikan, Alaska, two or three miles from the nearest outlying houses, we watched our driftwood burn low, talking little, mostly just looking out across the water toward Prince Rupert, British Columbia—a tiny spot of light on the horizon, between two small islands flanking Reviligado. We'd almost finished our jug of wine. We hadn't yet touched. I'd started to reach toward her several times, only inches away, reclining against the same log, but stopped as if shackled. She moved only with her eyes. My own age, she'd already had more lovers than I could imagine. She seemed willing, interested. Yet I would have to touch her first, before anything could happen. I had to throw the ball, without knowing the batter, the count, or even the rules of the game, because, hell, it wasn't a game. I didn't want a game. I'd refused to play the dating-game, back in high school, and had hated it the few times I'd tried in college. At the same time, without a game, without rules, I again felt that overwhelming impotence, a sense of inability to do anything but wait out the count, bunt, and run.

Night, during an Alaskan summer, lasts about three, maybe four hours. We'd been there so long the grey dawn began, with eagles and ravens stretching in the trees behind us, occasionally swooping out over the low waves in search of breakfast, though most people had barely gone to bed.

In hitting the curve, I realized, in reading difficult books, in running for distance, in enduring pain, poverty, and dangerous work, I'd taught myself discipline and control to the point of suffocating all spontaneity despite my love for the sensual. I'd feared spontaneity as a weakness; yielding to each emotional impulse, I could never have held my stance in the batter's box, confident the curve would break before splitting my head open. Nor could I have digested Augustine without falling asleep, or remained content eating only oatmeal, potatoes, bread, and cheese. I could not have kept my intellect alive through 10-hour shifts at the Ketchikan pulpmill, my first post-college job, doing work invented with human robots in mind. But I'd not have turned twenty-one in prison, either. To develop superhuman capacities in one phase of life required developing all phases, just to keep balance.

The girl waited. I saw the curve of our friendship vanish into uncertainty, sure to emerge an instant later as either boredom or what I made it. I reached.

And felt contact, not sharp and hard but warm and firm, demanding abandonment. Loss of control. Loss of identity, no longer number 7 for Fuji, no longer unconditionally released, as I'd been soon after my strike out; rather, unconditionally accepted.

We didn't make perfect contact, not just yet. But as the sunlight first struck the beach, with a chill breeze giving us goose bumps and scattering sand in our deserted clothing, I discovered again the exploding curve. Only this time I neither slammed it away nor made it dip off to nothing. This time we held and shared it. Prison collapsed into open sea and sky.

I turned up the ballgame after the national anthem. The black Reviligado sand and red Santa Clara dust are both far behind me. The exploding curve remains, in the thrust of Pamela's breasts, the arch of her back, the line of her leg and smooth plane of her belly.

She will be home soon.

99

JAY FELDMAN

There Ain't Enough Mustard

YOU PROBABLY READ about that little fracas at Yankee Stadium the other night, where some of the fans got all excited and tore up a concession stand. I guess a dozen guys spent the night in the can, but fortunately there was no serious injuries—just a few busted noses, and like that.

But if you noticed in all the stories in the papers and on TV, nobody could say for sure who or what started the fuss in the first place. So that's what I'm here to tell you—'cause it was me.

I should start by saying right away that I am not a violent person. My motto has always been, "Live and let live," and I like to keep a low profile, if you know what I mean. Oh, sure, I been in a few scrapes—who hasn't? Like the time on the subway in the morning rush hour when that very tall guy in the mohair overcoat was reading *The Wall Street Journal* on my head. But even then, I politely asked him two times to kindly remove his paper from my head before I got physical. And there was that other time with the City health inspector, but he definitely asked for it. And maybe a few other incidents when I was younger, but not for a long time now. I've mellowed, as my kids would say.

I admit I can have a temper. See, the thing I learned early is that when you're five-foot-one-half-inch, you better be able to take care of yourself, 'cause a lot of guys are gonna try and push you around, and if you don't let 'em know where to get off, you're gonna wind

101

up as a doormat, if you know what I mean.

When I was a young man, I grew a mustache. It grew real slow, and it took about three or four months before it got to looking half decent. So, these friends of mine, they were gonna play a little joke on me, see, so they jumped me and held me down while one guy shaved off half the mustache. I don't have to tell you, I was pretty burned up. So this guy gets finished shaving half my mustache off, and all of a sudden the rest of 'em realize they can't let go of me or someone's gonna get his head handed to him. So, here's five guys, all bigger than me, sitting on top of me, and looking at each other, trying to figure out what to do next. I'm not saying a word, but they could see the steam coming out of my ears. Finally someone says, "Hy. . .uh, Hymie. . .uh, listen, don't get sore. We're sorry. We shouldn't have done it. Please don't do anything crazy, OK? Awright?. . .Listen, we're gonna let you up. OK, when I say 'three,' everyone let go. One. . .two. . .three." And then, let me tell you, you never saw five guys scatter so fast in your life. And you can be sure they never pulled anything like that again.

But one thing I can honestly say, and I swear this is true: I never went anywhere *looking* for trouble. Sure, I never backed down to no one, but I never went looking—you can ask anyone who knows me. And that's the difference between me and a guy like Billy Martin. You gotta understand the distinction here. A guy like Martin, he's always looking for trouble; me, I'm always trying to stay invisible. I never had a chip on my shoulder, I never had a big mouth, and I always minded my own business—unless someone tried to push me around. And then I took care of myself. And that's the truth.

I also want to go on record here as saying I'm strongly opposed to all the fan violence they have in the ballparks these days. I think it's terrible. This little incident I'm talking about, though, was a whole different kettle of fish, as I'm about to tell you.

See, my kids wanted to take me to a ballgame to celebrate my retirement, which took place last month. I decided a long time ago that I wasn't gonna be one of these guys that drops dead on the job, if you know what I mean, so the day I hit sixty-two, that was it. Goodbye and good luck. See ya later.

There Ain't Enough Mustard

I used to be a big baseball fan, but I ain't been to a game in quite a few years. I'll catch a game on TV or radio, and of course, I still read the sports page. But that's about it any more.

I was a Brooklyn fan, and after they left for the coast, I kinda lost interest. I followed the Mets for a while when they came in, but it got to be too big of a schlep to get out there to Shea, so I gave that up. I never did like the Yankees much, and particularly since this shmuck Steinberger took over. I mean the guy just plain rubs me the wrong way. For one thing, when it comes to baseball, he don't know shit from Shinola. Tantrums he knows from. Royal proclamations he knows from. But baseball? Nuttin'. Zero. Zilch. He knows as much about baseball as Harold Cosell knows. The two of them would probably get along just fine.

The other thing that soured me on baseball is the crybabies they got playing the game now. Guys that won't play if they got a little boo-boo on their pinky finger. Guys that won't cross the street unless they get paid for it. The hell with 'em. I'd rather go down to the neighborhood park and watch five-year-olds play.

But this time, my kids really wanted to take me to the Stadium. My younger son Andy is a lawyer who works for a bigshot that buys a season box for a tax write-off. The kind of a guy who goes to a ballgame in a three-piece suit and leaves after a couple of innings. You know the type—hates baseball. Anyway, Andy notices that nobody's using the tickets for this particular twi-night double-header, so he grabs 'em, and him and his older brother Jerry worked on me till I said OK.

I love a twi-night. Always have. You go to the park, it's daylight; you see six, seven hours of baseball, and you never realize that it's gotten dark because of the lights and because you're so involved in the action—it's like going to another land, if you know what I mean—but when you leave the ballpark it's night time. And you never saw it happen 'cause you've been in that other country the whole time.

So I let the boys talk me into it. I even dug out my old Brooklyn Dodgers cap for the occasion.

Driving up to the Stadium, I have to admit that I got pretty excited. And walking from the car, I was really getting caught up in it, you know, it'd been such a long time since I'd been to a ballgame. And when we got inside and I caught sight of the field, I felt like a little kid again, if you know what I mean. The white lines on the green grass always did it to me.

The seats, it turns out, are right behind the third-base dugout. Hey, going in style. You gotta remember that I'm a guy who always sat in the bleachers with the lumpken proletariat.

Man, was that ballpark packed! Which figured, of course, since the Yanks were playing the California Angels, and Reggie Jackson is always a good bet to fill the house.

On the way down to our seats, I hear some kid saying, "Whyncha go back where ya belong, ya freak! Go back to Boston!" I look down, and here's this brat looking up at *me*. And the little pissant looks me right in the eye and says it again: "Go back to Boston, ya bum!" Boston? What the hey? And then I notice he's looking at my cap—the little creep can't even tell the difference between Brooklyn and Boston. I tell you, we're living in strange times.

So we get seated, and I'm all tingling, you know, from the field and the crowd and everything. It'd been so long, but it was like just yesterday. Richard Merrill comes out to sing "The Star Spangled Banner," and buddy, I heard it like I never heard it before. I always did suspect that the national anthem was really about baseball.

Jo-osé, can you see,
By the dawn's early light,
What so proudly we hailed,
At the twi-night's last inning.
Whose sport stripes and bright stars,
Through the Berra-less fight,
And the ramparts we watched,
Were so gallantly screaming.
And the rockets' red glare,
The bombs bursting in air,
Babe Ruth through the night,

That our flag was still there.
José, does tha-hat star spangled
Ba-ha-na-her ye-het wa-have,
O'er the la-hand of the freeeeee,
And the home of the Braves—PLAY BALL!

A couple of rows behind us there's a guy who's got a thing for Reggie Jackson. Now, Reggie ain't my favorite player either, but this guy had a real thing. Every time Reggie comes in from right field, this guy has something to say, and with one of those voices that could stop traffic on Times Square. "REGGIE, YA COULDN'T SHINE TED WILLIAMS' SHOES," or "REGGIE, YA COULDN'T CARRY JACKIE ROBINSON'S JOCKSTRAP," and stuff like that. Reggie struck out his first three times up, and this bigmouth was having a ball. Every time Reggie comes back to the dugout, he's checking the stands to see where this guy is sitting. In the eighth inning, Reggie comes up with the score tied and the bases loaded and belts one into the third deck in right field, and stands there at the plate watching the ball disappear into the crowd. I was reminded of that remark some ballplayer made a few years ago when a reporter asked him if he thought Reggie was a hot dog. "Is Reggie a hot dog?" the man said. "Let me put it this way: there ain't enough mustard in this world to cover Reggie Jackson." So Reggie circles the bases real slow, and on his way back to the bench, he stops and looks up at this bigmouth who's been giving him the business, and points right at him and sneers and spits between his front teeth.

By the end of the first game, we're all good and hungry, so I offer to go and get some eats for all of us. When I get up to the concession stand, though, it's mobbed. I mean there's a crowd like New Year's Eve on Times Square. And no lines, just pushing and shoving. I never did like that sort of thing, but when you live in New York, you get used to it, I guess. So I wade into the crowd, and after ten minutes, I've worked my way up to the front.

Behind the counter is this moose of a college kid—like about six-foot-three and 250 pounds. At first I figure I'll be polite and wait for him to look at me, but soon I realize that if I don't speak up, I'm gonna be here all night.

So I say simply, "Six hot dogs, please," but the moose doesn't hear me and serves someone else instead. OK, so after he's done, I try again: "Six hot dogs." Again he doesn't hear—or else he's ignoring me. Now why should he ignore me? Must be he didn't hear me, what with all the noise and him being two heads taller than me, so after he's free, I speak up once more. And once more he waits on someone else. So, now I'm sure he's giving me the old brush-off, and I take a quarter out of my pocket and start tapping on the counter with it. This gets his attention. He looks down at me. "Listen, shrimp," he says, "why don't you bang with your head?"

Now, "shrimp" is a form of address that I've never taken kindly to, especially from a big guy. The last fella that called me "shrimp"— and I'm talking like thirty years ago—ended up apologizing to me. So I probably don't have to tell you that I'm getting pretty hot. My first impulse is to go over the counter and rearrange this jerk's face. Instead, I count to ten, and say loud and clear, "SIX HOT DOGS!"

The moose looks down and says—and you can tell he thinks he's real clever—"Why don't you go back to Boston, Pops?" There it is again! Insult to injury! Another snotnose who don't even know the difference between Brooklyn and Boston! This kid needs to be taught a lesson. He's definitely got it coming to him.

Right in front of me on the counter is one of those giant-size mustard containers—like about two gallons worth. I'm fuming, but very calmly and slowly, I unscrew the plunger-top and lay it on the counter, and wait for my chance.

The moose is filling an order—his back is turned to me. When he turns around, his hands are full of hot dogs, and he leans forward to pass the order across the counter, at which moment I reach up with one hand, grab his jacket at the collar, yank him towards me and turn over the mustard container on his head. Then I pull him up over the counter and, holding him by the lapels, I yell in his mustard-covered face, "It's Brooklyn, not Boston, you igno-ramus! And next time you think about calling someone a shrimp, you better think twice!" And with that, I push him back over the other side of the counter.

And whaddya know, but sitting right there on the counter in front of me is the hot dogs the moose dropped when I grabbed him. And would you believe it, there's six of 'em. So I gather up the hot dogs, and when I turn around to go back to my seat, the scene is like one of those western movies where everyone in the saloon is swinging at somebody. I'm telling you, it's a regular brawl, a brouhaha.

A guy could get hurt in a mob scene like that, so quickly and carefully, I pick my way through the uproar and head down to our box. On my way, I notice that everybody's rubber-necking towards the top of the section, trying to figure out what all the commotion is about.

"Hey, just in time, Pop," says Andy when I reach my seat. "The second game's gonna start right away. What took you so long? We were starting to worry about you."

"Big crowd," I say, passing out the hot dogs.

"What the hell's going on up there?" asks Jerry. "Sounds like a riot."

I shrug my shoulders. "Who knows. I didn't see nuttin'."

"Hey, Pop, you forgot to put mustard on these hot dogs."

As far as the rest goes, you probably know as much as I do—I read about it in the papers, same as you. The concession stand got torn up pretty good, I guess, and they threw a few guys in the cooler for the night. Otherwise, no big deal. The moose that I gave the mustard facial must have been too embarrassed to admit that a sixty-two year old shrimp got the best of him, 'cause when the cops tried to sort the whole thing out, nobody could say for sure how it started.

Which is just as well with me. I don't need publicity. I like to keep a low profile. I ain't no hot dog, if you know what I mean.

WILLIAM T. STAFFORD

The Professor and the Chicago Cubs

WHEN THE PROFESSOR looked at his watch, he saw that it was precisely 1:07. Wait five more minutes, he said to himself, and you can make your favorite stool at The Wagon just as the game begins, have lunch there during the first two or three innings, stop back by the office long enough to look at the mail, and, if nothing pressing has come in, bike on home and watch the last few innings of the game. He noted that it was exactly 1:15 when he left his desk. When he returned, it was 2:15. At The Wagon he had eaten a bowl of chili, with slaw on the side, and had had two Old Style drafts, followed by a cup of black coffee. When he left, the Cubs were 2 up on the Dodgers at the end of three. It was great, he thought, seeing the Bull back on first at Wrigley. Durham had been injured ten days before the All-Star break, and this was his first return to the field. In his first at bat he had lined a screamer to the shortstop, who let it pass between his legs, and although it was a clear hit, it was ruled an error. The Professor, like the other regulars at The Wagon, thought it a bad call. But it didn't matter; the Bull had scored a run, even if unearned. With no afternoon mail, the Professor was about to leave for home when his assistant came in with a manuscript in his hand. Its problem, however, was simple; the Professor at any rate made it simple: He told his assistant to take care of it. As he closed his office door, the time was 2:51.

He was biking up his shared driveway beside his house when

his neighbor came out and yelled: "Home early again, I see. You'd better hurry. The Dodgers have just tied it up in the sixth." As he rushed into his study and flipped on the set, he noted the time as 3:07.

Before the set cleared, he heard the familiar gravelly voice of Harry Caray and knew the game was at least in the seventh. Harry always called the first three innings on WGN, Milo Hamilton the second three, with Harry returning for the rest of the game. Steve Stone, the best of the trio, was the color man throughout. While in the kitchen filling up his tall plastic cup with ice water, he heard Harry's voice come flooding back, "Ahh right . . . EV-VR-BODY . . . . Let me HEAR you—AH ONE . . . AH TWO . . . AH THREE," as the off-pitch, off-time crowd boomed "Take Me Out to the Ballgame" through his set, the Professor grunted a sigh of satisfaction and settled in his swivel chair. The seventh-inning stretch had begun at 3:10.

The game could hardly have ended with more excitement. During the eighth, ninth, and tenth, the Dodger lead-off man had gotten on base. Sometime during the eighth, the Cubs had brought in their second short-reliever, Big Tim Stoddard, and he was in trouble all the way: Dodger runners at first and second, in the eighth; runners at first and third, with one out, in the ninth. Lasorda's mistake was in the ninth when he pulled his star pitcher Alejandro Peña for a pinch hitter. Peña had given the Cubs fits all day, having allowed only five hits after Moreland's double in the first that had driven in the Cubs' only other run. A classy double play, Cey to Owen to Durham, 5–6–3, had gotten Stoddard out of one jam; a pop-up to the catcher out of another. And Stoddard had fanned the pinch hitter sent in for Peña. Yes, the Dodger mistake was not in its pinch-hitting; it was in removing Peña from the mound. Although the Cubs didn't score in the bottom of the ninth, they hit Niedenfuer, the Dodger reliever, pretty well. And when young Ryne Sandberg came to bat to begin the tenth, the Professor simply felt the Cubs were going to win. The moment came on the fourth pitch. The count was two strikes and one ball. The fourth pitch was high, but right over the center of the plate. WHAP! "It could be," Harry shouted. "It may be! It . . . is! Ho . . . l . . . y Cow!" The game was over. Cubs win 3–2. The Professor looked at his watch. It was 4:24.

Baseball had come to the Professor late in his life. (Thank God it had, he had often said to himself; otherwise, he was fond of remarking to his youngish stepson and son-in-law, he would still be an untenured assistant professor, if not an instructor.) It had come, he more publicly said, as a bonus with his second wife, along with her new outdoor grill, her beautiful wool couch, and the Tiffany lamp that she brought with her when they were married three years before. The truth was, however, that his interest in the game had had its first prod while he was still married to his first wife. It was at least five years ago, perhaps six, while he and she were spending a few days in Chicago—to do some shopping, to see a show, to eat in some good restaurants—that they had decided to go to a Cubs game. Neither had ever seen a big-league game. And when they were told, at some office in the Loop, that no tickets were available there but that they could surely get them at the park, they hopped on a bus headed for Wrigley Field.

It was a beautiful, clear summer day, temperature in the mid-70s, and the ballpark only about half filled. While they were standing in line at the ticket window, a pleasant young man walked up and asked if they would like to buy two box seats in the seventh row right behind third base. The young man said that he was a Scoutmaster from Winnetka, up with a troop of fourteen. But two of his scouts had not been able to make the trip at the last minute and if the couple did not mind sitting in the midst of some ten-to-twelve-year-olds, they would have, he assured them, excellent seats. They were.

Wrigley Field unfolded before the Professor as one of the most beautiful sights he had ever seen. He could never have imagined that it could be so small, that the ivy and grass could be so green, the field, the lines, the bags, so geometrically neat, the players so unbelievably close. Ron Cey, then third baseman for the Dodgers, had an intensity on his face unlike any the Professor had ever seen with glove extended in some kind of frozen readiness that unfroze with magical rapidity the moment the ball was hit. And he was only a few yards away. Dusty Baker, like Cey now no longer a Dodger, was fluid grace as he charged in from left field towards a pop-up behind third or a drive through third. He was much less intense, far more loose than Cey.

The only Cub player the Professor could remember well from that game was the shortstop Ivan DeJesus—and that probably was as much for the way the announcer pronounced his name—EEE-von D'Hey-Zus—as for the way he played. He vaguely remembered that Billy Buckner was also in that game, at first base, memorable perhaps as much for the ovation he received every time he came to bat as for anything he actually accomplished in the game. He was at that time the Cubs' star hitter. He was eventually traded.

The Professor and his wife rooted of course for the Cubs, as the closest thing they had to a "home team," and the fact that they lost that game did not spoil it one bit for either of them. It had been a splendid outing. They had both drunk a couple of beers and eaten hot dogs. The Professor had even ordered and consumed a box of Cracker Jacks, savoring their crunchy taste with a remembered taste bud that had not been resatisfied since he was a child, although a bag of sugar-coated peanuts in Paris had once come close.

Although the Professor knew nothing about baseball but what he remembered from playing the sandlot variety as a child—didn't they, back then, call strikes first, balls second, the opposite of the way the professionals called them?—his ignorance didn't stop him from pontificating to his first wife about the finer points of the game. She tolerated several of these remarks without responding. She then reminded him that when they had first met, some twenty-five years previously, she had been dating a professional baseball player, albeit one in a single-A league from southern Alabama, and that she had sat through scores of games. The Professor shut up following that reminder, although he was later to remember remembering, with some sly satisfaction, that the baseball player she had then dated was named after President Roosevelt, that he had been called Delano, "Deno," for short, and that her father used to complain about how uninformed Deno was, how he never read anything in the papers but the sports pages, unlike the Professor, who in those days was deep into current events. This small contretemps notwithstanding, they both had a good time—and promised themselves they would certainly do it again. But they never did.

After their divorce two years later, the Professor occasionally wondered why they had never returned to Wrigley Field. He still was not into baseball, not in the way he had recently become, although after that first visit to the Friendly Confines, he did watch an occasional game on the tube; and he could remember an instance or two when his first wife had been annoyed after he insisted on seeing a late-afternoon game concluded before they had dinner.

The reputed long-standing interest his second wife had in baseball, especially in the Cubs, was, he subsequently discovered, more legend than fact, although she had for years listened to Cub games on the radio. Moreover, she had visited Wrigley Field many times; she had even on occasion sat in the bleachers with her son, himself a fervent fan, and some of his friends. She knew the history of the Cubs fairly well, knew of most of the players by name, and became the Professor's prime resource person as his interest in the game began to intensify. (On occasion he had had to pitch his questions, when they became too arcane, to a graduate assistant— as when he asked her if it is really legitimate for the Cubs' manager to prescribe the color of shoe tongues an opposing pitcher could wear when he played in Wrigley Field. It is, he discovered.) Even so, he had been frankly impressed during that first game they saw together with the mystifying hieroglyphics she produced on the scorecard as the game progressed. She must teach him how to score, he had said to himself.

For a long time he associated his second wife with baseball. There was nothing much, he had been convinced, she enjoyed more than their frequent weekend trips to Chicago to see the Cubs play: the always comfortable ride up on Amtrak; the quick taxi-ride to one of the weekend-special hotels around Michigan Avenue; the hurried check-in and quick glance at and quick drink in their room, before walking over a few blocks to the crowded subway out to Addison. The Professor always choked with anticipation as they descended the rickety stairs at the Addison stop before pouring out into the street only two or three doors down from the main entrance to the park. The smell of hot dogs and beer, the cries of pennant and visor vendors, the whistles of the cops on the corner, and, most of all, the jostling, happy-looking crowds—all ages, all classes, all colors, with attire running the gamut from cut-off jeans without shirts or shoes to three-piece pin-stripes, from loosely knotted halters with bikini-brief hip huggers to long flowering dresses topped with wide-brimmed hats. The Professor always wore his old safari khaki—possibly because of its plethora of pockets, four alone on the jacket, into which he could conveniently pack his pipe, tobacco, cigarettes, and cigars—not to mention notebook, pen, hotel and house key, lighter, checkbook, and, when they didn't forget it, three or four packets of mustard in case the dogs they bought in the stands did not have enough. They almost never did.

Although the Professor and his wife traveled extensively everywhere, to Santo Domingo one spring break, to Arizona one cold January, to Utah one May, even to Budapest one August for an international congress, he enjoyed none of them more than their two to three visits to Wrigley Field every summer. He had begun slowly to watch the Cubs on TV—but only when it was convenient to do so, away games at night when he had nothing else scheduled, weekends when rain prevented him from playing golf, week-day afternoon games when chores were slack at the office.

He developed no interest whatsoever in the teams in the American League, although one of his daughters who lived outside of Washington had herself become a Baltimore fan, went to the games there frequently, and had even somehow secured tickets for the 1983 World Series for those games that would have finally been played there had Baltimore not wrapped up the Series away from home. The Professor professed absolute disdain for the American League, with its impure DH rule, which even his Oriole-loving daughter agreed was a stain on the game. Much too often he had repeated to friends, "Everyone gets his turn at bat—except in the American League." In fact, he developed an interest in other National League teams only as opponents of the Cubs and as potential or actual rivals for the league championship.

He was especially, even ostentatiously, indifferent to the White Sox, which, until 1984, most of his cronies down at The Wagon had designated as "their" team. He had on occasion joshed with an in-law who had grown up and lived on the South Side near Comiskey Park and who considered the Cubs a team only for the effete. The in-law once said to him that even the so-called Bleacher Bums were all rich college kids—or professors. The Professor had once been given a White Sox cap by a colleague who thought his single-minded devotion to the Cubs somewhat silly, whereupon the Professor wore the cap into The Wagon one lunch time during the summer of 1984 so that when asked what in the world he was doing with a Sox cap he could reply, "As a long-time Cub fan, I am uncomfortable when not wearing the hat of a loser."

But the feigned indifference to the fortunes of the White Sox was simply a minor infield joke. After two or three years the Professor's interest in other National League teams and even in some American League ones expanded somewhat as Cub players he had come to know were traded to them. At base, however, he remained a single-minded devotee of the Cubs, his interest in any other team or baseball activity determined solely by how it impinged on the Cubs, whether they won or lost. He was a one-team fan.

Late in the summer of 1984, when it seemed likely (or at least possible) that the Cubs could win the National League East, he discovered what he had heretofore called merely an "interest" was becoming an obsession. Until then he had honestly thought that his devotion to the Cubs was such that it would make little difference whether they won or lost. He had liked to think that each Cub outing he watched was like watching an exciting chess match, the eventual winner of less consequence than the strategy, the gambles, the goofs—the joy, in short, of observing the endless symmetries of the game with little concern for who won or lost. The fortunes and misfortunes of one club, he had decided, were sufficiently varied with highs and lows to last a lifetime. He should have known he had not been quite honest that afternoon of June 23 when Sandberg hit two home runs—the first with two outs in the bottom of the ninth, to tie the game 9–9; then, after the Cards tallied twice in the top of the tenth, to tie the game 11–11. He remembered saying at the time it didn't matter who finally won the game: the beauty was all in the comeback. Even after the Cubs did win 12–11, in the bottom of the eleventh, with Durham on third via a pinch single by Owen, he retained the belief that the final outcome didn't matter. When Whitey Herzog was reported in the papers next day as saying that Sandberg was the best player he had ever seen, the Professor still said that it was not the win that counted. But he probably knew otherwise.

How much otherwise was not totally apparent to the Professor until the end of the National League season, a high coming when the Cubs clinched the division title against Pittsburgh, followed by the higher high accompanying the lopsided scores the Cubs ran up against San Diego in the first two games of the league playoffs. The low that followed the subsequent three-game loss to the Padres was only slightly abated by Studs Terkel's comment, after that last game, that the Cubs were at their most lovable only when losing.

And in fact the Professor did look back on the '84 season as one that had rejuvenated his 60th year. He pasted a Cub logo on his office door, scribbled under it "Those Lovable Losers," and totally ignored the World Series.

But the Professor's obsession had only begun to intensify. During the off-season he scoured the sports pages every day for every scrap of news about the Cubs: whom were they trading or trading for; would they sign Sutcliffe, Trout, and Sanderson; and would they be permitted to install lights at Wrigley Field? When Sutcliffe finally signed, the Professor's joy was of an intensity that could only have been exceeded by the news that one of his three married daughters was about to present him with his first grandchild. And when he determined that his 1985 spring sabbatical would consist of a literary tour of the American Southwest, he must have known that his scheduled visit to the University of Arizona Library in Tucson was primarily a cover for visits to the Cubs' spring training camp at Mesa. (He saw them there twice.)

Between the Cubs' opening game against Pittsburgh on April 9 and their 56th game against Montreal on June 13, which included the suspended game against San Diego—Cubs up 4–2 at the end of six—which was scheduled to be concluded on July 10, the Professor had seen on TV at least part of every game televised, with one notable exception. He had had to schedule a three-day flight to North Florida, to visit his aged mother, sometime in June. He carefully arranged it for June 4 through 6 so that while there he could see two of the games the Cubs were scheduled to play against Atlanta, knowing that his mother's TV received WTBS out of Atlanta, although not WGN out of Chicago. He had been scrupulous in selecting flight hours that would get him there on June 4 before the 3:05 starting time, and in arranging beforehand to be free for the 1:20 game on June 5 and to be back home in Indiana before the 3:05 game against Pittsburgh on June 7. Those games all worked as scheduled, and he saw each of them complete. But, alas, he did have to miss the game against Pittsburgh on June 6—he couldn't even locate it on the Florida radio, as he could back in Indiana on the occasional days when the Cub games were not permitted to be televised because of network commitments. Even so, he did see highlights of that June 6 game, even on local Florida TV stations, as it was the only National League game scheduled on that date.

This obsession to see, or at least hear described, every game the Cubs played was beginning to create problems with the Professor's domestic, social, and professional life, although his wife made no great fuss when he insisted that they eat dinner in the TV room on days the Cubs played away from home early in the evening. She even tolerated very early dinners out so that they could see at least the last few innings of a game scheduled during the mid-evening hours. And although she rarely stayed up for those late, late games on the West Coast, she at least appeared to tolerate being awakened, sometimes as late as one in the morning, to be told how a particularly late game had come out.

She was sometimes not so tolerant, however, with the Professor's adamant insistence that they watch the game rather than one of the notable PBS nature or dramatic shows that they had often watched and enjoyed together. But the Professor quickly solved that problem by rushing out one afternoon and buying another TV set, having somewhat inconsistently refused to buy a VCR with the feeble but nonetheless firmly held rationale that taped-delay games were not quite the same thing.

His friends were somewhat less accommodating—at his invariably late appearances at cocktail parties on days the Cubs had late afternoon games, at his extremely early appearances (and consequent extremely early departures) on days of early evening games. The Professor was also an earnest and avid if not very accomplished golfer, had been one in fact six times more years than he had been a baseball fan. And although he customarily played in the morning and thus had no normal conflict there, he had on occasion played with colleagues on Friday afternoons. But now he would play with them only on those Friday afternoons that did not conflict with Cub games.

During most of the baseball season the Professor's university duties mercifully included no major conflicts with his viewing the Cub games. From approximately May 1 through the third week in August he did not teach, and although he was responsible for half-time administrative duties, these were flexible in their time and demands in a way that made them relatively easy to fulfill during the morning hours. Classes and seminars during August and September, however, proved troublesome. He had consequently gotten in the habit of requesting morning classes and once-a-week afternoon seminars, finally selecting Monday afternoons as the ones least likely to conflict with an important game. Only once, thus far, had he had the audacity to cancel a class for a game. It was sometime during September of '84, either during the division drive or the playoffs against the Padres. He had practiced no artifice, nor pleaded sick, nor put out tales of an ill wife or an invalid mother. He had simply told his class that it was cancelled because he wished to see a Cub game. The class of course was delighted; how his chairman would have reacted, had he heard about it, he didn't like to consider.

As the Cubs went into at least a six-game slump during mid-June of '85—having lost two to Montreal on June 12 and 13, three to the Cardinals at Wrigley Field on June 14, 15, and 16, and the first game of the season against the Mets in New York on June 17—he found himself saying that perhaps it would be better if they continued to lose. It would be nice, he and his wife said to each other, to go back to the good old days when there were no problems getting tickets to the Friendly Confines, when week-day fans rarely numbered over five thousand, weekend ones seldom more than fifteen or twenty thousand. They would not then really expect to win, would not groan as they had groaned, when the Cubs, who had played so spectacularly against the Cardinals on June 23 of 1984, lost 11–10 to those same Cardinals on June 14 of 1985 in a way that led even the Cub-owning *Chicago Tribune* to head its story of the game with "5 ERRORS MAKE CUBS LOOK SICK." Yes, indeed. In some perfectly honest ways, a losing team was more fun to support than a winning one. Perhaps the Professor had not been lying to himself when he maintained that his love for the Cubs had little to do with whether they won or lost. His intense joy at their spectacular win over the Cardinals in June of 1984 had been no more intense than at their spectacular loss in June of 1985.

Later in the summer of 1985 a discovery of sorts began to unfold. When the Cubs tied their previous straight-loss record of

13; when their escalating disabled list finally encompassed all five of their starting pitchers (Sutcliffe, Trout, Eckersley, Sanderson, and even Ruthven), not to mention at various times and for various lengths other players such as Dernier, Jody Davis, Durham, and Cey; when various young replacements, Dunston, Dayett, Hatcher, Engel, and Meridith, revealed their various incompetencies or were themselves injured; when in short the Cubs were effectively out of it by being thirteen games down at the middle of August— the Professor discovered that he was no less addicted to them as losers than he had been with them as winners. The drama and the comedy were no less intense.

He and his wife were at Wrigley Field on June 26, the day the Cubs ended their thirteen-game losing streak by defeating the Mets, and one would have thought, from their reaction and indeed the reaction of the crowd, that the Cubs had won the World Series. They, along with some 36,000 other fans remained in the stands a good thirty minutes after the game, still applauding. It was an exciting moment. Exciting in a different way was the reappearance of young Shawon Dunston, who was called up to replace Larry Bowa at shortstop when Bowa was released on waivers on August 12. It was fun enough seeing him and Sandberg collide and thus drop an infield fly during his first fielding play of the game, but the true comedy of the situation came only with manager Frey's comment after the game that the boy Dunston had to learn to stop running all over the field and remember there were other players out there. Comedy of a different sort was apparent on August 14 in a game against the Expos when the slumping Ron Cey hit a grand-slam homer to put the Cubs up 5–1, only to have Cub pitcher Ray Fontenot give up successive home runs in the top of the two-out fourth on two pitches to Butera and the Expos' pitcher Bryan Smith, neither of whom had ever before hit a home run. The Expos eventually won 8–7.

Although the Professor was to write a friend in mid-August that it was something of a comfort to find those lovable losers in their customary position near the bottom of the National League East, he was not sure that he honestly believed that. At any rate, he knew it for a conundrum that would not soon be solved. But it didn't matter. He had ten or, if he were lucky, perhaps fifteen or twenty more years to work it out. In the immediate meantime, he had only fifteen or twenty *minutes* to bike home, get his plastic glass filled with ice and water, and settle down in front of the set for the 6:40 start of the Cubs' seventh game of the season against the Braves.

JAMES KISSANE

Frankie's Home Run

Skylark, have you anything to say to me?
Can you tell me where my love may be?
Is there a meadow in the mist
Where someone's waiting to be kissed?

THAT WAS THE MUSIC in the air the summer I was twelve. A skylark I had neither seen nor heard; a misty meadow I would have thought a pretty dreary place, and a kiss a source of embarrassment. Hoagy Carmichael was a name unknown to me, and this song of his was just something I had heard on the radio. But its tune and certain of the words were so often in my head and took such unaccountable possession of me that they sang, and still do sing, the essence of my summer of 1942.

I see myself—or do I look out upon the world from within myself?—in dust-colored corduroys and a red baseball cap, standing in the weedy outfield of Overland Park, shagging balls for batting practice. I pound my fist aimlessly into the pocket of my glove and stare down at my new baseball shoes, a size too large because, being expensive, they were expected to last at least another season. The shiny aluminum toe plate on my left shoe is a bother. It keeps coming loose because the screws that hold it could not be so long as to punch clear through the sole, and its ostentatious signal that I am a pitcher makes me self-conscious. No one my size really needs baseball spikes, let alone a pitcher's toe plate; but when I had finally persuaded my mother to buy the shoes for my twelfth birthday, I had worked myself up to wanting the whole loaf. She pretended to agree that, as a precaution against scuffing, the toe plate made sense; and I must have supposed that having it would help me feel like a real pitcher.

The outfield is lonely and boring during the long ritual of batting practice; there is not another boy within yards of me. Though it is evening, the parched ground still seems to hold much of the sun's heat. Our ballfield is in the middle of the railroad yard and there is a certain desolation in the rust, the creaking metallic sounds, and the odor of creosote and cinders that seems to hover in the bright, oven-like summer air. I need a drink of water, but I would not want to be anyplace else. In a week or so this year's American Legion baseball squad will be chosen, and this is one of many try-out practices. I pick up a clod of dirt and toss it up for an omen. "If I catch this without its breaking," I tell myself, "that means I will make the team."

> *Skylark, have you seen a valley*
> *green with spring*
> *Where my heart can go a-journeying—*

I don't remember whether I caught that clod unbroken or not; I sought many such portents and some pointed to success, others to failure. As it turned out, however, I was chosen for the team.

I know there is nothing unusual in wanting to make a baseball team, even as desperately as I wanted to make that one. But in this case it really was supremely unlikely, and an almost freakish thing that I actually did. I do not say that out of modesty; it is simply the case that a twelve-year-old does not belong on the same baseball team with sixteen- and seventeen-year-olds. Seventeen was the maximum age. There may have been a few boys who were fifteen, and my brother, who was fourteen, was also trying out. The fact that he made it so young (I never imagined that he wouldn't) was considered a proud accomplishment; but for John Kissane's little brother of twelve to be picked for the squad along with him was, in the eyes of anyone who knew or cared, completely astounding.

Of course there were the particular circumstances, the reasons for my being picked as one of that summer's fifteen lucky ballplayers; but that summer, as I lived it, was one not of reasons but of feelings. Mainly, it was the war; a lot of older boys were busy in jobs created by the boom our town experienced. I was quite good for a boy my age, having played at pitching with my brother as the catcher all summer long since I was about four, but I owed my success chiefly to the manpower shortage.

Where are the words for the mixture of amazement and familiar recognition that was my mood as that early summer built toward the coming of something I should have known—indeed, did know—was properly several years off? In my town then we had no organized baseball expressly for twelve-year-olds. At twelve you dreamed about playing for the American Legion; at sixteen or so, if you were good, you actually made the team and got to play teams from other towns. I began that baseball season prepared to spend the whole summer dreaming. That would have been okay; I would have played catch with my brother as usual, in the cool of the morning and, if I didn't have any lawns to mow, again in the late afternoon when the shade from our house had reached out to where we had measured off the correct distance between a pitcher's slab and home plate. Sometimes Bud Piper, who lived up the street from us and who had pitched for the Legion for several years but now, as a high school senior, was no longer eligible for the team, might walk past and say hello. After all, it had been only a year since Bud Piper and Ray Swallow, who was a catcher, had seen my brother and me playing catch in Caldwell Park (where we sometimes went to break the monotony) and showed me how to throw a curveball.

So it would have been easy to dream away a few more summers, waiting to be really old enough to play and to wear an American Legion team sweater like Bud Piper's. There was some actual ball-playing kids my age might do, at least as substitute outfielders. That was called "the morning league," and I think it was three mornings a week that there was a chance for boys in our town to play baseball if they hadn't been picked for the real team or if, like me, they weren't yet old enough to try out.

The morning league wasn't like playing for a real team; there weren't any uniforms, of course, and the sides were chosen each time from whoever showed up that morning. But it was better than one-o'cat in the vacant lot, and it was more real than pitching to my brother in our side yard. We had gone to morning league several times the summer before, and sometimes I did get to play, which was exciting for an eleven-year-old. Of course they always put me in the outfield; there were plenty of bigger boys who wanted to pitch. Sometimes one or two of the players from the real Legion team—the "varsity," you might say—would come out to the morning league to umpire or coach and to receive our hero-worship. Once that previous summer, when I was eleven and when Bud Piper showed me how to hold the ball to throw a curve, Ray MacBeth came out to the morning league and played "pepper" with a bunch of us before the game started. Bud Piper and Ray Swallow were heroes to my brother and me, but Ray MacBeth— because he was a left-handed pitcher like I wanted to be—was a kind of god. He didn't live in our neighborhood, but you used to see him downtown, unmistakable with his dark curly hair and his lopsided left-handed look, wearing either a Legion sweater or the high school letter jacket (because he also played football). I'm not sure whether he graduated from high school in 1942, the summer I'm telling about, or the year after that. I know he played Legion ball when he was quite young. In any case, after high school Ray MacBeth went into the Marines and was killed in Iwo Jima or some such place.

As that summer I turned twelve began, the glory of actually playing serious baseball and being one of those ambling, self-possessed, admired young men wearing red sweaters with the letter 'P' on the front and the American Legion emblem on the sleeve seemed far in the future. My brother decided to give it a go and try out for the main team, though he was only fourteen and a half; and he assured me it would be all right if I went out to the practices with him and just hung around, not getting in the way but also ready to be useful if somebody needed a warm-up game of catch or if there weren't enough ball-shaggers for batting practice.

The try-outs consisted of three-inning practice games with some additional time given to such activities as batting and infield practice that would let everybody show his skills. My brother was still not very big for his age, but he was looking good at first base and as a catcher, and he had that rare and valuable gift in a young player of almost always being able to "get wood on the ball." The team manager, or coach, a middle-aged lawyer named Fred Tideman, was beginning to notice "Big Kissane." "Tidy," as we called Mr. Tideman, had never played the game himself, but he seemed to know everything about baseball that could be learned from a book. I think what he saw in my brother was the same thing that made me positive he would be picked for the team. "Big Kissane," though among the smallest of the serious contenders, always knew what he was doing. He caught on to everything without having to go through a period of awkward trial and error, and he always played "within himself"—a phrase I've learned from tennis, but which applied to my brother as a ballplayer.

One evening when I accompanied my brother to practice, hardly anyone else was there. It was one of those days our intermountain climate can produce in June, just before the baking hot summer arrives in earnest; raw and windy, even a bit damp. But the rain that had made the others decide our practice surely would not be held did stop; and when we got to Overland Park, the weedy baseball field that lay in the 'Y' where the Union Pacific tracks forked, Tidy and one or two boys were putting dry sand around home plate. A couple of others were having a warm-up game of catch, so my brother and I did the same. Perhaps the fact that it did not seem as if there would be a full-scale practice that day emboldened me, and when I "felt loose" I backed off to the regulation distance a pitcher stands from his catcher and began to "pitch" to my brother just as I would have in our side yard at home. In a while I heard Tidy yelling in his high-pitched way, but we were used to hearing him yell at his dog, Pete, who chased baseballs. Then one of the other boys nearer to me shouted too. "Hey, Little Kissane! Tidy wants you."

There was nothing in any sense official or formal, but after that rained-out practice I must have been a *bona fide* competitor for a place on the town Legion baseball team. That dawned on me only gradually, because all Tidy wanted was to tell me I ought to go up on the pitcher's mound and get the feel of throwing down from it to my brother behind home plate. Of course I had pitched to real batters in games of one-o'cat in vacant lots and school yards, but in those days softball was the organized game for younger boys, and I never wanted to pitch softball. "Hardball" took space and at least a catcher's mask, and—if you were serious about it—players enough for halfway-decent sides. So nearly all of my baseball experience as a pitcher up to that summer was throwing in our side yard while my brother caught and while I imagined (sometimes) that this game of catch was actually the centerpiece of a really important baseball game. This was well before the thorough organization of baseball for younger boys; likewise it was not an era, and certainly ours was not a town, of elaborate recreational facilities. Team baseball in my hometown was then a monopoly of the American Legion, and Overland Park was about the only place even laid out for the playing of hardball.

So when I accepted Mr. Tideman's kindly invitation to throw from a pitcher's mound, I was excited to be doing such a serious thing for what was virtually (except for maybe a furtive toss or two) the first time. As often as I had imagined doing it, I was nevertheless surprised by what a tremendous difference pitching off a mound seemed to make. Everything you do from up there works better and has more authority.

Of course Mr. Tideman wouldn't have known that was my first time on the pitcher's mound. In any event, he did not seem particularly impressed by the showing I made, and I'm not saying there was any reason why he should have been. He did, after a while, stand up at the plate with a bat in his hands to give me a target. Then he would ask me to throw it over the outside corner of the plate, or the inside corner, or down past his knees, or across his chest. Perhaps I should have taken that for a sign that the long, monotonous game of catch I had been playing with my brother since I was four was no longer a series of intense and heroic moments of make-believe that always came out the way they were supposed to. From now on what I was doing was working on my pitching. In those imaginary ballgames, every time the count on the batter reached three and two the next pitch produced a strike out. But now the point became how well I was "hitting the mitt" that my brother was learning to move to the corners of the plate and whether, when he signalled for a curve ball, he could accept what I then threw as the genuine article.

That first experience on the pitcher's mound seemed, at the time, important enough just as a thing in itself. How could I know that my true field of action had stopped being our side yard and the enormous but invisible stadium that surrounded it? Certainly Mr. Tideman gave no obvious signal that fortune smiled on me that chilly day.

At following practices, however, even I could tell that something had changed. Tidy began making sure I warmed up just as thoroughly as the older boys, those who were actually out for the squad. Then, when we had been some time at this routine warm-up game of catch, Tidy would toss a catcher's mitt to the boy I was paired with (if he hadn't already been using one) and say to me, "Go on now and pitch him a few." So I would adjust the distance between us to approximately that from pitcher to catcher and begin to throw more deliberately and with my particular version of those slow and graceful contortions that allow a pitcher to generate speed and deception.

Still I had no trouble keeping my hopes in check; it was easy to understand that Tidy was rewarding the dutiful regularity of my attendance at these practices by making them a bit more interesting, even if they could not have the consequences for me that they would for the others. But Mr. Tideman must have had a flair for the dramatic, or a taste for whimsy. Perhaps he was a sentimentalist. At any rate, his view of the game and of his function with respect to it, I can now see, was rather different from that of his modern-day counterparts who organize and manage young people's athletic teams.

It was a week or so later that the squad from which the American Legion team would be chosen played a "pre-season" game with a team from another town. Everyone who had been coming to practice would get to play, and everyone's chances to make the final team roster would be affected by the showing he made. Of course I was going. We would find out whether my brother would be a catcher or a first baseman, and, almost as important, the game was to be played at the ballpark of the local minor league club. This was the authentic playing field of a professional baseball team. The outfield was not weeds, but grass as genuine as what we mowed in our yard. There were dugouts for the two teams, and the game would be played at night, under floodlights. I was sure too that, since "Little Kissane" had virtually become a mascot, my presence in our team's dugout would be tolerated.

Despite its relatively impressive setting, it was a very ramshackle game. The other team had already been narrowed down to regulation number so they appeared in neat uniforms; the contenders for places on our local team outnumbered the available uniforms, so in fairness everyone on our side had to wear everyday play clothes. From the point of view of our team, the score was secondary. Our attention was on which boys were playing and on individual performance, for as the innings went by the starting players at most positions were replaced by substitutes.

Near the end of the game while our side was at bat, one of our players came down to the end of the dugout where I was watching. He had a catcher's mitt and a ball. Perhaps it was the floodlights that made him look pale, but I thought his manner spoke with a strange urgency.

"Tidy wants us to warm up!"

"Are you going in?" I asked. But I began to wonder if I was to be given the treat of playing an inning at some safe position like right field.

"I been in!" He sounded a bit impatient. "He said to warm you up."

"How?" I wanted to ask whether I was just to toss the ball or warm up out in the left field bullpen like a pitcher.

"Come on! Tidy said to take you out to the bullpen. I think he's going to put you in to pitch."

And that was what happened. I pitched two innings of that ballgame, an experience so delicious, and one that has been privately held so long, that it seems hopeless and absurd to write about it. Everyone should get to pitch. There is that instant—just the blink of an eyelid—when the ball you've thrown seems to hang over home plate as the batter takes his swing at it. You have put all you can into the pitch, but for just that instant you know the peculiar detachment of the ball's being indeed "out of your hands." If the batter misses, the ball will plunk into the catcher's mitt with a lovely sound; but you will still be feeling the ecstasy of having actually seen the ball and the bat pass right through each other. Then the ball that is returned to you from its miraculous adventure feels reassuringly solid; and somehow that constitutes the challenge, and gives you the heart to risk it again.

I did not strike out every batter, and I even gave up a couple of runs; but I did fool several of those much bigger and older players I had never seen before who came up to bat smiling at me in eagerness and derision.

When that game was over my serious hopes began. The baseball shoes were a birthday treat from my mother for having got to pitch, and for me they were a sign that I was really out to make the team. I knew that was still improbable, but I could not ignore the fact that my status had changed from that of hanger-on to that of some sort of player. So along with chasing balls during batting practice, I worked out with the prospective pitchers: bespectacled and scholarly-looking Teddy Bistline; big, blond, good-natured "Snapper" Ewing; and George Kyle, who acted lazy but could play any position on the field with effortless skill. What I remember most of all about those practices, however, was standing in the outfield while everyone took his "at bats," waiting for a ball to roll out through the junegrass, humming to myself or listening to the hot silence of an early summer evening, and imagining with a kind of happy wistfulness how it would be if I were chosen for the team.

What it did feel like when I actually had been chosen, I remember less distinctly. Certainly, when I was given my uniform and saw that it looked all right, even with the huge tucks my mother had to sew in it, I knew life was sweet. The games I got to play in confirmed that the spell baseball had cast during my summers of playing catch and daydreaming could be matched by its reality, by the rhythm of its slow and complex unfolding through nine innings and by the intensity of all the separate and unique duels between pitcher and batter. Ordinary times also shared the sweetness. At any moment, whatever I happened to be doing, I could know that I was enviable by bringing to mind the amazing fact of my pitcherhood. But to realize you are enviable is to know felicity at somewhat of a distance, merely on principle. To have reason to be happy is not, in my experience, quite the pinnacle of happiness. It is certainly better than most ways to feel, but it is not the same as letting yourself succumb, briefly but immoderately, to an unlikely hope.

But I loved the practices, and the few little trips we took to our games out of town were like nothing I had ever done before. I knew that the other boys thought me an oddity among them, but most appeared to overlook what must have seemed to them my relative babyishness. I accepted their teasing as a way of being noticed, and I suppose they took it easy on me because of my big brother, who never seemed protective but must have been.

The days I am now remembering feel like they stretched almost unendingly through that summer; actually, they cannot have amounted to more than a few weeks. The end of vacation, even the end of our season of Legion baseball, was still quite far off when the summer as I have remembered it all the rest of my life came to an end. It was a very small incident that marked the ending, and even at the time I think I must have realized that I should have expected something of the sort might happen. Yet, the truth is I was not prepared, unless those reservations about good fortune I have referred to were after all a preparation.

132

I remember it as in the morning. My brother and I were in Caldwell Park, a square "city block" of grass and trees near our house. Perhaps we were on our way home from downtown; perhaps we had been playing croquet. Anyway, we were at the drinking fountain, a rusty bit of convenience that stood where all the paths through our little park converged to form an often muddy oasis. As we paused to drink Frank Pulos sidled up to us with that smile on his face. Frank was my age, a smaller boy, but tough and knowing. He went to another grade school, but we would be in the same junior high in the fall. I knew him only a little, through a good friend who had moved to my school from Frank's neighborhood. Without any particular reason, I didn't much like Frankie Pulos; he was pretty callous for a twelve-year-old, but there was really nothing objectionable about him. Except that he was always smiling in a way that made you feel he was seeing right through your ordinary human crust into the soft vulnerable center. It occurs to me now that it wouldn't have been a bad thing if I had known Frankie better, or if I had known more people like him.

"Well, Kissane," Frank Pulos said. "I hear you got suction with Tidy and made the Legion."

That was right out of the blue, and I wasn't even sure I understood. "What?" I asked, but something inside me had already gotten the message.

"You're a suck-ass, Kissane. Everybody knows you don't deserve to be on that team."

If Frankie had been a friend, I probably would have challenged him in one way or another; had he been a long-standing enemy or rival, we might have even fought about it. But being a comparative stranger, from another neighborhood, he was somehow unanswerable. It was as if he spoke the world's judgment; I could not see him then as a particular grinning twelve-year-old boy, acting on an urge of venial malice or maybe just caustic playfulness.

As it happened, I took my cue from my brother, who may not even have heard what passed between me and Frankie and who in any case has always had an almost perfect indifference—perfect in its total lack of arrogance or vanity—to what other people think.

"Come on, Jim," he said to me. "Let's go home for our mitts and play some catch."

I could simulate such indifference, but I never could attain it. So, leaving aside the alternative of rubbing Frankie Pulos' face in the dirt—or having my face rubbed in the dirt by Frankie—I suppose, instead of walking docilely home to our game of catch, I should have sought comfort and enlightenment from my brother. What form that might have taken, I hardly know; but just to have aired the incident with my brother, or with anybody, would have done me no harm and perhaps much good.

As it is, I am destined to keep remembering that summer and to keep asking—as if it were Hoagy Carmichael's skylark—whether it has anything to say to me. What is there to say about so sweet an attainment having resulted in a hurt that still makes me flinch? What has it to do with the habitual way I meet even my most trifling success: as if I must hurry to belittle it before someone else can do so ahead of me? Does it explain why it has been my working hypothesis—so mean and unjust—that people are by and large more inclined to envy than to good will?

Are there other secrets hidden in my skylark summer? I have wondered whether some of them might be unriddled by considering the other two characters who have figured materially in this reminiscence, my brother and Frankie Pulos. Suppose either of those two were telling this story of that summer: What would the story then be like?

But of course the obvious point is that neither of them would tell it; for them it was never anything to remember. My brother had his own triumph that summer, he too made the team. You might say his represents success on a normal scale, accepted and enjoyed in a moderate and matter-of-fact way. Why would he not suppose that summer was much the same for me as it was for him? He loved the game itself no less than I did, but I think he never made it the stuff of persistent daydreams or lost any sleep over it. For Frankie my little catastrophe was simply a case of getting some natural resentment off his chest and letting it go at that. What would be his feelings if he knew what a telling blow he had struck that morning at the drinking fountain? Amazement surely, and healthy contempt, most likely.

Frankie's point of view and my brother's would be the reasonable ones, but the story is only mine—about a summer when I won an American Legion baseball sweater that I could never bring myself to wear.

LUKE SALISBURY

Jack Wolf's Try-Out

M Y FAMILY USED TO SPEND summers on Lake Ontario on a stretch of shore that was white and sandy, like the Caribbean. There was a row of cottages ("camps" if you were local) on a bluff which overlooked the beach and faced west so every night the red ball of the sun set into the lake, which is why the place was called Sunset Bluff.

Jack Wolf was my best friend at the lake. I met him on the beach when we were both thirteen and I needed another player for a team which had challenged the nearby Salvation Army camp to a softball game. Jack was from Belleville, a little town about seven miles inland. His family had taken a cottage for a week. Anyway, he played shortstop and we won the game.

We liked each other immediately. Jack wasn't put off by the fact that we lived in the suburbs of New York City, or that my grandfather, who'd built one of the first cottages in 1925, was supposed to be rich. Jack seemed to like the idea. I soon learned that boys he went to school with thought he was a "city slicker" because he lived in a town and his father wasn't a farmer. Jack's father ran an appliance store in Adams, which was bigger than Belleville, but nothing compared to Watertown, which was a "city" boasting a population of 25,000, and a square that had more stoplights than any area of equivalent size in New York City, or so I was told.

Every summer Jack and I played whiffle ball, softball, and hard ball. His family either took a place, or he got a ride down to the lake, and we played and talked baseball. He liked to talk baseball. He was the only good athlete I ever knew who really enjoyed talking baseball. I wasn't a good player. Whiffle ball on the beach with over-the-bluff as a home run, and girls strolling at water's edge were my games. I never enjoyed the feeling of the horsehide coming at my head or bouncing through my legs. By the age of eleven I knew I wasn't going to be a baseball player. Jack was different. The older we got, the better he got.

I went away to school in the ninth grade. Athletics were compulsory so I was forced to perform on JV teams in moldy gyms and suffered the yearly indignity of being cut from the baseball team. Summer was particularly fun because girls were around. I didn't have the nerve to speak to them, but at least they were near; and Jack and I, and several other kids whose families had places on the bluff, played whiffle ball, softball, and sometimes hard ball on the field at the Salvation Army camp, late in the afternoon, when the campers were swimming.

The summer we were sixteen Jack got his Junior license ("A Junior's license he called it) and could drive during the day. He used to come booming off Route 3 and slide onto the dirt roads that led down to the lake shore. He had the use of a '57 Chevy wagon his father no longer took to work. The Chevy was a marvel of engineering and fantasy. The wagon was ostensibly a family car—it was big enough for eight people, port-a-crib, chaise lounge, golf clubs, cooler, and hoola-hoops, but the engine was a pure product of American make-believe. The wagon had a 348 cubic inch motor. Today one can only shake his head at the excesses of this blue and gray, shark-finned, gas-guzzling monster; but a 1950's American father could purchase the machine secure in the knowledge that his family had been taken care of while secretly delighting in the fact that he could take his two-toned guided missile out on the highway and hot rod the devil out of it. Jack could be seen barreling down those dirt roads raising dust and kicking up stones two miles away. My father used to say his car was like an Arab caravan making its way across the desert.

Everything changed in 1964. We were seventeen. Jack had taken Drivers' Ed and could drive at night. I returned to the lake with a Beatle haircut. My hair must have been an inch and a half long but it was brushed down in front rather than back, like the lines of that Chevy. Jack was amazed. "Nobody around here's got one," he said, as I got into the Chevy that first chilly night we were back. I wrinkled my forehead, accentuating how far down the hair could go. I shook my head and smiled. I had been a tall, skinny fellow with pimples and a crew-cut. It took a cultural phenomenon like the Beatles to shake me out of that crew-cut. I had suffered through those lonely, pimply, boys' school years of 1961, 1962, 1963, convinced I was destined to be an intellectual and a dork, rather than cool and wild, but the Beatles changed that. Jack ran his fingers through his short black hair. He wore glasses and combed his hair back on the sides while keeping it short on top. Occasionally someone would say he looked like Elvis Presley, but no one really looks like Elvis Presley. Jack did look a little like Buddy Holly.

"Jesus," he said, looking at my hair. "Let's get some beer."

I nodded, and the tone of the summer was set.

"I didn't know you drank," said Jack.

"I've only been drunk once and threw up. It was awful. Gin. Let's stick to beer."

The drinking age was eighteen and neither of us had an ID so we went to a little store outside Adams. Jack kept urging me to go in and try to "buy." "Nothing happens if he asks for your ID. You say you lost it. Nobody knows you here. Now go ahead and try."

That night, at that little place where the beer was located between popsicles and fishing rods, it worked, and I got a six pack of Genesee®. Genesee® is one of the worst beers I have ever had, but that summer, when two beers made us high and four drunk, it was a marvelous illegal elixir. Radio advertisements boasted of a "Genesecret" and extolled the virtues of "pure Hemlock Lake water." "What's the Genesecret?" I used to ask Jack, and he would invariably say, "Don't know. You got to be eighteen to find out." The next summer, when we were eighteen, and drank all the time, both drinking and Genesee® lost their charm, but in '64, when I sported the first and perhaps only Beatle haircut north of Oswego, it was great.

We drove to a hill in the middle of a field and saw the lake over the trees in the moonlight. We each had two beers. One of the pleasures of seeing Jack every year was hearing how he'd done in sports. He was the quarterback of a six-man football team at Belleville Central School where 400 kids, kindergarten through twelfth, received the legacy of Horace Mann. Jack captained the basketball team and played baseball. He wasn't conceited about his exploits. "It's a small school. I don't know how I'd do in the city," but Jack knew he was good and said pressure brought out his best. Jack had had a great season. The year that brought me out of a crew-cut doldrum had been good to him too.

"I hit .571. Can you believe that?"

We drank that Genesee® and he told me about his season, game by game. "I can hit anybody. They can't get the ball by me. It's the wrists. I always make contact. Only struck out once and that was in Mannsville where the background is all trees." That impressed me. The average might be some kind of small school fluke—what did other people in the Pioneer Conference hit? But striking out only once in an eighteen-game high school schedule impressed me. I asked about home runs. "Hit three," he said, and launched into a beery analysis of idiosyncratic ground rules which had robbed him of "at least three more." Jack was bursting with confidence. He said he could talk freely with me because I knew he wasn't bragging and "therefore" could brag as much as he wanted.

"I got a letter for a try-out."

Jack produced a worn blue and white envelope that contained an equally worn letter on Dodger stationery requesting his presence at a try-out camp on July 17, 1964, at Robert Pendleton Field in north Syracuse. "I got that 'cause my coach sent my name. I can't go. Probably wouldn't make it. My mother won't let me. She doesn't want anything to interfere with college."

"Jack," I said, "you've got to go."

Mrs. Wolf thought something was up when we left. She was a small woman with hard features whose hair was always frosted into a permanent. Bett Wolf was the sharp-tongued edge of small town respectability. She knew everything, told everything, and was keen enough to figure out what no one told her. "Where might you boys be going?" she said, with a knowing smile.

"Well," I said, smiling mischievously. Mrs. Wolf liked that. She thought my family were local gentry, and with her rigid sense of caste and shame, liked the idea that I was a young man from a good family itching to get into trouble. She knew I read books and went to prep school, and until that summer, thought I was a good influence on Jack. There was another reason I bore watching. Jack had a girlfriend named Carol. Carol had been his girl for three years of high school, and everyone in town assumed they'd marry ("whether they have to or not," Bernie Sampson said), just as everyone assumed Jack would someday be the coach at the Central School. Jack and Carol were a fixture except in the summer. Then he was "down to the beach" and both his mother and Carol worried about what could be found among the summer people.

"Well," I said in the slightly sexual Tom Sawyerish voice Mrs. Wolf always got out of me, "we might pitch a tent over on Chamberlain's land and . . ."

"And get drunk with some girls down there?" said Mrs. Wolf, feigning her best Methodist moral indignation. The woman was a snoop but a good sport.

"Can't," said Jack, in the cocky, self-assured voice he used with adults. "We're under age."

"Since when has that stopped you?" Mrs. Wolf gave Jack a playful cuff, and we left. He spun the tires with oedipal glee and we headed out of town. I was glad Jack's mother hadn't said anything about the try-out because he might not have been able to lie to her. At the time I thought pretending we were off for drunken adventures in a tent was a clever cover; but now I think she knew exactly what we were doing and understood that it was part of the games a seventeen-year-old plays with both his parents and the adult he will be. I was glad Jack's father wasn't there. He was not a man to cross. Mr. Wolf was a lot like Jack. He was short, stocky, and meant business in a compact, competitive way. Mr. Wolf had been a tail gunner in the Second World War and liked to say, "There was nothing but plexiglass between you and disaster."

We roared down Route 81 on a bright Friday afternoon. The radio was on full volume and I remember hearing a song I heard all the time that summer and haven't heard since, "You're The One," by the Chartbusters. We heard it once on WNDR, then on WKBW, the prodigiously powerful station from Buffalo, and finally on WOLF, a Syracuse station that didn't penetrate the North Country.

Route 81 was a new highway, one of those divided four lane "super highways" that, along with Elvis Presley, are a lasting legacy of the 1950s. No longer is a traveller consigned to the crowned, two-lane blacktop of rural America. Dwight Eisenhower, in his wisdom, saw that what America needed were coast-to-coast drag-strips: wide-big-shouldered-straight-as-the-horizon-well-manicured highways where the American male could take his oversized, fantasy car and rocket down a straight-a-way forgetting his suburb, his kids, and his wife's girdle. On the super highway, Americans could be Superman.

Jack and I were never happier. He was going to try out for the Dodgers. I was leaving an old self. The highway was straight, the tank was full, the radio was loud. We heard "My Boy Lollipop," "My Guy," "The Shoop Shoop Song," "Memphis" by Johnny Rivers, "Rag Doll," "Don't Worry Baby" which I still think is the best Beach Boys song, "Every Little Bit Hurts," "Walk On By," "A World Without Love," and a medley of Beatle songs culminating in "Hard Day's Night" which, as the disc jockeys liked to say, was about to sweep the charts.

We talked baseball. We both thought Tony Oliva might be the best player we'd seen come up. Ted Williams had been my boyhood idol, and since his retirement, I'd been waiting for another high-average hitter with power.

"That boy's got a great swing," said Jack. "Best Cuban ballplayer that ever was."

"There's nothing like a good left-handed hitter."

"Hell," said Jack, one hand on the wheel, the other hanging out the window. "The best hitters are always left-handed. Except me."

"I like Tony Conigliaro," I said. "He's only nineteen. Can you believe somebody only nineteen is playing in the big leagues?"

"He's the first guy almost our age," said Jack. "Gives you a funny feeling, doesn't it?"

Jack decided to "bury the peg," which meant making the Chevy go as fast as it could. He was a very good driver, but the speedometer was registered to 120 MPH and burying the peg meant getting and holding the red tip of the needle against the little peg under 120. We sometimes went a hundred on straight local roads but "burying the peg" required a stretch of Dwight Eisenhower's interstate fantasy system.

"Here we go."

Jack floored it and the Chevy went from 70 to 80 to 90. We roared down the highway and the eleven-foot white lines blurred into one straight, hard line. The flat farm land went by in waves like an angry green sea. We broke 100, a magical barrier. There was a palpable sense of breaking through, breaking away, just plain breaking—giving into the anarchy of the road, the trance of speed, the anger of 348 cubic inches straining to make the world spin. Gerry and the Pacemakers were singing "Don't Let the Sun Catch You Crying," which was a big favorite at the Friday night dances where records were played out of the back of a truck and Jack used to introduce me to girls. But the song was lost in the rush of air. We were beyond music. We were beyond baseball. We were in the white world of speed, and the Chevy didn't stop at 100. Jack kept it floored and the needle crept towards 110. The rear ends of cars rushed up at us. We passed a big eighteen wheeler and the driver's mouth was open. Good Jesus, the world was ours when we hit 120.

We found Pendleton Field and checked into a nearby motel. The field was big. We walked the perimeter. There was a diamond at each end and two Little League games in progress. A snow fence separated the outfields. We were in a working class suburb. The houses were one- and two-story white clapboard. Some of them needed painting, others had aluminum storm doors, and a few had cars parked in the front yards. It was the sort of neighborhood where men build additions to their own houses. The people were not what my mother would have called "nice."

"That fence'll be gone tomorrow," said Jack. He walked slowly. "They'll have us throw, take infield, and hit. The best guys'll pitch." He wasn't exactly talking to me but at the field and suburb which must have seemed like a cramped, alien world. "So this is the city?" he said, and I didn't say that north Syracuse wasn't exactly my idea of a city. "No wonder all these people want to come up and take a camp." He made a gesture that took in the horizon of ballfield, houses, and a junior high school at the end of the block. "The field's OK," he said, as we went back to the car. "It's smooth. It's OK."

"No ground rules to keep you from getting home runs," I said.

The motel room had yellow walls and cheap yellow-gold curtains. Jack turned on a rusty air-conditioner that jutted in from a window. The machine clanked but barely moved the air in the hot room. He tried opening the glass louvers in the door but the handle was stuck. I put a quarter in Magic Fingers and lay on one of the beds. After a brief rumble it quit and I laughed but Jack didn't. He methodically unpacked an old suitcase, hung his baseball uniform in the closet, and put his spikes under the uniform like a businessman preparing his clothes for an important meeting. "Don't worry," I said. "You've got the wrists." Jack's father used to say big league scouts were looking for "the arm behind the barn" and Jack always said he had "the wrists behind the fists."

"I'm hungry, goddamn it," Jack said. "Let's eat."

We went out on foot and found a Carrol's a few blocks away.

Carrol's got to upstate New York before McDonald's, but other than red and white decor, and the slogan "A serving a second," the food and shopping center ambience were the same. Jack picked at a cheeseburger and complained that his fries were overdone. That summer was the first time I saw a McDonald's style restaurant and for two months thought the food was delicious. So did Jack.

"I don't know why I'm nervous," he said. "All that can happen is I don't make it."

"We'll see."

"Then everybody'd be happy."

"The Yankees are playing the Tigers tonight," I said, and talked about the possibility of the Yanks losing the pennant. We both disliked New York but the idea the Yankees could lose was practically heresy. They hadn't lost since '59, which in my life was the summer before the onset of libido, and might as well have been in the ice age.

"How the hell can they lose?" said Jack. "They've got Mantle and Maris and Ford. Those guys don't lose."

"Aparicio and Robinson can do it," I said.

"Like hell they can."

Jack saw the girls first. They came in a white Falcon with a dented right fender. They were both heavy and wore pink lipstick. One was almost pretty. She had short brown hair and a cute nose. The other was plain and heavier and had much bigger breasts. They both had small black purses with black fringe, wore the same lipstick, and chewed gum. They stood outside for a minute and looked over the customers. Jack got up. Neither of us was any good at "picking up" girls. Under normal circumstances we'd goad each other, think of ten opening lines, and the young ladies would be gone long before we did anything but laugh at each other. Jack went right over to them. I followed a few respectable but unbelieving steps behind.

"What do you think of his hair?" Jack asked the prettier one. They giggled. "I thought everybody had hair like that in the city."

Jack bantered with the girls. The heavier girl, Diane, wanted to touch my hair. This generated enough coyness to establish a conversation.

"I don't suppose either of you girls are eighteen?" Jack said.

"'Course we are," said Bobbi, the prettier one.

"Prove it," I said.

"Oh," said Diane, "he's one of those boys that want you to prove everything."

"She didn't say she loved him," said Jack. "She just said she was eighteen."

Diane proved she was eighteen by buying a pint of rum. I bought a six pack of Coke and we went riding in the Falcon. Jack didn't drink. I told the girls he was trying out for the Dodgers. I was very proud of that. I don't think they believed me. I drank too quickly. After a nervous quarter hour I was laughing and telling stories. Diane had read *The Catcher in the Rye* and was impressed when I told her I went to prep school. She had also read *Lord of the Flies*. When the rum hit me I told her what a great ballplayer Jack was. I said he had "the wrists behind the barn." Bobbi talked about the Beatles and said she was going to go to *A Hard Day's Night*, when it opened at a drive-in, "even if I have to screw somebody," and then said, "Oh, I shouldn't have said that," and we all laughed like hell. The girls liked us. They were older and they thought we were funny. Maybe they liked the way we looked, or maybe they wanted to pick up some guys no one knew and do something no one would know about. Maybe they were the easy big city "makes" Jack dreamed about and I used to tell him populated city streets.

Bobbi let Jack drive the Falcon. We went by the field and Jack asked if "a lot of niggers" played there. Diane kissed me. She kissed me again and looked me in the eye. I kissed her and then we were wrestling and kissing in the back seat. This was one of the best

146

times. This was license. I was a stranger in a strange city on the verge, perhaps, of entering that strange and most familiar land. I'd never "made out" (has any phrase ever meant so much and so little? You could get everything or a whiff of perfume and have "made out") with an older girl. I drank and Diane drank but she drank at the easy confident pace of one acquainted with liquor, not the spastic haste of a hoyden showing off.

The next bottle was a fifth of Bacardi and we told them we had a motel room. "Just like you're trying out for the Dodgers," said Bobbi. She seemed offended and moved away from Jack. He drove for a while and then looked over his shoulder. "What's goin' on back there?" and jerked the car to a stop. "There're laws against that stuff, or there ought to be."

"Keep driving," said Bobbi.

"Yes, ma'am," said Jack, and peeled out leaving "rubber."

We drove around in the twilight. What was happening in the back seat seemed to frighten Bobbi and bother Jack. They stopped talking. I knew Jack was drinking. He drove with one hand and had the fifth in the other. I played with a thin gold chain around Diane's neck and the world smelled like chewing gum. At first, I thought she was on top of me so I couldn't get my hands on her tits which felt so big and hot on my chest; then I wondered if she wanted me to go under her pink sweater and undo her bra with one deft hand, like a burglar cracking a safe. I didn't want to go any farther. We were hot strangers and nothing had been tried that hadn't been invited. I was happy. This was as much as I'd ever gotten and it was as much as I deserved. I wasn't experienced enough to demand more for ego's sake. I was happy trying to get the gum out of her mouth while feeling the thin pink sweater stretched so tightly over her broad back. I also knew, with the unfailing intuition of the amateur, that when the car stopped, it would be over because we wouldn't be strangers. I knew we would never get back to that level of fumble and intoxication, so I said, "Keep on driving, Jack," and didn't say anything about his drinking.

"Slow down," said Bobbi.

"Can't this thing take it?" said Jack.

"Christ," said Bobbi.

In back, I fondled and grappled. We shared neck, shoulder, and mouth. I got on top and my hands got around to the front where they met minimal resistance. We went up and down in a helpless, fully clothed bump and grind. I remember thinking this is enough. The undiscovered country can wait—I just want this excitement, this thrill. I'd been let into the club of hot, limited teenage passion—that Saturday night world where I thought those who didn't go to prep school spent a happy portion of their adolescent lives—and where I had travelled only as a dreamer, not even a voyeur, but a dreamer learning through books, gossip, fantasies, boys' school lies, and at that moment, in that car, I can't say if sex or the excitement meant more. It wasn't love and it wasn't really sex but it was wonderful. I thought I was paying a debt that had to be paid. Now, years later, the debt seems to be part of a past which I'm afraid will slip away and die in some country of its own.

The ride ended at the motel and the evening changed. Had we all gotten the room together, or pretended to be married, or even lied to the desk clerk together, it might have been different. We actually had a room and Diane and Bobbi were unimpressed. There was something premeditated and sleazy about it. Unpremeditated sleaze might have been fun, but our rusty yellow and gold twelve dollar room, with its odor of mildew and glass door which was missing a slat, could have been rented by two salesmen paying ten-year-old boys to take their pants down. I tried to get Diane to sit on the bed and kiss me but some essential innocence had been lost. Bobbi said they had to go to a dance. "Don't go," I said, and the situation was almost saved when Bobbi spotted Jack's Belleville Central uniform hanging in the closet with a pair of blue baseball socks neatly folded next to his spikes. "You really are going to try out," she said.

"What the hell do you think we came down here for?" said Jack.

"Maybe you'll have better luck with the Dodgers," said Diane.

"Have a drink?" I said, holding up the half empty rum bottle.
"No," said Bobbi.

"Give me that," said Jack, and grabbed the bottle. He took a
long drink. No one told him not to. Bobbi looked at Diane and
Diane looked at me. Jack took another drink, wiped his mouth, and
said, "Shit." I finally said, "You can't play with a hangover."

"Who says I can't?"

"Don't do it."

"Why not?"

"It's stupid."

"You saying I'm stupid?"

"Jesus, Jack."

"Come on," said Bobbi, taking Diane by the shoulder. "Let's
get out of here."

"Please don't leave," I said.

Jack snapped the TV on and switched channels until he found
the Yankee game.

"Let's watch something else," I said.

"I thought you just read books."

"The girls . . ." I said.

"Fuck the girls."

Bobbi started to leave. Diane said something about seeing me
again but before she finished, Jack locked the door. "You're so
smart," he said to me. "You figure out how to get out."

"He's drunk," said Diane.

"He's an asshole," said Bobbi.

I got up even though I had no idea what to do. "Come here, hot
shot," said Jack. "You want to see the wrists behind the barn?
Come here. Play slap and I'll open the door. Don't worry, girls. The
prep school gentleman'll get you out."

The girls looked at us with anger and distrust. Anger made
Bobbi seem younger. She looked girlish and frightened. Diane's
anger made her look older and stern, a vision of the woman she
would become. I put out my hands, palms down. Jack put his
small, strong hands under mine. The girls watched in disbelief.
Slap, as the name implies, involves putting your hands on someone

else's, and he tries to slap you before you can move. If he misses, you get to try to slap him. Jack immediately slapped my right hand with his left. As soon as I put my hands down, he slapped both of them before I could move. He got my right with his left, then he got my left with his right. When I looked him in the eye, I got slapped, and when I looked at my hands I got slapped. When I tried to move, I got slapped, and when I didn't move, I got slapped harder. It went on like that for at least ten slaps. He'd fake or look at me and while I was trying not to flinch, I'd get slapped.

"You're not trying. You never try."

"Fuck you."

"They don't leave until you try."

"I'm trying."

The backs of my hands were red. They hurt but I wasn't quick enough to get out of the way.

"Try this." Jack slapped me across the face. He stumbled as he did it, so perhaps, as he said later, he didn't intend to hit me so hard. I was more shocked than hurt and then he almost burst into tears. "I'm sorry, buddy. Jesus, I'm sorry." I turned away. I was in no mood for an apology.

Jack went to the door. I believe he intended to open it, but he slipped and his hand went through it. He was cut to the bone.

HENRY H. ROTH

The Cinderella Kid

H OW MUCH DO YOU WANT TO KNOW?
Better, how much do I want to know or tell?
I grew up with colored and Spanish kids. All were
in the same lousy boat and I saw right away most kids
stink and those that are brave and smart keep their mouths shut and
noses clean and hope for some guy or lady with a magic stick to get
you out of the Home. Believe me it was no real home but a Home
for Orphans; you never forgot how you owed everything to the
Sisters, the social workers, and all citizens who paid taxes. There
was a kid in my cottage whose old man was killed robbing a bank.
Well, as he grew up his only aim in life was to be a bank robber. I
mean that's all the past history he knew, so he grabbed that. He was
so sad I don't know if I wanted him to make it or not.

As for me I had no memory of parents, so I picked out what I
could understand, which was sports. I knew the world didn't give
a shit about me and if I made a mistake they would put me in worse
places than the Home so I was goody goody until it became a habit.
While my buddies got into more trouble as they got older I stayed
clean but no one called me chicken shit because I was real big and
strong. The joke is that the kids didn't really see they were different
from other kids, while I knew I was just pretending to be a human
being.

I pretended so long that I got lucky, very lucky for a while. Like
the little guys at the Home who prayed each day they might get

adopted or somehow their parents would show up in big cars and drive them away to a fancy house. I also dreamed. It was some lumpy shape waving something. It wasn't scary though; it was like the kind witch in the *Wizard of Oz*, or sometimes it was a man like a prince—shit I never told anyone, they would've put me away. But when my luck came and they nicknamed me The Cinderella Kid at the training camp in Florida I wasn't surprised. For a while I was The Cinderella Kid.

The only way I could get off of the Home grounds was sports. So I went out for everything. I played a lot of basketball and football but it was boring. Baseball was my game right away. It couldn't begin or end without me because I was the star pitcher, a real king of any hill. My arm was my golden button to everything. By my junior year in high school scouts were calling up my cottage or asking to speak to the chief administrator. Coach Sutton always treated me like a person, not like some freak who could do one thing great. He handled the negotiations. Everyone in town started noticing and singling me out. The Home girls are ready to screw from twelve on; it was about the only exciting thing we had to do there. But now the town girls were saying hello, I was like the star quarterback of a high school I never went to. After twelve no-hitters, I was even invited to the mayor's house. At the end of my senior year, with plenty of local publicity, I signed for $25,000, payment to be spread over five years.

Most of the diary I kept the first February in Florida is gone but I still keep the few pages left near my draft card and birth certificate.

. . . first day in Florida. It's fucking cold. I share a room with one guy, *one guy*. All the hot water and food you can ask for. Curfu is ten o'clock. Don't worry I'm not going to screw up here.

. . . when I finish batting practice some coach walked over patted my head and arm and said not to throw so hard tomorrow. Just like Coach Sutton but this is the majors.

. . . my roomie is a pitcher too, he's been looking at me real funny. He should I'm faster and only throw strikes . . . some reglars on the team had supper with me ... I didn't say a fucking word just like when I was at the mayer's house.

... last night I walked round the beach barefoot kicking sand into the Atlantic. My best dream was never one million as swell as whats happening. Pitch three innings tomorrow.

... two hits no runs no walks six strikeouts. My roomie caught a cold. Tough.

... wrote Coach Sutton this morning. Took a dip in the pool for the first time. First time someone didn't tell me when to come out of the pool. Pitch again Friday.

... my buddy was sent to the farm team camp. I don't mind his empty bed I've never been in a room alone. Four innings today three hits no runs two walks four strikeouts. A writer did a whole artacel on me. Last night I woke up crying, glad that prick wasn't there. He had a terrific control problem.

... club still carrying plenty of guys over the limit but I'm still one of them. One coach is my pal, even if it's bullshit I like it. Wish I knew how to talk better but I don't want them to laff at me. Some wise guy said I'm not any Cinderella Kid but the Humbel Kid. Some day I'll put him down with a better knickname meantime I brushed him in batting practice.

... we're out of Florida and the veterans say it wasn't as good wether as other years. Nuts, it was paradize. From now on we go 6 innings each start ... hell I can go 66 innings. My new roomie is a catcher rookie like me and we go over all the hitters. Imagen talking about how to get Willie Mays out, it's so crazy like figring out how to screw Kim Novak. I mean anything is possible.

... supposed to go seven today. Charlott last stop. next the big City. My roomie split a finger he's really wurryed they won't carry him now.

During my first trip north, I had pitched so good I was still with the varsity. Look I was a big strong wiseassed kid who wanted everything right away. Charlotte was the next to last game before opening day; I felt tight warming up but I knew it would loosen up.

153

But it didn't. I was very wild, lucky to last the first two innings; I walked three in the first, two in the second. Manager was giving smug fishy looks. He didn't say anything but I could see our bullpen warming up. My arm felt lead heavy, the ball was like a snowball I couldn't really grip. I was scared and mad. There was no chatter from the infield, everyone was waiting for me to fold, to blow sky high. I walked the first batter in the third then I shook off my catcher when he signaled a fastball, and again shook him off for a curve and nodded for a slider. Christ the catcher was pissed. Also I forgot to hold the runner and went into a full windup. "Steal!" the second baseman yelled. In the middle of my motion I caught myself and aimed the ball to the plate real fast. A line drive right to the third baseman who had an easy doubleplay. By the time I got back to the dugout I was trying not to cry. I'll never forget that bush fire running through my shoulder into my hand and killing my fingers. I couldn't believe anything could hurt like that and I kept looking at my arm. I couldn't believe it was still there.

In time the arm got stronger but when it came to pitching I was feeble after ten minutes of lobbing batting practice. I had to throw three quarters and there was no sign of any fast ball, the ball headed toward the plate with little or no spin. From Charlotte they sent me down to Tennessee, where I would faithfully warm up each day, toss the glove high into the air, then crouch in the smelly dugout. Most nights I would end up on the grass half drunk, listening to a pretty little river that split the town's main street and led nowhere and served no purpose except to calm me down.

That was my whole summer, dressing but not playing any-more. And me only eighteen. Labor Day, my joke season finished, I went back home. Another bad joke. The Home was a real home for losers. I returned because there was nowhere else to go. I still had my car and no one could take away the bonus, but my arm, my rocket to other worlds, was out of fuel. Coach Sutton let me help him in football, basketball, and wrestling, and then it was time for another spring training.

That season I was in three towns. They kept sending me around, hoping that sun and dry air might heal the muscles. I only got hotter and drier and the desert towns were like jails; the arm hurt so bad I really began to have a real drinking problem; it was all I could manage by myself. There was no future for me; if not for the bonus I would be pumping gas at a nearby Esso but even with money what else was I qualified to handle? Coach Sutton suggested I try college, our community college accepted anybody with a high school diploma which I did have. The final push was a form letter from the ball club stating that *my contractual obligation for the next three years would entail only showing up for spring training and determining whether there had been any significant improvement in my condition.*

The parking lot at the Community College could have been for an A&P except there were plenty of trees plus instructions all over the place. Area reserved for faculty—reserved for maintenance—reserved for students—no parking any time. Wow, I should have left my car on the damn grass because I sure didn't belong there. The guidance man looked like he agreed except it was his job not to agree and I did have a high school diploma.

"We wish to help you," he said, "we've begun a Seek program to help the dis. . . ."

I knew the word. "Disadvantaged, you mean." Boy was he ever right. Yet he was a nice guy, really turned on, really interested.

"Eddie Sutton has spoken to me."

"He's a great guy."

After a while the guidance man sucked on his pipe and said, "You know, you're a very interesting and determined young man."

I wish I hadn't answered. "And scared."

That he really liked—a scared disadvantaged.

"You speak very well," he said.

I wanted to smash him, shout at him, yell so fucking loud he'd fall right off his swivel chair, the bastard. But he was nice. So far it's taken me twenty years to speak at all. I never talked much at the Home but not because I was shy or had nothing to say. I just wasn't going to growl and curse like those other apes. So I kept quiet like some of those monks, and I watched TV news and all the broadcasters, Brinkley, Huntley, Cronkite. I watched them every day. I didn't understand much of what they said, but I saw how they paused a lot even sighed and they never said well or uh before talking. And they never cursed. I tried to copy them and still do. I knew my vocabulary wasn't much but Coach Sutton explained I would begin slowly at college and get special classes and help. Most important, he promised nobody would make me feel small.

"I can tell you're a very mature young man."

I flapped my dead arm. "I was a pitcher."

"Mr. Sutton told me. Very unfortunate. But I'm glad you're here. Our program is just beginning. We must both be patient."

He sounded like a pitching coach, only he smiled all the time. And then a girl came in who he introduced as my new coach. The greatest looking girl who shook my hand and led me to the library. And I have tried real hard to never let that hand get away.

I'll try to report one of our recent conversations. I was packing my suitcase to go south again for spring training.

"You would have never come here if you hadn't . . ."

"Yes ma'am, without a sore arm I'd be with nifty women and cars. The sweetlife."

She smiled so much better than any guidance man who ever lived and she's been smiling that way for three years.

"You know that song at the concert, 'Who Am I'?"

Now she began to look sad.

"Look, I'm happy and I don't know who I am. I am untapped, I am one of the untapped . . ."

"Don't joke."

"I'm not. After I hurt my arm I was drinking a lot. Then one day I remembered Benito who was growing up to be a bank robber like his old man. Coach Sutton was all over me about college and once I got to thinking about Benito, man I almost ran to the school in the middle of the night."

"I hate baseball."

"And I hate the word potential but I love untapped, like there's no end to it or me. If you win thirty games like McLain, that should be the end. He'd be better off to play the organ for the rest of his life."

"I don't understand baseball, you never talk about it."

"You don't want to hear."

"Unless you want me to."

"It's just another bad symbol of America."

"You're not even packing a glove."

I smiled. "You don't want me to."

"It's crazy. You're crazy."

"I'll tell you what baseball is, okay? The guy that can make all the routine chances sticks. Hard chances even the great stars only make less than fifty percent of the time. It's all in the stats. All you have to be is a machine, not messing up the usual everyday bounce."

She was looking straight at me now, neither happy nor sad.

"Till now I haven't ever had one routine chance and I'm not a star so every possible play stays that way. All the other kids at the Home are the same, we get no routine shots—we're all untapped. That sounds like school bullshit but it's true. Really."

"Who are you?" she joked.

The suitcase was locked up.

"If I die," I answered, "I leave my mind to you and my body to baseball."

When I got my $25,000, there were hundreds of other bonus babies all over the country, but I was the only orphan and was promptly nicknamed The Cinderella Kid. Five years later, I'm not worth a fillin note on a lousy rainy Florida day when there are not even any injuries or trade rumors to report. You know there was a writer who did an article on a ballplayer, once called a phenom, who had hung on as 25th man. Now at thirty he was about to be cut. The column was really good, so the local papers reprinted it in each town the club played on the exhibition schedule. This ball-player read the same story every day for two weeks; finally he cornered the writer threatening his life if he *wrote that fucking story one more day*. But I wouldn't get any such goodbyes. I hurt my arm so quickly that there's no possible interest five years later.

The management was of course furious, annoyed and tired of me. So for this last tryout I was assigned minor league quarters for the first time down there. I refused to report. The travel secretary screamed but each year I'm one of the protected players so they shouldn't try to deal that way with me. "It's the last damn year," he muttered but my accommodations were changed. I know they fired the scout who signed me, but he hooked on with another team right away. Hell when he first saw me I was worth every penny. The bastards didn't even give me a locker or uniform, still I didn't even bring my glove this year.

I called Janet every other day and wrote her daily, telling her about the book I was reading. Maybe she'd just found a dumb stud and was developing his mind but I didn't care. In the words of Lou Gehrig I consider myself the luckiest man on the face of the earth. Sometimes I think authors of books are talking only to me, telling me all their secrets. Words are magic, the rest is a game. Janet says I may turn out to be a writer. My chances of that are about as good as winning one game in the low minors. But I will be a teacher. You know I can't wait to teach at the Home.

The rain finally stopped and I'd gotten me a baggy uniform. The best thing happened. Jocko Gordon was down here. He was my manager the first year and the only guy I met who really loves the Game; he was still in the kid league, still happy to be seeing a ballgame every summer day. Jocko greeted me like a long lost son.

"Let's toss a few. Orders," he chuckled. "Toss me one or two and tell me what you've been doing. You look great kid."

I didn't toss any but told him my story. That grand old guy hugged me.

A clean white ball skimmed toward us, I slapped it into the stiff borrowed glove. "Let's go to work old man."

"Go right ahead."

I shut my eyes, raised my leg, kicked off, and threw straight and easy. The sun was really shining as if saying forgive me for the past few days. Boy what a warm mother sun. Sweat was rolling off my face and I felt powerful and very loose. I was having a real good time and I threw the ball back as soon as it was returned to me by the crouching Jocko. As usual the pitches were slow, straight as strings.

"You don't throw sidearm anymore?"

"You're kidding, I still do."

"You haven't been kid." His voice was funny.

I threw again, he was right, that god damn Jocko was right. It was five years ago, the old smooth-styled delivery.

"Try a curve," he shouted.

I did.

"Hurt?"

"No."

"Snap it off harder this time, don't be scared."

The ball rose then dipped as if shot.

He couldn't handle the pitch and retrieved it on his hands and knees. "I'll be damned I'll be damned," he muttered.

A bat boy came over to us. "Jocko, someone wants to seeya."

"Later."

"C'mon Jocko they're waiting."

"You better go. I'll be here. Don't get our front office mad."

Jocko backed away, eyeing me very funny.

Meanwhile I did a few windsprints, I wasn't in bad shape and right now I felt giddy and light and stupid. This practice field banks down to the back of a high school. I still had the ball in my pants pocket, I slid down the hill and suddenly was all alone. There were trees bunched together. I aimed for the middle broadest one, throwing as hard as I could. The effort and the pain that immediately followed sunk me to my knees. Meanwhile the ball was ricochetting back. In my dizzy state I thought the tree had been bent back. And the pain was gone as quickly as it had arrived. I threw again, the tree definitely shuddered. There was no pain at all. The ball banged halfway back and I ran to greet it.

I got back unnoticed, did some more windsprints, and then headed for the clubhouse. I avoided Jocko until supper when he joined me.

"How are ya?"

"Fine Jocko, just fine."

But Jocko was mean and serious.

"I'd like to catch ya again tomorrow. Okay?"

"Sure." I was still smiling.

He tried to match me but he couldn't. "I've been bounced."

"You're kidding?"

"They gave me a scouting job."

"Those bastards."

"The league may fold, they're getting tired carrying young kids and old men."

"I thought that was baseball."

"Look they cudda cut me off completely."

"Wonderful."

"I gotta tellya something else."

"Shoot."

"I followed ya."

"Huh?"

"I was up on the hill watching, my eyes are still very good kid."

"Well . . . ?"

"See ya tomorrow morning. Get a good night's sleep."

Jocko as he promised was waiting. He crouched and my heart went out to him, I thought his body would break in two. This was no position for a man close to sixty. He took his cap off; it was crazy how his few hairs pointed up to the sun—an old ball hawk who still loved to sweat.

As for me, I felt like a stranger living on somebody's credit card. I was a one-in-a-million look-a-like for someone else. I was the twin of a dumb strong kid in one of those John Tunis novels making a comeback from a crippling arm injury. I looked at the number one worshipper of false idols, and told Jocko I accept all legends—Hornsby never went to the movies and I hated every pitcher, Rabbit Maranville ate goldfish, Ty Cobb was mean, and Walter Johnson never cursed. But hell no, Jocko, I won't go. And it's not the generation gap. For I go even further back to the short pieces of O'Henry, not fashionable now, old Jocko, but very big a long time ago. And I take coaching from him.

When I looked again a faceless guy with a tiny glove was going to try and catch me. Balls! So I knocked Jocko flat with a live rising fastball. He took a long time getting up. He was definitely excited. I waited in vain to spy happiness and understanding; there was only greed and lust. He was a company man no matter how much the Company screwed him. Next I gave him the full windup and knuckle balled. Then I flipped another toward him; the ball made it in one nutty bounce. Jocko walked toward me.

"C'mon, kid, stop fooling around."

I've heard that voice most of my life. From impatient social workers, teachers, bored cops, even my own inner voice. But that life style is no more. Jocko is not my man. My spiked cleats are pinching. I point to the right arm. "I should have told you yesterday I can throw real hard once or twice a day, then it's bad as before. I shouldn't have teased."

Jocko wasn't buying. "Let's try some more."

One of the coaches walked over, he hated me because I would never be any use to him. He hated Jocko because Jocko could get *his* job one day. And right now he was bored and boss.

"Okay, kid," he joked, "let's see the high hard one that cost us twenty-five big ones."

I blew kisses at my enemy, grunted, and made it to Jocko on two big bounces.

The man laughed a while. "Jeez, Jocko, can't you find a better way to goof off?"

Jocko was about to say fuck you to one of us. But true baseball man, hypocrite, he just chewed his gum.

Before I left the field and before I left Florida, I returned to my victory scene. There might be spies in the trees, so wisely I carried no baseball. I did pace off sixty feet six inches and I did pitch one classic of a game. A few fouls but that was all. I was carried off the field by my proud teammates; with their cheers and the papers proving my worth I felt neither guilty nor sad calling an airline and arranging a flight. Hell The Cinderella Kid had made it all the way back, you couldn't ask for more than that.

JOHN HILDEBIDLE

His Big Chance

OH, JIMMY WAS A PIP; everyone knew it. It helped to be a Fontaine in a town where the hotel that family had bought and named for itself loomed a story higher than anything else on Main Street. And it helped that he was clever, and tall, and had just *that* smile. But what topped it all off was baseball. When he went off to college, he was still, as his mother liked to say, a little ahead of himself; but after a year of schoolwork and ballplaying (whenever the ground was dry enough) and three jobs on top of that (there wasn't enough of Grandpa's money left to pay the way), he'd really grown into something, tall as ever but now broad across the shoulders too, and the arms that used to dangle as if they were looking for a place to hide had turned hard as two-by-fours.

Jimmy was supposed to spend that summer learning the hotel business, but before long he was playing ball all the time. He certainly could show those farm boys a thing or two, mostly with the bat; but he was no slouch behind the plate either. What could be better? Good exercise and fresh air and good money when you added it all up, and there was no harm in having a hero in the family, either.

So with one thing and another, Uncle Ralph's daffy idea made a kind of sense, at first. No one believed him when he bragged about connections; Ralph was always saying that, but all his connections had never gotten him further than two steps from the poorhouse. Still, you could read in the papers that some people actually made a good living playing baseball, and nobody could ignore how these days money got tighter and tighter, and maybe it was just some kind of luxury to have Jimmy off in college for most of the year. Grandpa was beside himself when he first heard. When he wanted to be the first college man in the family, he couldn't argue with what the ledger said. But he told himself that maybe college would be just a tryout, with Jimmy squeezing in some schoolwork during the winter.

The first surprise was that Uncle Ralph did seem to know somebody, maybe not Connie Mack or Christy Mathewson, but enough of a somebody to answer his letter. It was miles and miles to any big-league team and the letter Ralph got didn't offer any train fare, but it did mention that there were scouts who came that way every so often.

Whatever Ralph lacked in common sense, he at least had an eye for drama, and he knew that just letting Jimmy show up some town-team from Nashua or Concord might not be enough to capture the hard eye of a scout. The House of David team usually came through late in the summer but that was too long to wait; so off went another letter, to another somebody who handled a barnstorming negro team; and before Grandpa could even begin to point out how silly the whole thing was, it was all set: The posters run up (on speculation) by a job-printer Ralph had taken fishing a few times, and the mayor, once he was promised he could umpire, convinced him he could dig up the money to add some fireworks afterward.

Of course it didn't take all that just to draw a crowd for a ballgame, especially once Ralph, now convinced he was Mr. Ban Johnson himself, managed to put together a roster of the best players from all the teams for miles around, and hired a fellow from Manchester who'd had a few so-so years pitching for the New York Highlanders and who could still throw a baseball, and even had some control of it—when he was sober. Before long everybody—not just Ralph and Jimmy and of course Grandpa—looked upon it as a great occasion, and the selectmen, without being asked, hired some of the high-school boys to take the worst bumps out of the playing field and give the wooden stands a new coat of whitewash.

Jimmy made a point of telling himself this was all just a lark, but he couldn't keep his hopes from rising. The morning of the game he was awake well before sunrise, and he nearly cried when dawn revealed heavy clouds and a wind that promised rain. Uncle Ralph was certain he had all the necessary charms working, however, and the two of them sat down in the dining room to a huge breakfast. By late morning it looked as if he were right; the rain held off and then the clouds broke and it was as fine and hot a summer day as you could wish for.

Most of the town went down to the station to see the visiting team come in, but Ralph got all his players together early at the ball field and put them through their paces. The big pitcher, whom Ralph had kept under a teetotal eye for three days, looked grumpy but ready. He let Jimmy warm him up a little, and the fast ball had a sweet little hop to it. Jimmy tried to talk about signals but the pitcher said he'd throw the first couple quick, up and in, and "Then those duds will just wave at anything else I throw anyhow. They're like that."

By noon the crowd was building, every seat full and people standing well out along each foul line, and the fellow from the general store doing quite a business in scorecards and lemonade. The visitors had marched down Main Street like a drill team and then sat together in center field, eating box lunches. They didn't look like much; their uniforms didn't quite match and hung on them as if they were borrowed, and the only one who looked big at all had a roll of fat around his middle. When they started to loosen up, though, the uniforms somehow began to fit better; and there was something in their gestures that suggested that they were on good terms with the scuffed baseballs they threw around. The fat guy caught; it was surprising how quickly he could raise all that weight out of a crouch. But the pitcher looked like a bad joke: thin, squeaky-voiced, coffee-colored, with flapping sleeves and shoes about three sizes too big. He was lobbing them up like wedding invitations and every time he tried to throw a curve ball it bounced at least twice before it got anywhere near home plate. Jimmy almost felt sorry for him.

Ralph and Grandpa had fine seats right behind home plate, and beside them were two strangers, with straw boaters and flashy ties and little slips of paper they kept looking at and writing on, whom Jimmy supposed were the scouts. The point of all of Ralph's plots and plans could hardly have been kept secret, and when the mayor shouted "Play ball," Jimmy had the warm feeling of being the object of every eye. Ralph had conceded last ups to the visitors, and Jimmy, who was of course batting fourth, was convinced he'd get an early chance to show what he could do. But the skinny pitcher wasn't lobbing any more, and it took him ten pitches to set down three batters, only one of whom managed so much as a foul tip. Still, that just made it seem more of a challenge, and Jimmy crouched down behind the plate with his confidence intact. It was his day and he knew it.

The first batter hit from a deep crouch and the hired pitcher did just what he said he would; his best fast ball came just behind the batter's head. The batter didn't move an inch; and when the next pitch came in—a pretty fair curve, down and away—he stepped into it and sent it on a line back over the pitcher's mound and nearly took the pitcher's ample belly along with it. But the pitcher was, in his way, a man of principles, and it took four more hitters, two runs, and an out that came only because the center fielder was even luckier than he was fast, before he began to realize the high-and-tight fast ball wasn't the key to success. Jimmy went out to talk to him but he just turned his back.

The crowd was still pretty noisy but somehow you could hear a skeptical edge begin to take hold. On the next pitch Jimmy knew he was in trouble; he could see the ball jerk and twitch, the spit flying off of it, and all he could do was go to his knees to try to block it, which he did but with the part of his body that hurt the worst. He lay face down next to the plate telling himself first to breathe, then to stand up, but his body wasn't listening. By the time he could see or hear another run had scored. He went out to the mound again, very slowly, and said he'd need to know when the spitball was coming, but the hired pitcher just said, "Maybe I should roll it in?"

By the end of the inning Jimmy was still a little woozy; he wasn't sure whether five or six runs had scored, and he was beginning to suspect it might not matter. The skinny pitcher didn't take any warm ups. "No use wearing it out," he said to the crowd, which by now knew where the entertainment was. But they let out a healthy roar for Jimmy, their own boy. Jimmy couldn't find a bat that didn't feel like a wagon-tongue. When he finally got himself settled at the plate, he saw the pitcher smile at him: "Hey College Boy, I hear you're really something." Then the ball came right at him, and although his eyes told him it was a curve—it must be, it had to break, his body broke first and he felt himself back away and wave as—sure enough—it broke over the plate. "Don't you be nervous, College Boy," the pitcher said.

Jimmy watched, or rather heard, one fast ball. Then he fouled off another one, and he knew he'd just about measured it. All his preservation instincts made him give up on another curve that started out straight for his head; but the mayor had some local pride left and called it a ball. "Merry Christmas, College Boy," the pitcher said. He tried another fast ball, outside, but Jimmy was ready and got most of it, his swing just the slightest bit late but the ball still went singing down the right-field line, barely foul. "My, my, I *am* impressed," the pitcher said; and went into the longest wind-up Jimmy had ever seen, topped off with a head-jerk that looked like a bee had just stung his neck. Jimmy kept his eye on the ball the whole time and he was ready this time to turn the fast ball into two bases. The ball floated and floated, visibly slowing down and Jimmy just couldn't hold back; as he finished his swing he could see the ball still coming. "That was Mr. Restful," the pitcher said; and the crowd, all on his side now, cheered.

From the bench, Jimmy got to watch one more strike out and a sad excuse for a pop-up; and then, from behind the plate, he had plenty of time to admire what the visitors could do with a bat. The fat catcher could hit the ball so far he hardly had to run; and the skinny pitcher would announce just where hits would land. "You got to study this game, College Boy," he said to Jimmy, whom he'd made his interlocutor. By the third inning no one even bothered to announce the score. The skinny pitcher started alternating which hand he'd throw with, and the fielders did about every trick you could think of, catching balls behind their backs and what not. The mayor did his best to get the home team some base runners by calling balls when the pitches were obvious strikes, but it didn't do much good. Meanwhile the hired pitcher had disappeared and Jimmy found himself catching a bright-eyed farmhand who had volunteered from the stands.

It was still a lovely day but there were shadier places to enjoy it, and the crowd dwindled rapidly. Ralph and Grandpa and the two scouts stuck it out, of course; and so did the mayor's wife, who was more or less obligated to, and a crowd of younger brothers who enjoyed laughing and the old fellows who usually napped on the hotel porch. By the time Jimmy got to bat again even the skinny pitcher's good humor had started to wear out, and he threw one hard one at Jimmy's belt buckle, just to put things on a serious footing, and then the curve ball one more time. But Jimmy had by now fallen back on sheer desperation, which was stronger even than the reflex which told him to back away.

He knew exactly where the ball was headed and got his whole body into it and could tell without looking just what a beautiful arc the ball described as it rose out toward the creek that was beyond the left fielder. As he rounded first he saw the outfielders still chasing it, and he decided there was nothing on God's green and ample earth that could keep him from going all the way around. Past second he could feel the ache in his groin start to deepen but he kept his legs moving. The third baseman tried to decoy him, crouching down as if a throw was on its way, but Jimmy went right by him and on toward home, where the fat catcher stood in the way.

Jimmy was no midget himself and went head first into the catcher just as the throw finally arrived. The two of them rolled toward the dust-covered plate. Jimmy reached out with one hand but the catcher's knee pressed down on his belly and held him fast; and Jimmy could see the ball, absurdly small in the catcher's hand, as it came toward his chin, where it hit with a resolute thud. "No sir," the catcher said, quietly but clearly, "No sir, you're on my property." Jimmy's hand was still a foot from the plate; just far enough to break utterly his last weak grip on common sense.

Before he was even aware he'd moved, Jimmy was up and swinging wildly at the catcher, who bobbed away from the punches, smiling. Still Jimmy swung, again and again, so enraged by it all that no one dared to try and stop him, although he could vaguely hear the mayor making conciliatory noises. Suddenly a wiry arm grabbed him and turned him around; it was the pitcher shouting. "Out is out, College Boy." Jimmy stopped in mid-swing and looked around at what was left of the crowd, all staring hard at him, some even cheering him on; all except the two scouts, who seemed mostly interested in the one or two clouds overhead. "Game called," the mayor announced; and Jimmy, all his energy now spent, limped over to the bench to collect his gear.

Grandpa was gone, but Ralph, who after all knew a good deal about failure, kept an only slightly worn smile on his face as he brought the two scouts over to shake Jimmy's hand. They were polite, of course, and explained that just now the big club was neck-deep in catchers but they'd keep him in mind. Ralph walked the two scouts down to the train station, gabbing the whole time, as if it were all still a matter of charm and careful pre-arrangement. Jimmy walked home, his groin aching badly, his chin swollen, his knuckles raw and his belly bruised.

Grandpa, a poor loser but a gentle winner, had a hot bath

waiting for Jimmy, who let the water soak through his aches while the fireworks rumbled in the distance. His appetite wasn't bruised, and Grandpa made sure the kitchen did its best for him. Afterward the two of them took a walk, Jimmy limping along at the old man's usual sedate pace, up Main Street, out past the Methodist Church and all the wide-porched houses, where people resting in the cool evening nodded and sometimes even said kind things about how far that last hit had gone; and then down the other side of the street, the hotel gliding closer to them in the twilight, the town at ease. As they climbed the two steps on to the hotel porch, where his usual rocker waited, Grandpa finally said, "So. College I guess."

"Yeah. College," Jimmy said.

DAVID NEMEC

Browning's Lamps

I N JANUARY OF 1974, a writer named Howard Gammill was interviewing Goober Talbot, the old outfielder, in a hotel room in New York. This is not really the beginning of the story, but it was Gammill's first inkling there might *be* a story. More of one, anyway, than Talbot could tell him.

Talbot had once led the National League in batting, but that had been during the Second World War when most of the better hitters were in uniform; in later years Talbot had trouble hanging on as a mere pinch hitter. Unlike most of the old-timers Gammill had interviewed over the winter, Talbot bore no grudge toward baseball. "Ol' country boy like the Goob," Talbot kept saying between nips at the pint of rye in his lap, "jes glad he got to play up top as long as he did." He reposed on the bed, his shirt unbuttoned to the waist, his feet up, eyeing the tape recorder as if he had never seen one before. He was a fat, nearly toothless hulk who bore no resemblance to the cherub face that had once adorned bubblegum cards. *No more than sixty*, Gammill thought, *and already he's fallen apart; sad the way these guys let themselves go when they're done playing.*

Gammill's book would be called *Day of Gold*. Each of the former players Gammill was interviewing had performed a single, solitary super feat during an otherwise mediocre career. Gammill didn't much care for the book's title or the idea behind it, but his editor was convinced there was another book or two to be mined from the lode

Kahn's *The Boys of Summer* had uncovered a few years back.
Gammill's last literary endeavor had been a string of folksy interviews with a dozen pitchers who had faced both Cobb and the Babe.
It had sold fifty thousand copies and brought him some recognition—but not the kind the men in his book had enjoyed in their day;
that would forever be beyond Gammill's reach. Talbot could look
back on his former glory—the batting title, fluke that it was, still put
him in the limelight for a few moments now and then. Gammill's
book would provide yet another such moment for Talbot, and he
seemed grateful for it. Some of the others—Hunnefield, the pitcher
who'd lost a Series no-hitter on a broken-bat single, for one—
wouldn't agree to come to New York, though all their expenses
would be paid and they'd get a grand or two besides. To talk to
Hunnefield, Gammill had to make a hideous bus trip from Miami
airport to a sugar mill town in the Florida interior. Even then
Hunnefield, now a foreman at the mill, wanted Gammill to find him
a job in baseball as his price for talking, and when Gammill couldn't
promise this, the interview dissolved into a blast at the game: *a
ruthless business.* Can't find room for an old star, but willy-nilly pays
millions to kids fresh out of Little League who don't even know how
to hold a runner on first base . . .

Gammill was thirty-five in 1974 and still in reasonably good
condition. In college he'd once gone three-for-four against a pitcher
who later won twenty games for the Red Sox. It was his own
personal day of gold. And he wanted to believe that he could have
hit in the major leagues if he'd had the chance. Oh, maybe not .300,
but at least a solid .270 or .280. Earlier in the winter he'd let this
fantasy slip out while interviewing Gusty Gayles, whose twenty-
nine saves in 1953 still held a Cardinal record, and Gayles had
laconically said, "Try .080," and then led him into a field back of the
Gayles' homestead. It had been a raw day in November and
Gammill had worried about the bat stinging his hands when it
made contact, but Gayles, at fifty-four, still had a slider that was so
wicked, Gammill had all he could do to scratch out a couple of weak
ground balls.

That, rationally, should have been the end of it. The sensible man would have resigned himself to writing about baseball, realizing that was about as close as he could ever hope to come to the game, but Gammill knew that for him there could be no easy end to the dream. The five-year-old who had stood up in front of his kindergarten class and announced he was going to be a ballplayer had become a thirty-five-year-old who would gladly trade all the glowing reviews that *Day of Gold* would bring to see his name, just once, in a major league box score. So he made up his mind to get into something else as soon as he finished the book. Talking to men like Talbot only rubbed salt where the skin was still too thin. He was worried that Talbot could sense this. That was perhaps why Talbot kept gloating, "A man that's played in the big leagues, he's done something proud."

"No regrets?" Gammill said.

"Exceptin' maybe that the Goob ain't around for this designated hitter gimmick. Ol' Goob coulda had another bat title, he didn't have to go out to the field and make a clown of hisself."

"You did alright all those years as a pinch hitter."

"Once a game. That was all the Goob could swing. Shoot, hardly enough to get the blood warm."

"Who do you think the best pinch hitter you ever saw was? Besides yourself, of course."

In bringing the pint bottle up to his mouth, Talbot paused to wag his head self-effacingly. "The best? Naw, that wadn't ol' Goob. Goob was all right, but there was better."

"For instance?"

"Waahl, guy down in one of those cotton-pickin' leagues ol' Goob played in when he was no more'n a taddy. Guy you prob'ly never heard of. Pless. Pinch Pless, they called him. Worst glove ever, couldn't catch a pea in a bushel basket. Made ol' Goob look like DiMaggio out there in the pasture—but stick a bat in his hand, man, that sucker coulda hit a apple seed blowed off a barn roof."

In such ways do writers learn there are stories better than the one they are telling. Listening to the tape of the interview later,

173

Gammill heard the catch in his voice when he asked, "What league was this, do you remember?"

"Somewheres down there in 'Bama or Kentuck. Maybe Tennysee. Played in those dogpatch leagues a lotta years before the Phils took attention that ol' Goob was always good for his .350. You oughta look up the Goob's complete record sometime. It wadn't jes those eight years in the majors."

But Gammill wasn't interested in the Goob any longer. Somewhere, in one of his talks with the old pitchers, he seemed to recall the mention of Pless, a few seconds on the order of ". . . toughest hitter I ever faced, tougher even than Cobb, was back in the bushes. Little tubby guy named Pless. Never even made it up to A ball, from what I remember, because there was no place he could play in the field where he wouldn't kill himself. But Christ! Best pure hitter you ever saw!" Gammill hadn't even included this bit of memorabilia in his book, or rather he had, simply recording everything verbatim and then letting his editor weed out what didn't seem of interest. He'd been very lazy in his approach to that book, and he'd been going along about half asleep on this one, too. But he was waking up; the second reference to Pless triggered a nerve at the back of his mind.

He wondered if Talbot remembered the exact year he'd played against this Pless. Talbot thought it was the early thirties, after taking a moment to gaze at the ceiling as if calculating something. His true age, probably, as opposed to his baseball age.

"Say '31 or so?" Gammill heard his own voice on the tape straining to sound mild.

"A while before the war, anyway," Talbot said. He sounded tired. Small wonder—the pint bottle had been empty by then, and he'd dragged his suitcase from under the bed, looking for another. Getting off the bed to shake hands when Gammill was leaving proved embarrassing to both of them.

The next morning Gammill ran through his taped talks with the old pitchers until he found the one he wanted. The description of

Pless was about as he'd remembered it, and there was an odd lilt in
the pitcher's voice, as if the memory brought him pleasure. Every
player wanted to believe he'd been up against the best at some
point, so perhaps this Pless really was something. Still, Gammill
was prepared for a disappointment when he started digging through
old *Baseball Guides*. It was too hard to believe Pless could have been
much good and still been buried all those years in the lower minors.
Gammill was browsing through the final averages for the Smokey
Mountain States League in the 1932 edition when he came across
Pless for the first time. Pless was listed by his full name, as was the
Guide's custom: Pless, Walker B." Scanning the page, he took in
Pless's statistics unbelievingly; in 108 at bats Pless had accumulated
forty-nine base hits and fourteen homers. In the entire league only
one other player, someone named Rice who'd batted over 400
times, had more homers and no one was within a hundred points
of Pless's .454 average. Delving farther back, he discovered in 1928
Pless had hit an astounding .483 with twenty-six homers in less
than 200 at bats. Over the course of that season Pless had managed
to play enough games in the outfield to have his fielding average
listed too; it was actually lower than his batting average and looked
so absurd—thirty-five errors and only twenty-eight put outs—that
Gammill would have been sure it was a misprint if he hadn't
recalled Talbot's ". . . couldn't catch a pea in a bushel basket."

He picked up a paper and pencil and began making columns of
Pless's batting achievements, going all the way back to 1921. When
he had finished he caught his breath. Pless had an average in
organized baseball of .447 and once had led the Bluegrass League
in homers and triples despite having fewer than 100 at bats. His
incompetence in the field had kept him from ever moving out of the
lower minors, apparently. It was a different game then. No club
wanted only half a player. Smead Jolley, who hit a ton everywhere
he went, was ultimately squeezed out of the majors because of his
fielding mishaps, and the Cubs had once dropped a player named
Babe Twombley after he hit .377. You still had to wonder, though,
if there weren't more to the story: a drinking problem, or perhaps
some bizarre physical defect like that Pete Gray who'd played with

only one arm.

Gammill placed an ad in *The Sporting News*, requesting anyone with knowledge of the whereabouts of Walker B. Pless, nicknamed "Pinch," former minor league slugger, to write to him. For a month after the ad ran, he checked his mail each day but without any real hope anything would come of it: Pless had played too long ago; he'd probably been dead for years. One morning, however, an envelope came, bearing a postmark that, near as Gammill could make out, was of a town in Kentucky that began with "G." In the envelope was a single sheet of cheap tablet paper with a few pencil-scrawled lines on it. The gist seemed to be that the writer had once been a teammate of Pless's. "You ever get down to Gloam," Gammill was told, "just come around the general store in the day." The signature was unreadable, and there was no return address. Gammill found a Gloam in the atlas; it was about a hundred miles south of Louisville, which meant another miserable bus ride, and on top of it the expenses for the trip would have to come out of his own pocket. What could he tell his editor? "Nobody wants to read about a guy who never even made it out of Class C," the editor would say.

He got to Gloam late on a Wednesday afternoon. The writer in him tried to feel on the verge of a story, but the dryness and shaking in his hands felt more like the day he'd gone into the field with Gusty Gayles. Gloam had three stores and he started with the one that looked the least prosperous, following the principle that had carried him through most of his literary enterprises: when in doubt as to which way to point your nose, seek the smell of failure.

An old man in a flannel shirt was behind the counter. Gammill watched him a while from the doorway. There were several customers in the store, but the man paid little attention to them. His eyes seemed to be focused on something in his mind. He had a frail, wizened, stooped profile—nothing about it to suggest an erstwhile ballplayer. Still, Gammill sensed that this was his man. Nearly all the ex-ballplayers he had interviewed had those turned-inward eyes, as if the only events that mattered were memories. He approached the counter with the letter in his hand. The man's eyes remained out in space. Gammill saw that the flesh on his face and neck hung in loose folds, as if it had once encased the head of a much heavier man, and he knew then ("... little tubby guy") that he was, in all probability, looking at Pless himself.

He stood at the counter, waiting for the man to focus his eyes on the present. After the better part of a minute the man turned and started to move off. So there was nothing for Gammill to do but speak. "Mr. Pless? Walker Pless?"

For an instant the man appeared to be startled. Then Gammill saw his shoulders steady and straighten, a movement that Gammill took to mean he would not be caught out so easily. "Who're you?" the man said flatly.

"Howard Gammill." Gammill held out the letter. "It said I'd find you in the general store."

"Lemme look." The man took the letter, pressed it flat on the counter, then stood well back as if he needed the extra distance to see. "Uh huh ... I remember this. Thing in *The Sporting News* said if anybody knew Pless. I knew Pless."

"Matter of fact," Gammill said matter of factly, "you are Pless, aren't you?"

The man laughed in a short, humorless way, as if he were being polite. "People hereabouts call me Carter. Joe Carter."

"But you played as Walker Pless." If Gammill had learned anything as a writer, it was how to persist.

The man laughed again and shrugged slightly. "When I played as anybody."

"Look, I just want"—Gammill shot a sharp glance over his shoulder—"I mean, can we go someplace where we can be alone?" he said more quietly.

"Here's good enough."

"All right, then, what I want to do is talk to you about your tremendous hitting ability. I mean you had some of the highest averages in the entire history of baseball." He was conscious that Pless's eyes were fixing on him now. "There'll be some money in it, of course. Several hundred dollars."

"Don't care about money. Store brings all I need."

That was either a lie or else Pless had the skimpiest needs

humanly possible. "Well, will you agree to just talk to me, then?"

"It's what we're doing." Dry as Pless's words were, his tone held no hint of irony. Everything was being said in the same flat voice.

"The question in my mind is why you never made it out of Class C. It must have made you a little bitter to post those fantastic averages year after year and never move up."

"No place I could move. There wasn't such a thing in those days as a man could just pinch-hit. Johnny Fredrick, Red Lucas, Sheriff Harris—they all had a position to play."

"How was it that you were such a terrible fielder? It would seem you could have learned, like you learned to hit."

"Nothing to learn there. Hitting came natural. Playing in the field, running them bases, just couldn't ever pick it up. Tried, hell— Christ, did I try, but it wouldn't come."

"Tot Pressler said you were the toughest batter he ever pitched to. Even tougher than Cobb."

"They'd say the same thing now, I was playing. Nobody around could get me out steady. Getting down to first base, though, that'd be something else. I'd have to hit it out to the wall even to get a single."

"You're telling me you could still hit?"

"For damn sure. Maybe nothing what I did when I was younger and had more shoulder, but near .300 anyway."

Gammill had heard things like this before from other old-timers, outrageous protestations that even at seventy they could play the game as well as the kids. Usually he had to restrain himself from grinning, but now he felt his whole body undergo a peculiar tightening. Pless's eyes held a dark and steady light in their centers. The rest of the man looked ordinary, even a little below ordinary; his shoulders drooped so much they almost touched the counter, and his pipe-stem arms didn't look strong enough to hold a bat, much less swing one. But those eyes looked as if they might contain something special. "Hornsby always used to make claims like that," Gammill said invitingly.

"Hornsby was good, but I was better. Still am."

"Come on. You must be over seventy. You mean to tell me you

could hit Ryan, Seaver, all those hard-throwing kids they have now?"

"Satch Paige threw as hard as any of 'em. Two years ago he came through here and I had a little get-together with him out on the high school field." Pless's mouth made an effort to smile naturally, but it escaped into an old man's nervous quivering of the lips. "About five pitches, Satch gave up. 'Never could get one by you,' he said; 'never will.'"

"Paige must be nearly seventy himself."

"Still throws mean, though. Legs ain't there to give him much follow-through, but the ball still comes."

They had arrived at a juncture where Gammill could no longer deny his motives for coming there. Still, he had to pretend, if only to himself, that he wasn't taking any of this seriously. *I'm not from Missouri, Mr. Pless, but you're still going to have to show me* was the sort of thing he wanted to say, light but to the point. Instead he found himself coming out with it like a kid would, as a challenge. Pless irritated him, under all; it was that damn could-not-care-less attitude, as if he knew how helplessly Gammill was his captive.

"I'm not Paige," Gammill said, "but I still remember how to throw what used to be a pretty fair nickel curve. Go you any amount from a beer to the price of a month's supplies for your store that you can't hit anything off me but air."

Pless could easily have laughed this off, but Gammill had begun to sense that the man, for his own reasons, was a captive here no less than he. "Not much good light left," Pless said. "Don't get dark till around six, but the old windows never did like them shadows. So you get back here in under a hour with your gear, and maybe we'll have us time for a few swings."

"I'm ready now. My glove's in the car, along with a bat and a couple of balls."

"Need more'n a couple. Field here's got a crick running back of right field. Good lefty batter's gonna hit a few out in it. Can't be helped."

"I'll take my chances."

"Waste of time, two balls. Nobody out there shagging, they'll roll in the crick first two swings. You get yourself down to the sporting goods, get a good dozen or so. Maybe dig up a kid to chase. Meet me out to the field in an hour."

Two boys were on the high school field knocking flies when Gammill got there. For a coin or two they probably would have agreed to shag for him, but instead he gave them each five dollars to go home. Whatever was going to happen here, he wanted no witnesses to it. Besides, the creek, at a glance, looked about four hundred feet from the plate. He sat on the grass beside the backstop, waiting for Pless to come along. In his lap was a Louisville Slugger, Hank Aaron model, and a gloveful of new balls, American League, Joe Cronin's signature on them. Pless didn't get there until after five o'clock; he took a squint at the sun down low behind third base and said, "Got about ten pretty fair minutes. Couldn't find no shaggers, eh? Well, get yourself ready to do some chasing out yonder."

Pless was wearing the same flannel shirt and trousers he had on in the store. Other than rolling up his sleeves, he made no preparations. He merely picked up the Aaron bat, hefted it two or three times, then shambled toward the plate.

"Stick okay?" Gammill said. He had rather expected Pless to bring his own bat and himself to have to go through some shenanigans to check that it wasn't loaded or coated with nails or some such thing.

"It's wood, ain't it?" Pless was setting himself in the open stance of a slugger. On him, though, with the stick arms and baggy clothes, it looked like a scarecrow turned sideways.

Gammill would have liked a few warm up pitches, mainly to make certain of his control so he wouldn't bean Pless, but he felt ridiculous not being ready when Pless, more than twice his age, obviously was. Looked impatient, in fact. He kept hefting the bat, then stepping out of the box to rub his eyes and take a fresh squint toward third base with them while Gammill toyed with the mound.

Satisfied at last with the footing, Gammill went into a perfunctory windup and delivered a medium-range fastball belt high.

Pless's eyes seemed to bug out of his head and his arms to quiver like jelly before he managed to launch the bat in a kind of schoolgirl swing, but the result so stunned Gammill that he felt his own eyes widen to their full size. The noise—bat against ball—made his eardrums tingle, and peeling his head over his shoulder, he was just in time to see a hectic blur ripple the underbrush that separated the creek from the outfield.

"'Lean on the cripples,' mama always said," Pless called humorlessly.

Gammill stood still as ice, frozen in the thought that he was in the dream of his life. To make sure it could not be punctured he started a more elaborate windup, resolved to let his arm all out on the next pitch, but Pless was out of the box again. Doing some more eye rubbing. Then Pless hopped back in, and he was cocking his wrist to break off a vicious curve.

The ball snapped sharply down and toward Pless's knees. It wasn't a major league pitch, but it didn't miss being one by much. Most batters would have let it go by as slim pickings, taken the strike. Pless took a stuttery step toward first base, though, and golfed it down the line, a man-sized double in any league.

The next pitch, on the outside corner, was sent on a line to dead center, and the fourth, fifth, and sixth were scattered to the deepest parts of the outfield, missing the creek only because they were not pulled quite hard enough.

"Ain't getting around on you a'tall. Old shoulders don't have that good snap no more." Pless sounded almost apologetic.

Gammill had two balls left; he would soon have to do some retrieving. The first hit, in the creek, was definitely gone, and some of the others might not be found either. He had only brought half a dozen more balls, despite Pless's injunction. His breath was coming nearly as hard as Pless's now, though not because of any physical effort. He was in a state of tremendous excitement and unbelief. He watched Pless hold the bat between his knees while he dug at the corners of his eyes. Pless had done this same routine now before each pitch. It could have been only an old ritual Pless had picked up, a habit like Harry Walker's taking his cap off and putting it on again or Rocky Colavito's stretching the bat behind his back to flex his shoulders, but it could have had other meanings. Maybe Pless didn't believe what he was seeing, either.

Gammill tossed the ball idly in his hand, but his mind was not idle. "Lights going on you, Pless?" he said finally. The man had taken an especially long time since the last pitch.

"Dust in the old windows," Pless muttered. He took a handkerchief out of his pocket and shook it out in a vastly exaggerated gesture. Gammill had the distinct impression that this was all part of a show to get him to ask the question that had been crabbing away in his brain for the past several minutes.

"What would happen if you didn't rub your eyes? If you just got in there and hit?"

Pless put the handkerchief away and squared himself at the plate again, as if he hadn't heard. Perhaps he really hadn't, or hadn't wanted to.

"What about it, Pless? You putting some kind of trick drops in them or something?"

For an instant, only the barest instant, Pless's shoulders jerked, and Gammill remembered in the store when the man had been caught off guard. Only out here it seemed he was acting as if he wanted to be caught. Gammill felt a tremor of recognition across the back of his own shoulders as it occurred to him that the events in the store might have been staged, too. He had been meant to see quickly through the play-role of Joe Carter, slothful storekeeper. Now he was intended to see that Pless had a secret to hitting. Those eyes were it. In them, somewhere. There'd been Ted Williams with his 20–10 vision, so acute he never swung at a pitch that was so much as a hair out of the strike zone. Pless's eyes looked to be even keener, for distances anyway. In the store Gammill recalled how Pless had held the letter well away from him to see it. An old man's eyes, when it came to reading. Or perhaps that too had been an affectation. Gammill was beginning to arrive at the notion that Pless could actually read Cronin's signature on each ball before he swung at it. If he could read at all. If he had ever learned how. Goober Talbot recognized his favorite brand of rye by the picture on the label, and Pless didn't look much swifter in the head department. By God, though, with Pless's ability to hit, even a cretin could make the majors these days. Gammill himself would become a Hall of Famer. He understood now the foolishness of the hope that had brought him here. He had wanted to divine the secret of Pless's wizardry with a bat and acquire it for himself. But the secret wasn't anything that could be told. It was a gift, Gammill was convinced, a gift of vision, and there was no way he could acquire that.

And then, as it happened, there suddenly was a way. Pless, in swinging at the next pitch, went down in a heap beside the plate and lay very still. The ball squibbed off his bat along the ground toward Gammill, who followed its course a moment or two before he observed that Pless had fallen. Racing to the plate, he found Pless's eyes open and blinking but the rest of his face gone awry, as if he had been struck in the head—clubbed from behind. Gammill had seen this once before on the ballfield; in 1948, as a nine-year-old, he had watched Don Black, of the Indians, topple after swinging hard at a pitch, the victim of a cerebral hemorrhage. Bending over Pless, he asked if he could be heard. When Pless only blinked some more, he shouted he was going for a doctor and ran for his car.

In the hospital the improbable fragments that had been shaken loose and stirred amok all those weeks ago in that New York hotel room tumbled at last into the mosaic of a firm and final plan. Pless was diagnosed as having sustained a massive stroke and put under around-the-clock observation. According to the doctors, he might pull through but more likely he wouldn't; in any case, he would never again be more than basket material. All this Gammill was told after identifying himself as Pless's nephew. He was taking a risk that Pless had no other living relatives, or at least none who cared enough to impede step one of the Gammill Coup. Around midnight, left alone briefly with Pless, he got a pen into the man's putty-jointed fingers and sat beside the bed, pretending to doze while he waited for the nurse to return. On the bed sheet, within reach of Pless's hand, was a single spidery line of scrawl: "I leave my body to my nephew, Howard Gammill, to do with as he wishes." Pless's signature was even more wispy than the will itself, and Gammill trusted no one would examine it too closely, for he had started to write *Pinch* before catching himself and scratching *Walker* over it.

No one wondered unduly how long Pless had managed to eke out a will although pretty much paralyzed, but a few days later, when Pless fell into a coma that spelled the end, Gammill's request that Pless's eyes be transplanted into his own head got some odd looks and an argument. What did a young man with quite service-able vision want with the eyes of a bummy cabbage-head? Gammill produced a tale of hereditary blindness at age forty, noting that Pless alone of the males in his family had been spared the dread affliction. All the doctors Gammill spoke to had the same reaction. To a man, they did not want the responsibility for any operation such as Gammill was suggesting. One eye—well, perhaps, but never both. There was Holzapple, though, up in Louisville, an ophthalmological renegade who'd put his mother's eyes in a mole for the sake of experiment.

Gammill found Holzapple to be much older than he'd antici-pated. Close to Pless's age, in fact, with hair growing out of his ears and indeed out of the edges of every orifice except his eyeballs. These listened intently to Gammill and then appeared to blur with doubt.

"Why not just swap the corneas? Be much safer. Corneas I can do just like putting in a new windowpane."

"The whole eyeball," Gammill said. "It has to be. The disease affects the retinas."

"Oddest thing I ever heard. Only attacks the males, you say?"

Gammill was afraid Holzapple would continue to probe until the story was shown up for the sham that it was, but Holzapple stopped short of that. He seemed willing to allow Gammill his lie if Gammill in return would sign a waiver releasing him of all culpability in the event the operation failed. Gammill's plan had included a clause that he would get his own eyes back if Pless's didn't work out. They could be stored somewhere, couldn't they, while the results of the operation were awaited? No such luck, Holzapple said. There was no going back; the tissues wouldn't absorb further surgery for weeks afterward, and in the meantime Gammill's eyes would be worthless. As yet, human organs weren't like spare auto parts that could be kept on the shelf until needed.

Hearing all this, Gammill suffered a violent qualm, but it passed in the glaze of remembering Pless's artistry with a bat. The chance that those seventy-odd-year-old eyes in his thirtyish body could make him overnight into a Rod Carew . . . the mere chance! That they could also reduce him to a walker of guide dogs, a toter of tin cups was swept quickly out of mind by a picture of himself in a major league uniform. And the voices of sportscasters all across the country saying, "Howard Gammill, oldest Rookie-of-the-Year ever, at thirty-five, four times a batting title winner, today was elected to the Baseball Hall of Fame in a landslide vote. Gammill, who compiled a .386 lifetime average in his brief but incredible career . . ." Later for the stuff of dreams. For now, it was enough that he had a shot at making them come true. He signed the waiver, entered the one hospital in Louisville that still granted the controversial Holzapple surgical privileges under the name of Harold Traynor (getting a kick out of the fact that no one of the staff recognized the real monicker of the immortal Pie) and as a show of faith gave his own eyes to a teenage girl who had blown her face apart with a can of hair spray.

Coming to consciousness after the operation, Gammill found his entire head swathed in bandages and wished only to sleep until the day they could be removed. Thus he swallowed voraciously all the Valiums and Darvons he was given and sought extras from his fellow patients, bargaining away dishes of rice pudding, slabs of steak, occasionally slipping a bill or two into a hand that could not see what it was getting any more than his own could see what it was giving.

Days passed on. On one of them Gammill turned his face toward what he was told was the window and tried to see through the bandages. It was his only moment of impatience. The afternoon

Holzapple announced they'd try a test or two was a murky one. Anyway, that was how it looked when Gammill unsealed his new eyes and took a glance into space. There wasn't much of it—that was his first impression, and his second was that his room must be underwater. A lot of fishy items were out there swimming around, some of them so close he could have reached out and grabbed them, if he'd been able to locate his hand when he looked down where it used to be. In its place was a wad of fuzz, and another was off to his left talking to him in Holzapple's voice.

"See anything, Gammill?"

"The bottom of a rain barrel."

"Excellent. Most transplants come up blank."

"Now you tell me."

Gammill waited for Holzapple to tell him that his sight would get better. Holzapple didn't. The bandages went on again, and the day following Gammill saw the same spectrum of murk. A moment occurred, however, when it lifted and the world he remembered emerged as if from behind a curtain. He felt reborn, in a way. Certainly not the same man. Holzapple predicted there'd be other such moments of clarity, and that one day they'd begin outnumbering the periods of murk. As soon as the riot in his vitreouses ran its course.

In late May there came a morning when the bandages came off and stayed off. The eyes were still bloodshot and more blurry than not, but Gammill did not feel he could wait any longer before conducting a few vital tests of his own on them. One in particular. He chose an interval when he was unobserved, closed his right eye and lifted a finger to the corner of his left. He could not rub hard, the flesh there was still too tender for that, but he did get in a few light swipes before a throbbing started.

The throbbing was severe enough to make him blink, but he would have blinked anyway. He couldn't have helped himself. For what he saw over the next few moments nearly stopped his heart. His left eye was fixed on the nurse where she stood at the window arranging the blind to let in the morning light. At first everything that occurred seemed in the realm of the ordinary—her back arched and her hand closed on the cord, tugging to secure it. But as she turned from the window, matters started to get weird. She looked as if she was having trouble bringing her head around; and yet—no, it wasn't just her head, it was all of her body. None of her movements looked right; they were the right movements, and in their natural order, but something about them was way off. Gammill's hand went to his eye reflexively to rub some more, then dropped with astonishment to his side as what was happening dawned on him. The nurse was moving as if she had been put into slow motion! It was taking her forever just to get away from the window and cross the room to his bed.

In another movement, however, she seemed to be running at him, and then she was there. "What's wrong, Mr. Traynor? Are you all right?"

"Fine. Never better." He ought to repeat the process immediately so he would know he hadn't imagined it, but the nurse wouldn't stop hovering over him.

"You look so pale, and your eye—why is it closed like that? Does it hurt?"

It was his left eye that was closed now, against what it had seen. The right one was moving around the room a little wildly, for it was his now: the secret, the trick to hitting .400. To hitting 1.000 if he wanted to be gluttonous about it! Jim Palmer's curves would have no more menace than clots of cotton candy. Wilhelm's knucklers might never reach the plate in this millennium.

"Nothing hurts. I feel great. It's just being here. I'm getting edgy."

Holzapple released him from the hospital at the end of the week. By then he'd learned that the rubbing stunt worked equally well on both eyes, and that no matter how hard he rubbed, the slo-mo phenomenon lasted at most only a few seconds. All of this was knowledge gained under indoor conditions, lying flat on his back in bed. Out of doors remained an unknown until he hit the street. There, with the hospital looming behind him, he stood on the corner waiting for the traffic light to change. When it seemed to be taking too long, he realized what he had done. In stepping out of the hospital into the dazzling sunshine, he had performed by instinct some brushing of the eyes to protect them. It could be brought about quite by accident, then. He wondered what other quirks he had yet to discover. Refining his act was undoubtedly going to take a while. Not terribly long, though, he hoped, because the baseball season was already well underway and he'd have to debut soon to have any chance at Rookie-of-the-Year.

In his musing he had missed the light change. No problem. A pass at his eyes and approaching cars were reduced to the pace of giant snails. He stepped off the curb and started across. In a moment he was reeling backwards, lunging for the curb again. His legs, walking, weren't carrying him anywhere near as fast as the cars. In bed he'd had no occasion to notice how his own movements slowed to correspond to the world around him. A whole world of snails and himself one of them. A world of time interrupted, if only for a few moments here and there. It was all illusory, but then, what wasn't?

Tinkering with something cosmic was what he was doing. Pless had done it for years, and nothing untoward had happened to him, except your standard old man's graceless death. One thing he had done some stopping to think on while in the hospital was how Pless had come into possession of these eyes. Perhaps witchcraft was behind them. How else to explain the similarity in method between summoning their magic and the genie in Aladdin's lamp? With that strangely thrilling conviction, Gammill hailed a cab and went directly to the airport, rehearsing the sick-relative story he would spring on his editor to account for the long silence from his type-writer.

The Indians, going nowhere as usual, let him travel with their club while he supposedly worked on a baseball version of Plimpton's *Paper Lion*. The players ribbed him mercilessly and kept suggesting such titles as *Wooden Indian*. His editor had made a deal with the Cleveland management whereby he would be put on the active roster after the twenty-five-man limit was lifted on September 1, and thrown into a game or two as a pinch runner. The prospect of putting him up to bat, though, was nigh into nonexistent. The game was still smarting from Veeck's use of a midget years ago and wanted no more sideshow ventures, even under the catch-all guise of literature.

That, on short notice, was the best Gammill's editor had been able to do for him and then only under enormous prodding. In his professional view he gave a very low value to the theory about Gammill's needing an insider's look at the game before he could make *Day of Gold* credible, especially since rival publishing outfits were coming out with baseball books all the time by poets and feminist journalists who had no more idea that "hit-and-run" in baseball parlance was not a criminal offense, then they did that a steel cup was not for drinking but an item of protective apparel. "The trouble with Bouton, Brosnan, and the rest of them," Gammill said, "was they were really company men at bottom. If you thought they made feathers fly, put me in the clubhouse for a few weeks and you'll see the real lowdown on what makes a bunch of men run around in pajamas."

Gammill actually took no notes at all, though he did make a display of hanging around a lot and nodding wisely to himself each time one of the subs uttered in his earshot some *bon mot* about the game. The Indians' manager meanwhile ignored him, as did most of the regulars. From time to time, however, one of the rookie pitchers, a lefty named Tybender, came out to the park early in the morning and threw a few minutes of batting practice to him in return for some tutoring in the art of writing. Tybender was keeping a diary of his first season and hoped to become a novelist when his playing days were over. That could be soon, for pitching to Gammill began invidiously to undermine his confidence. At the outset Gammill limited his eye gimmick to one or two pitches a session, but gradually he stepped up the tempo until he was smoting the rookie's best offerings effortlessly out of the park. Word of Gammill's unlikely prowess in due order reached the Indians' third-base coach, who lurked in a corner of the dugout one morning, pretending interest in the bat racks. Both Gammill and the rookie knew he was there, and both were nervous. The rookie, thinking he was on trial, blazed his first pitch high and tight, and Gammill, having decided to take a straight look at a toss or two before going into his eye-throttling routine, narrowly missed decapitation.

Tybender next served a curve that started in on Gammill's hands and broke like a comet at the last instant over the inside corner. That, at least, was how the pitch might have appeared to the coach. To Gammill's genie-invoked eyes it was a moon on a platter, and he hit it into the upper deck.

A groan escaped Tybender, and in the dugout there was a clatter. Glancing over his shoulder, Gammill saw a bench had fallen and the coach was now up on the steps.

Mixing frequent cap adjustments with the cleansing of perspiration from his brow, he kept time on the field in a state of near perpetual suspension while he rattled balls off the fences like buckshot. He was careful not to overstimulate the coach, sometimes deliberately missing pitches he could easily have clobbered. Once he even switched for a few moments to batting righthanded and looked foolish. The coach was meant to believe he was treating the outing as pure fun and that he took nothing he did too seriously. Like an aspiring film actor, he must not toot his own horn but let the director discover him on his own. He finished the workout with a shot over the center field fence that struck at the base of the bleachers, territory no Indian had reached in years. Locked into downshifted motion still, and a little dizzy, he turned from the plate to amble toward the dugout. The coach was creeping out on the field to greet him, arms waving like windmills on a breezeless day. The coach's words tumbled out at normal speed, though. Sounds, oddly, were not affected in the slightest.

"Pretty fair stroke there, Gammill, for a guy sits behind a typewriter all day. Stick around. Maybe Klosterman will chuck a few to you when he comes out to do some photos for *Sport*."

Klosterman was the team's ace, a righty fireballer who already had nine wins despite it being only June. The closest thing to Feller since Feller himself. "Well, I don't know if I'm up to anything like that," Gammill said. "My God, I'm just out for a little exercise."

Self-efface at every opportunity. Overdo, if necessary. What a clod the coach was. Could barely keep from choking on the wad of chewing tobacco in his cheek over what he'd seen, but still trying to play it coy. As Gammill watched, the man's coma ended and the arm gyrations quickened. That was the way it went, one instant the world spinning in turtle time and then everything back to its usual pell-mell self.

"Your life insurance is paid up," the coach said, directing a stream of tobacco juice at a point midway between his feet and Gammill's. "Besides, Klostie needs some work on his breaking stuff against lefties."

The coach was getting intrigued by him. When he'd pounded Klosterman around, the manager would be next. The Indians desperately lacked a reliable designated hitter. They lacked at a number of other positions, too, but Gammill's fantasies did not extend to filling any of them. In the field he'd discovered, as Pless must have, that slowing down the flight of a ball hit his way did not help much; he was missing the instinct and the footspeed necessary to get him to where it was going. On the other hand, standing stationary in the batter's box, lining himself up to tee off on an object rendered almost ponderous, was a matter he could have mastered in his sleep. Well, actually not. The eye gimmick would not work in the dark or under artificial light: Gammill did not know why that was. It seemed to have something to do with the sun; on a cloudy day, for example, he couldn't get his eyes focused clearly. He remembered Pless's obsession that there be good light for batting and his continual squinting into the setting sun, which he had regarded at the same time as part of the act. Of late he had begun feeling unaccountable impulses to gaze into the sun himself. The brighter it was, the more he was drawn to it. Thus far he had refrained from indulging those urges. The sun was dangerous to the naked eye; moreover, things that did not . . . *belong* sometimes materialized if he were out in it too long. There had been those queer ads for toothpowder and chewing tobacco on the outfield wall a few days ago; and just this morning Tybender had been wearing a baggy uniform of a style that had been the norm in Goober Talbot's day.

Klosterman finished his photography session with *Sport* shortly after eleven. He held no great interest in Gammill but agreed to toss a few pitches to him in lieu of his normal workout the day before a scheduled starting assignment. Gammill pretended to shake in his shoes as he stepped up to the plate, to be playing the clown. He settled in, the bat resting on his left shoulder. Directly overhead the sun glared, nearing noonday intensity. Behind him the coach hunkered in the dugout; a few other players, subs out early for a little extra practice, took up positions on the field. Falling in with Gammill's mock festive spirit, one of them stationed himself at shortstop with a catcher's mitt, and another trotted out to first base wearing his cap backwards. This man went flying heels over head when Gammill's first swing caromed a liner at him so hot it tore the glove off his hand.

"Better bear down, Klostie, get a man killed out here," someone shouted. Unobtrusively Klosterman dug a deeper foothold for himself at the edge of the rubber. Gammill peered at his obdurate, arrogant profile, trapped in the throes of time half-frozen. Suddenly the profile seemed to grow in size, to move closer, and over its shoulder Gammill saw the shortstop was now playing barehanded. Craning his head judiciously to the right, he watched the man on first smooth his hair and replace his cap. The maneuver was standard, one he'd seen a thousand times on the playing field, but the cap was a different matter. He had never seen one like it anywhere. Definitely it was not the red felt job the man had on his head up till a moment ago. Matter of fact, it was brown. So was the rest of the man's uniform, including the socks, which also bore wide yellow stripes. And in place of the first baseman's glove he had been wearing was a skin-tight contraption that resembled the hand protectors used by golfers and horsemen.

Klosterman, under average height, rather stocky, now seemed positively elongated. He too had on a brown uniform. His pitch came plateward from below his shoulder, jerkily sidearm, with hardly any windup. Thoroughly unnerved, Gammill could not get his bat off his shoulder even though he had what must have been a good five seconds from the time it left Klosterman's hand.

But it was no longer Klosterman out there. The face that stared back at his was gaunt and sallow. Then of course it disappeared and Klosterman's sneering mouth and ruddy cheeks floated in front of him again.

He backed hastily out of the box and scraped some dirt over his hands. Klosterman's call to him was low-pitched but giggly with amusement. "What happened, Howie? Too much smoke on that one?"

Gammill wanted desperately to assume this was all some effect of the light on his still not-quite-healed eyes, and that at the same time was precisely his dread. The sun even this moment was attempting to pull his eyes up from the ground. Now it was much more than curiosity that impelled him to wonder what he evoked each time he performed his Aladdin ritual. However, his dogged determination asserted itself at this point. He would forge ahead. A hand on his forehead, thumb and middle finger stroking gently at the corner of either eye, and the earth's rotation slowed, an action so deftly managed that it would have seemed only a moment's brow-mopping to the casual onlooker. Anyway, all the attention was on Klosterman, who was cranking his arm for another high, hard one.

Except that Klosterman's pitch once more came in sidearm, and with so little steam on it he could literally have counted the seams on the ball. A queerish ball it was, too, having no league stamp on it and a trifle lopsided, more a melon shape than exactly round.

He swatted grimly at it and watched it scoot out over second base where it was speared on the run by the shortstop with his bare left hand. Pausing to right himself, the man heaved the ball across to the first baseman, who awaited it with both feet straddling the bag.

Throughout this performance Gammill stood stock-still. Whatever was going on out there reminded him more of a vaudeville act of baseball than baseball itself. No one in his right mind played first base with his feet anchored like that, but then no one played barehanded either. Not in this day and age.

Nor, for that matter, in Pless's day. Hence the possibility, which was just now occurring to him, that *these eyes might retain pictures of the past, along with their other supernatural qualities,* could not be rejected out of hand.

Or now, wait a minute.

Gammill again felt a curious desire to look skyward and reluctantly succumbed to it.

He saw nothing unusual up there, but the mere fact that he wanted to stare into the sun and keep on staring was in itself unusual.

"Whattaya, crazy? Burn your lamps out, you keep doing that." Klosterman's voice was derisive, but the words sounded as a familiar melody to Gammill.

Someone else had referred to eyes as lamps, once. Someone long ago, in the infant days of baseball.

The Gladiator. He who, legend had it, used to stand on the street each morning upon emerging from his hotel and stare for moments on end directly into the sun. Gave the old lamps energy, he said when queried about his habit, and though his logic was thought to be the height of madness, who could argue with its results?

The Gladiator. For years the scourge of the old American Association.

And there it was. Gammill's jaw sagged. And as he tore his eyes away from the sun, he experienced at first a fantastic suspicion, then a sudden pulsating conviction. Unhurriedly he backed away from the plate and bent down as if to tie his shoe while he thought more. But his nonchalance now disguised as panic: it was horribly clear to him that these eyes had not originated in any Walker B. Pless.

The American Association. The Beer-and-Baseball-on-Sunday League. Those drab brown uniforms out there a few moments ago, those absurd block caps, the awakening, confused images of another century versus the gaudy red and white Indian outfits he saw all around him now: two kinds of appearance and no reality at all.

He wished with all his heart that he had the capacity to tell himself otherwise, but he knew beyond any doubt that he had been in the company of the fabled old St. Louis Browns. The elongated pitcher, that had been Scissors Foutz who still held the all-time record for the highest lifetime winning percentage. None other than the Old Roman, Charlie Comiskey himself, at first base. The rest of them scattered out over the diamond he didn't know by name, but they were all there. The boys of Chris Von Der Abe. For a moment his terror was overcome by a blade of fancy. Oh, the book he might write if he could somehow get them to stay long enough to talk to them!

But then his own psychic plight numbed him to any sensations of nostalgia, and he began trembling. All that looking into the sun the Gladiator had done hadn't been to store up energy but for quite another purpose.

He yearned to find some other explanation of events, but he knew he could not. In a surge of self-pity, he wondered whether anyone in all the world was as unlucky as he. He had the secret to becoming the greatest hitter in the history of baseball, and unlike Pless, who had lived in a day when hitting alone couldn't vault a man into the majors, he had nothing to stop him from exploiting it. Nothing except the complete knowledge of his doom if he did. It seemed all too clear to him that the Gladiator hadn't acquired his lamps by accident but had bargained for them hideously and then had somehow maneuvered to pass them on before he was called to account. Pless too had managed to escape the fate sealed in their centers.

Of course, at least some of this could be the product of a panicked imagination, but could he afford the risk? Could he gamble that whoever was luckless enough to have the eyes when the lights finally went out in them would not be made to pay the full electric bill?

Backing out of the batter's box, Gammill understood at last the difference between obsession and mere desire. For someone truly obsessed there would have been no decision to make now: the risks were never greater than the possibility of reward. But for him there was nothing in his mind but decision.

He pulled his face away from the sun and ran for the dugout.

In Louisville the following morning, he was unsurprised to learn when he looked up Pless's death certificate that the B. stood not for Babe or Bingo but for his mother's maiden name. Holzapple could tell him little of the early history of eye transplants but agreed to check the reference books. One of the first on record, it turned out, was performed in the same hospital where Holzapple now had surgical privileges. In 1905 a six-year-old boy who was blinded in a factory accident had received the eyes of his dying uncle. Neither the boy's name nor that of the donor was recorded in medical annals, but Gammill had only to check *The Baseball Encyclopedia* to fill in both with deadly accuracy.

The boy had been Walker Browning Pless, and his uncle had been Louis Rogers Browning.

Old Pete. The Gladiator.

Gammill would never know under what circumstances the original pact for the incredible eyes had been made. Nor would he ever discover whether Pless had known the awful secret of the eyes and schemed mightily to get them out of his head. But then no one had to know anything of his own brush with sorcery.

Holzapple charged him a thousand dollars for the eyes of a toothbrush salesman who had fallen off a motorcycle, and what with the efforts of the two operations, his vision was only eighty percent of what it had once been. But Gammill would settle for seeing the world at normal speed, no matter how dimly.

By the middle of fall he was back at work on *Days of Gold.* Holzapple never told him what he had done with the bewitched eyes, and Gammill never asked. It is said, though, there is a mole in Louisville now that comes out of the ground at dawn and lies about the rest of the day, staring at the sun.

196

AUTHOR'S STAT SHEET

Irwin Chusid is a freelance writer/editor and radio producer residing in Montclair, New Jersey, who lists his occupation in the SABR (Society for American Baseball Research) Directory as "Renaissance Man."

Merritt Clifton operates Samisdat Press in Vermont and has authored dozens of baseball stories, including the widely praised underground novella *A Baseball Classic* (1978).

Robert Coover, one of America's finest contemporary novelists, is perhaps best known to baseball fans as the author of one of baseball literature's finest novels, *The Universal Baseball Association, Inc., J. Henry Waugh, Prop.* (1968).

Jay Feldman writes prolifically about baseball (for *Sports Illustrated*), organizes annual "Baseball for Peace" ballplaying tours to Nicaragua, and publishes the "Baseball for Peace" newsletter in California. Plays in an over-30 hardball league; still can't hit the curve ball.

Leslie Woolf Hedley operates the literary publishing company, Exile Press, in California and sustains an active love–hate relationship with what has become of baseball.

John Hildebidle teaches literature and creative writing at M.I.T., which is almost like devoting oneself to crafting World Championship rings for the Boston Red Sox.

W.P. Kinsella is the award-winning author of two of baseball's best-loved novels, *Shoeless Joe* and *The Iowa Baseball Confederacy*, and is perhaps the most dedicated present-day practitioner of the baseball short story as a distinctive literary genre.

James Kissane teaches in the Department of English at Grinnell College, Iowa, and contends that his only intention in writing "Frankie's Home Run" was to record "absolute truth"—

an admission which puts him right up there in a class with Leo Durocher and Yogi Berra among baseball philosophers.

David Nemec is the author of three successful novels and four non-fiction books, including *Great Baseball Feats, Facts and Firsts* (New American Library, 1987) and *The Absolutely Most Challenging Baseball Quiz Book, Ever* (Macmillan, 1977).

Jay Neugeboren is one of America's most prolific fiction writers and author of perhaps the finest basketball novel written to date, *Big Man* (1966), as well as one of baseball's most memorable novels, *Sam's Legacy* (Holt, Rinehardt and Winston, 1973).

Henry H. Roth, who teaches English at CCNY, has published 150 short stories in literary magazines. His novel, *Cruz Chronicle*, is being published by Rutgers University Press. Having grown up within walking distance of Ebbet's Field, he still hasn't gotten over the departure of the Dodgers.

Luke Salisbury is Vice President of the Society for American Baseball Research and author of one of baseball's best recent trivia books, *The Answer is Baseball* (Times Books, 1989).

William T. Stafford is Professor of English at Purdue University and long-time editor of the academic journal *Modern Fiction Studies*, as well as one of the most die-hard among contemporary Chicago Cub fans.

Tom Tolnay is a magazine editor and small press publisher residing in New York who has remained a silent partner in creating this present volume of stories celebrating our national pastime.

Lawrence Watson teaches in the Department of English at the University of Wisconsin, Stevens Point, and is also an accomplished author of numerous stories and poems in literary journals and of one major novel, *In a Dark Time* (Scribners, 1980).

ACKNOWLEDGMENTS

The following previously published stories appear with the generous permission of their original publishers or authors, to whom we are greatly indebted:

"McDuff on the Mound" (Robert Coover), from *The Iowa Review* 2:4 (Fall 1971), 111–120. Reprinted with permission of *The Iowa Review*, the author, and his agent Georges Borchardt, Inc.

"The Zodiacs" (Jay Neugeboren), reprinted with permission of the author.

"A Rookie Southpaw, With Talent" (Tom Tolnay), originally appearing as "The Rookie Southpaw and the Portland Clams," in *The Saturday Evening Post* (October 1983), 66–69, 104–108. Reprinted with permission of *The Saturday Evening Post* and the author.

"The Glory of Their Haze" (Irwin Chusid), from the *Star–Gazette*. Reprinted with the permission of the author.

"The Day God Invented Baseball" (Leslie Woolf Hedley), from *Pig Iron, No. 9* (Baseball Issue), 1982: 66–68. Reprinted with permission of *Pig Iron Press* and the author.

"Pinstripe" (Lawrence Watson), from *Arete: The Journal of Sports Literature* 2:2 (Sprint 1985), 111–123. Reprinted with permission of *Arete* and the author.

"The Professor and the Chicago Cubs" (William T. Stafford), from *Arete: The Journal of Sports Literature* 4:1 (Fall 1986), 171–179. Reprinted with permission of *Arete* and the author.

"Frankie's Home Run" (James Kissane), from *Minneapolis Review of Baseball* 7:4 (1988), 46–54. Reprinted with permission of the *Review* and the author.

"Exploding Curve" (Merritt Clifton), from *Pig Iron, No. 9* (1982), 88–89. Reprinted with permission of Pig Iron Press and the author.

"The Cinderella Kid" (Henry H. Roth), from *New American Review*, reprinted with the permission of the author.

"Browning's Lamps" (David Nemec), from *Twilight Zone Magazine* (June 1982), 23–34. Reprinted with permission of the author.

The stories by W.P. Kinsella, Luke Salisbury, Jay Feldman and John Hildebidle are appearing in print for the first time in this volume and are published with the permissions of their authors.

Baseball's Dozen Best Adult Novels

Carkeet, David. *The Greatest Slump of All Time.* New York: Harper and Row Publishers, 1984 (New York: Viking Penguin, 1985).

Charyn, Jerome. *The Seventh Babe.* New York: Arbor House Publishers, 1979 (New York: Avon Books, 1980).

Coover, Robert. *The Universal Baseball Association, Inc., J. Henry Waugh, Prop.* New York: Signet New American Library, 1968.

Graham, John Alexander. *Babe Ruth Caught in a Snowstorm.* Boston: Houghton Mifflin Company, 1973.

Greenberg, Eric Rolfe. *The Celebrant.* New York: Everest House, 1983 (New York: Viking Penguin, 1986).

Harris, Mark. *The Southpaw (by Henry W. Wiggen, Punctuation Freely Inserted and Spelling Greatly Improved by Mark Harris).* Indianapolis: Bobbs–Merrill Publishing Company, 1953 (Lincoln, Nebraska: The University of Nebraska Press, 1984).

Harris, Mark. *Bang the Drum Slowly (by Henry W. Wiggen, Certain of His Enthusiasms Restrained by Mark Harris).* New York: Alfred A. Knopf, 1956 (Lincoln, Nebraska: The University of Nebraska Press, 1984.)

Herrin, Lamar. *The Rio Loja Ringmaster.* New York: The Viking Press, 1977 (New York: Avon Books, 1978).

Kinsella, W.P. *Shoeless Joe.* Boston: Houghton Mifflin Company, 1982 (New York: Ballantine Books, 1983).

Kinsella, W.P. *The Iowa Baseball Confederacy.* Boston: Houghton Mifflin Company, 1986 (New York: Ballantine Books, 1987).

Malamud, Bernard. *The Natural.* New York: Farrar and Giroux Publishers, 1952 (New York: Avon Books, 1980).

Roth, Philip. *The Great American Novel.* New York: Holt, Rinehart and Winston, 1973 (New York: Viking Penguin Books, 1981).

Fifty Recommended Baseball Novels

Ardizzone, Tony. *Heart of the Order*. New York: Henry Holt and Company, 1986.

Asinof, Eliot. *Man on Spikes*. New York: McGraw-Hill Book Company, 1955 (New York: Popular Library, 1955).

Bell, Marty. *Breaking Balls*. New York: Signet New American Library, 1979.

Bowen, Michael. *Can't Miss*. New York: Harper and Row Publishers, 1987.

Brady, Charles. *Seven Games in October*. Boston: Little, Brown and Company, 1979.

Browne, Robert (pseudonym for **Marvin Karlins**). *The New Atoms' Bombshell*. New York: Ballantine Books, 1980 (previously published as *The Last Man Out*, Englewood Cliffs, New Jersey: Prentice-Hall Publishers, 1969, by Marvin Karlins).

Burch, Mark H. *Road Game*. New York: The Vanguard Press, 1986.

Craig, John. *All G.O.D.'s Children*. New York: William Morrow and Company, 1975 (New York: Signet New American Library, 1976).

Craig, John. *Chappie and Me: An Autobiographical Novel*. New York: Dodd, Mead and Company, 1979.

Cronley, Jay. *Screwballs*. Garden City, New York: Doubleday and Company, 1980.

DeAndrea, William L. *Five O'Clock Lightning*. New York: St. Martin's Press, 1982.

Donohue, James F. *Spitballs and Holy Water*. New York: Avon Books, 1977.

Everett, Percival L. *Suder*. New York: The Viking Press, 1983.

Frank, Morry. *Every Young Man's Dream—Confessions of a Southern League Shortstop*. Chicago: Silverback Books, 1984.

Geller, Michael. *Major League Murder*. New York.: St. Martin's Press, 1988.

Gethers, Peter. *Getting Blue*. New York: Delacorte Press, 1987.

Fifty Recommended Baseball Novels

Gordon, Alison. *Dead Pull Hitter.* Toronto: McClelland and Stewart, 1988.

Gregorich, Barbara. *She's on First.* Chicago: Contemporary Books, 1987 (Toronto and New York: Paper Jacks Limited, 1988).

Harris, Mark. *A Ticket for a Seamstitch (by Henry W. Wiggen, but Polished for the Printer by Mark Harris).* New York: Alfred A. Knopf, 1956 (Lincoln, Nebraska: The University of Nebraska Press, 1984).

Harris, Mark. *It Looked Like Forever.* New York: McGraw–Hill Book Company, 1979 (New York: McGraw–Hill Paperbacks, 1984).

Hays, Donald. *The Dixie Association.* New York: Simon and Schuster, 1984 (New York: Warner Books, 1984).

Hemphill, Paul. *Long Gone.* New York: The Viking Press, 1979.

Honig, Donald. *The Last Great Season.* New York: Simon and Schuster, 1979.

Hough, John, Jr. *The Conduct of the Game.* New York: Harcourt Brace Jovanovich, 1986.

Kahn, Roger. *The Seventh Game.* New York: Signet New American Library, 1982.

Kluger, Steve. *Changing Pitches.* New York: St. Martin's Press, 1984.

Kowet, Don. *The Seventh Game.* New York: Dell Publishing Company, 1977.

Lardner, Ring. *You Know Me Al—A Busher's Letters.* New York: Curtis Publishing Company, 1914 (New York: Vintage Books, 1984).

Littlefield, William. *Prospect.* Boston: Houghton Mifflin Publishers, 1989.

Mayer, Robert. *The Grace of Shortstops.* Garden City, New York: Doubleday and Company Publishers, 1984.

McAlpine, Gordon. *Joy in Mudville.* New York: E.P. Dutton Publishers, 1989.

Morgenstein, Gary. *Take Me Out to the Ballgame.* New York: St. Martin's Press, 1980.

Morgenstein, Gary. *The Man Who Wanted to Play Centerfield for the New York Yankees.* New York: Antheneum Books, 1983.

Neugeboren, Jay. *Sam's Legacy.* New York: Holt, Rinehart and

Winston, 1974.

Peuchner, Ray. *A Grand Slam.* New York: Harcourt Brace Jovanovich, 1973.

Platt, Kin. *The Screwball King Murder.* New York: Random House Publishers, 1978.

Plimpton, George. *The Curious Case of Sidd Finch.* New York: Macmillan Company, 1987 (New York: Ballantine Books, 1988).

Pomeranz, Gary. *Out at Home.* Boston: Houghton Mifflin Publishers, 1985.

Quarrington, Paul. *Home Game.* Garden City, New York: Doubleday and Company, 1983 (Toronto, Ontario: Doubleday Canada Limited, 1983).

Rice, Damon (pseudonym*). *Seasons Past.* New York: Praeger Publishers, 1976. (*actual authors are **Svein Arber**, **Harold Rosenthal**, and **Ford Hovis**)

Ritz, David. *The Man Who Brought the Dodgers Back to Brooklyn.* New York: Simon and Schuster, 1981.

Rothweiler, Paul R. *The Sensuous Southpaw.* New York: G.P. Putnam and Sons Publishers, 1976.

Schiffer, Michael. *Ballpark.* New York: Simon and Schuster, 1982 (New York: Signet New American Library, 1983).

Small, David. *Almost Famous.* New York: W.W. Norton and Company, 1982 (New York: Avon Books, 1983).

Snyder, Don J. *Veterans Park.* New York: Franklin Watts Publishing Company, 1987.

Stansberry, Domenic. *The Spoiler.* New York: Atlantic Monthly Press, 1987.

Stein, Harry. *Hoopla.* New York: Alfred A. Knopf, 1983 (New York: St. Martin's Press, 1983).

Tennenbaum, Sylvia. *Rachel, The Rabbi's Wife.* New York: William Morrow and Company Publishers, 1978.

Willard, Nancy. *Things Invisible to See.* New York: Alfred A. Knopf, 1984 (New York: Bantam Books, 1986).

Wolff, Miles J. *Season of the Owl.* New York: Stein and Day Publishers, 1980 (New York: Stein and Day Paperback, 1984).

Baseball Literature Anthologies

Einstein, Charles, Editor. *The Baseball Reader—Favorites from the Fireside Books of Baseball*. New York: McGraw-Hill Publishers, 1980.

Einstein, Charles, Editor. *The Fireside Book of Baseball*. Fourth Edition. New York: Simon and Schuster, 1987.

Gardner, Martin. *The Annotated "Casey at the Bat": A Collection of Ballads About the Mighty Casey*. Chicago: The University of Chicago Press, 1982.

Graber, Ralph S., Editor. *The Baseball Reader*. New York: A S. Barnes Publishers, 1951.

Greenberg, Martin H., Editor. *On the Diamond: A Treasury of Baseball Stories*. New York: Bonanza Books (Crown Publishers), 1987.

Grossinger, Richard, Editor. *The Temple of Baseball*. Berkeley, California: North Atlantic Books, 1985.

Grossinger, Richard, Editor. *The Dreamlife of Johnny Baseball*. Berkeley, California: North Atlantic Books, 1987.

Holtzman, Jerome, Editor. *Fielder's Choice: An Anthology of Baseball Fiction*. New York: Harcourt Brace Jovanovich, 1979.

Kerrane, Kevin and Richard Grossinger, Editors. *Baseball Diamonds—Tales, Traces, Visions and Voodoo From a Native American Rite*. New York: Anchor Books, 1980.

Kerrane, Kevin and Richard Grossinger, Editors. *Baseball I Gave You the Best Years of My Life*. Third Edition. Berkeley, California: North Atlantic Books, 1985.

McSherry, Frank D., Jr.; Charles Waugh and Martin H. Greenberg (Editors). *Baseball 3000*. New York: Elsevier-Dutton Publishing Company, 1981.

Shannon, Mike, Editor. *The Best of Spitball, The Literary Magazine of Baseball*. New York: Pocket Books (Simon and Schuster), 1988.

Thorn, John, Editor. *Armchair Book of Baseball*. New York: Charles Scribner's Sons, 1985.

Thorn, John, Editor. *Armchair Book of Baseball 2.* New York: Charles Scribner's Sons, 1987.

Villani, Jim and **Rose Sayre,** Editors. *Pig Iron No. 9 (Baseball Issue).* Youngstown, Ohio: Pig Iron Press, 1981.

Critical Readings On Baseball Fiction

Angelius, Judith Wood. "The Man Behind the Catcher's Mask—A Closer Look at Robert Coover's Universal Baseball Association," *The Denver Quarterly* 12:1 (1977), 165–174.

Ardolino, Frank R. "The Americanization of the Gods: Onomastics, Myth, and History in Philip Roth's *The Great American Novel,*" *Arete: The Journal of Sport Literature* 3:1 (Fall 1985), 37–59.

Berman, Neil S. "Coover's *Universal Baseball Association:* Play as Personalized Myth," *Modern Fiction Studies* 24:2 (1978), 209–222.

Bjarkman, Peter C. "Bats, Balls and Gowns: Academic Dissertations on Baseball Literature, Culture and History," *The SABR Review of Books: A Forum of Baseball Literary Opinion,* Edited by Paul D. Adomites. Kansas City: The Society for American Baseball Research, 3 (1988), 89–104.

Bjarkman, Peter C. "Diamonds Are A Gal's Worst Friend—Women in Baseball History and Fiction," *The SABR Review of Books: A Forum of Baseball Literary Opinion,* Edited by Paul D. Adomites. Garrett Park, Maryland: The Society for American Baseball Research, 4 (1989), 79–95.

Bjarkman, Peter C. "Major League Hits From Minor League Players—Small Presses and the Baseball Book Industry," *Small Press* 7:3 (June 1989), 25–26.

Bjarkman, Peter C. "Baseball Novels from Gil Gamesh to Babe Ragland to Sidd Finch: A Bibliographical Survey of Serious Adult Baseball Fiction Since 1973," *Minneapolis Review of Baseball* 9:1 (January 1990), to appear.

Bjarkman, Peter C. *The Immortal Diamond: Baseball in American Literature and American Culture.* Westport, CT: Meckler Books, 1990, to appear.

Boe, Alfred F. "Shoeless Joe Jackson Meets J. D. Salinger: Baseball and the Literary Imagination," *Arete: The Journal of Sport Literature* 1:1 (1983), 179–185.

Candelaria, Cordelia. *Baseball in American Literature: From Ritual to Fiction.* Unpublished Doctoral Dissertation. South Bend, Indiana: The University of Notre Dame, 1976.

Candelaria, Cordelia. *Seeking the Perfect Game: Baseball in American Literature.* Westport, CT: Greenwood Press, 1989.

Cashill, John R. "The Life and Death of Myth in American Baseball Literature," *American Examiner: A Forum of Ideas,* Michigan State University, Volume 3 (1974), 24–37.

Cochran, Robert. "Bang the Drum Differently: The Southpaw Slants of Henry Wiggen," *Modern Fiction Studies* 33.1 (Spring 1987), 151–159.

Cochran, Robert. "A Second Cool Papa: Hemingway to Kinsella to Hays," *Arete: The Journal of Sport Literature* 4:2 (Spring 1987), 27–40.

Dodge, Tom. "William Kennedy's *Ironweed*: The Expiation of a Broken Ballplayer," *Arete: The Journal of Sport Literature* 4:2 (Spring 1987), 69–74.

Grella, George. "Baseball and the American Dream," *Massachusetts Review* 16:3 (Summer 1975), 550–567. (Reprinted in: *Sport Inside Out,* Edited by **David Wanderwerken** and **Spencer K. Wertz.** Fort Worth, Texas: Texas Christian University Press, 1985: 267–279.)

Harris, Mark. "Bring Back That Old Sandlot Novel," *The New York Times Book Review* 42 (October 16, 1988), 1, 44–45.

Harris, Mark. "Horatio at the Bat, or Why Such a Lengthy Embryonic Period for the Serious Baseball Novel?" *Aethlon: The Journal of Sport Literature* 5:2 (Spring 1988), 1–11.

Harrison, Walter Lee. "Six-Pointed Diamond: Baseball and American Jews," *Journal of Popular Culture* 15:3 (1981), 112–118.

Harrison, Walter Lee (1980). *Out of Play—Baseball Fiction from Pulp to Art.* Unpublished Doctoral Dissertation. Davis, California: University of California at Davis, 1980.

Hye, Allen. "*Shoeless Joe* and the American Dream," *The Markham Review* 15 (1986), 56–59.

Knisley, Patrick Allen. *The Interior Diamond—Baseball in Twentieth Century American Poetry and Fiction.* Unpublished Doctoral Dissertation. Boulder, Colorado: University of Colorado, 1978.

Kudler, Harvey. *Bernard Malamud's "The Natural" and Other Oedipal Analogs in Baseball Fiction.* Unpublished Doctoral Dissertation. New York: St. John's University, 1976.

Critical Readings On Baseball Fiction

O'Connor, Gerry. "Bernard Malamud's *The Natural*: 'Or, The Worst There Ever Was in the Game'," *Arete: The Journal of Sport Literature* 3:2 (Spring 1986), 37–42.

O'Donnell, James. "A Short History of Literary Baseball," *Crosscurrents* (Washington Community College Humanities Association Yearbook) 7:1 (1988), 4–6.

Randall, Neil. "*Shoeless Joe*: Fantasy and the Humor of Fellow-Feeling," *Modern Fiction Studies* 33.1 (Spring 1987), 173–182.

Reynolds, Charles Dewey Hilles. *Baseball as the Material of Fiction.* Unpublished Doctoral Dissertation. Lincoln, Nebraska: The University of Nebraska, 1974.

Roberts, Frederic. "A Myth Grows in Brooklyn: On Urban Death, Resurrection, and the Brooklyn Dodgers," *Baseball History* 2:2 (Summer 1987), 4–26.

Rodgers, Bernard T., Jr. "*The Great American Novel* and 'The Great American Joke'," *Critique* 16:2 (1974), 12–29.

Saposnik, Irving S. "Homage to Clyde Kluttz or the Education of a Jewish Baseball Fan," *Journal of American Culture* 4:3 (Fall 1981) 58–65.

Schwartz, Richard Alan. "Postmodernist Baseball," *Modern Fiction Studies* 33.1 (Spring 1987), 135–149.

Shannon, Mike. *Diamond Classics: Essays on One Hundred of the Best Baseball Books Ever Published.* Jefferson, North Carolina: McFarland Publishers, 1989.

Shelton, Frank W. "Humor and Balance in Coover's *The Universal Baseball Association, Inc.*," *Critique* 17:1 (1975), 78–89.

Smith, Leverett T., Jr. "Versions of Defeat: Baseball Autobiographies," *Arete: The Journal of Sport Literature* 2:1 (Fall 1984), 141–158.

Smith, Leverett T., Jr. "More Versions of Defeat," *Arete: The Journal of Sport Literature* 5:1 (Fall 1987), 97–114.

Solomon, Eric. "Jews, Baseball, and the American Novel," *Arete: The Journal of Sport Literature* 1:2 (Spring 1984), 43–66.

Solomon, Eric. "The Bullpen of Her Mind: Women's Baseball Fiction and Sylvia Tennebaum's *Rachel, The Rabbi's Wife*," *Arete: The Journal of Sport Literature* 3:1 (Fall 1985), 19–31.

Solomon, Eric. "Counter-Ethnicity and the Jewish-Black Baseball Novel: The Cases of **Jerome Charyn** and **Jay**

Neugeboren," *Modern Fiction Studies* 33.1 (Spring 1987), 49–64.

Solomon, Eric. "The Boy of Summer Grows Older: Roger Kahn and the Baseball Memoir," *Baseball History* 2:2 (Summer 1987), 27–47.

Stein, Harry. "Baseball on Their Minds—The Lure of the Diamond, the Pace of the Plot," *The New York Times Book Review* 40 (June 1, 1986), 9, 56.

Turner, Frederick W. "Myth Inside and Out: Malamud's *The Natural*," *Novel* 1:2 (1968), 133–139.

Wasserman, Earl R. "*The Natural*: Malamud's World Ceres," *Centennial Review of Arts and Sciences* 9:4 (1965), 438–460.

Wineapple, Brenda. "Robert Coover's Playing Fields," *Iowa Review* 10:3 (1979), 66–74.

ABOUT THE EDITOR

Peter C. Bjarkman is Chairman of SABR's (Society for American Baseball Research) Latin American Committee and author of a comprehensive study of baseball literature, The Immortal Diamond *(Meckler). Known as "Doctor Baseball," Bjarkman taught linguistics at Purdue University for seven years, and now maintains "offices" in the grandstands of Comiskey Park and Wrigley Field. Recently he has published illustrated histories of the Dodgers and the Blue Jays.*